Joan,

Sixty in Sarasota

We're so happy that your daughter is doing well.

George C. King

Sixty in Sarasota

George C. King

Copyright © 2005 by George C. King.

Library of Congress Number: 2004195163
ISBN: Softcover   1-4134-8026-8

All rights reserved. No part of this book may be reproduced or transmitted in any form or by any means, electronic or mechanical, including photocopying, recording, or by any information storage and retrieval system, without permission in writing from the copyright owner.

This is a work of fiction. Names, characters, places and incidents either are the product of the author's imagination or are used fictitiously, and any resemblance to any actual persons, living or dead, events, or locales is entirely coincidental.

This book was printed in the United States of America.

To order additional copies of this book, contact:
Xlibris Corporation
1-888-795-4274
www.Xlibris.com
Orders@Xlibris.com

27159

To the city of Sarasota and especially The John and Mable Ringling Museum of Art for its inspiration and permission to use the cover photo

Once upon a time there was a paradise beyond compare, where all forms of life might flourish. The air was always warm because the sun shone every day. The land cradled gold beneath its surface, and the waters of its lakes and streams promised eternal youth to all that drank. There was no personal income tax, and voting was conducted by absentee ballot to relieve the stress of election day. And so they came—the conquistadors and the Canadians, the retirees and the rattlesnakes.

PART ONE

ONE

The fidgety man in the somber black blazer, turtleneck, and slacks was probably the only member of the audience who couldn't concentrate on the performance. The setting was exquisite—an intimate interior embellished with graceful columns, pale green wall panels trimmed with gilt, and strategically placed cherubs—the Harold E. and Esther M. Mertz Theatre of Sarasota was originally built as an opera house in Scotland. The actors were professional, the acclaimed Asolo Theatre Company. And the spectators were rolling in the aisles.

He could've sworn when his wife ordered the tickets that she'd told him the play was a French farce entitled *He Peed in Her Rear*. He wasn't surprised by the title because you might expect something like that from the French. In fact, he'd discovered upon arriving at the theater that the play's correct name was *A Flea in Her Ear*. The subject matter of the comedy troubled him—impotence, infidelity, mistaken identities, revolving bedrooms. One of the characters had a defective palate and could only speak in vowel sounds. The audience howled every time he spoke, but the man in black remained befuddled because he couldn't understand a word the character was saying. He also hated drawing attention to himself. Wouldn't others notice his morose calm amidst the gales of laughter?

All of these misgivings served to strengthen his resolve. He could disappear during the first intermission, commit his crime while Act II unfolded, and return during the second intermission. He'd skipped acts before, complaining to his wife of restless legs, a stiff back, or boredom. She didn't care as long as he played escort and allowed her to relish the theatrics.

"I need to stretch," he said when the house lights came up. "Don't wait for me." She waved him on, then drew a hair-trigger compact from her purse, slung like a holster over her bare shoulder. He knew that she'd be just as happy to be seen without him. The high waist of her diaphanous black dress had plumped up her cleavage, and a single red amethyst hung like a beacon between her breasts. She would cast alluring glances into the sea of theatergoers and reel in any lecherous stares.

He wanted to leap into the aisle, but restrained himself so as not to arouse curiosity or suspicion. It was fortunate that he chose this course, or he would have bowled over a fragile woman shuffling along the green carpet with a walker. After cautiously sidling by her, he pretty much had a clear shot to the lobby. Most people were still rousing themselves from their seats. There was much coughing, clearing of throats, and honking of noses as accumulated matter was expelled from the audience's collective airways.

These eruptions frequently marred performances along with the interminable unwrapping of cough drops and breath mints. And there was always someone asking for a bit of dialogue to be explained or repeated. He blamed these intrusions on the age of the audience, at least five to ten years older than he and his wife, who were both sixty. He regularly experienced a deep-seated urge to scream at the offenders, but often he just walked out as he was doing now.

A few people were already milling about in the lobby, and a handful of smokers had begun poisoning themselves outside the theater entrance. He encountered a woman who, like himself, appeared headed for the parking lot.

"I left my sweater in the car," she said, smiling and clutching herself by way of explanation.

"I'm getting my wife's," he said. He would make good on the lie. She hadn't brought her wrap inside, and he would gain points through his thoughtfulness. Although it was early November, he judged the night air to be in the seventies. But the theater's air conditioning was cranked up so high that the patrons might just as well have been slabs of meat dangling in an abattoir.

He approached his car, parked deliberately distant from any overhead lights, and stealthily scanned his surroundings. Observing no one, he opened the trunk of the beige Lexus. First he grasped the large safety harness and wrapped it around his waist several times before securing it. Next he stuffed the inside pockets of his jacket with the tools he would need for the job: gloves, a heavy mallet, a chisel, and a can of white spray paint. He closed the trunk, buttoned his jacket, and studied his chest. No one would be the wiser unless he was searched.

The theater, which was part of the Florida State University Center for the Performing Arts, was situated a few hundred yards northeast of the Ringling Museum of Art. The museum itself stood at the head of University Parkway where it intersected U.S. 41, also known as Tamiami Trail, or simply the Trail. Besides the art museum, the grounds included a circus museum, a café, exotic plants and trees, and the recently restored John and Mable Ringling mansion—Cà d'Zan, "House of John" in Venetian dialect.

He had to admit that the mansion was impressive, especially after the $15 million restoration approved by the state. But now one of his neighbors, a moron named John, kept referring to *his* home as the "Cà d'Zan." It was enough to drive him to sabotage, he thought, as he strolled in what he hoped was a casual manner toward the museum grounds. But the mansion was not the object of his displeasure—it was a sculpture in the museum courtyard whose features he could no longer endure.

A local street, Bay Shore Road, separated the parking lot from the museum attractions. Beyond this lane a chest-high wall broken by a few gates bounded the property. The gates were all closed, but the wall acted as only a minimal barrier. He quickly surveyed the enclosure, choosing a segment out of range of the street lamps and shaded by a clump of small oaks. After hoisting himself over the obstruction and clearing a hedge on the other side, he brushed off the evidence of his contact with the rough masonry.

~

Will Baker had been added to the Ringling Museum security staff after the 9/11 attacks. A retired New Jersey police officer, he welcomed the work, which wasn't full time. He'd been filling up his days with fishing and golfing for two years, but even he had to admit there was more to life than snook and par threes. The nose-dive in the stock market had put a crimp in his and his wife's spending as well.

So guarding the museum's treasures had enlivened his routine and added money to his bank account. Sometimes he worked at the main entrance checking bags for weapons or bombs, though he didn't really think that the art gallery was a likely target for terrorists. He drew night duty occasionally—he'd agreed to it to ingratiate himself with his employers—but as a part-timer, he didn't have to carry the load.

Tonight he was driving the tram route between the museum and the Cà d'Zan, pleasant duty in the cooler air. And quiet since everything was closed. He'd worked overnights in Atlantic City that left him gasping for air—a friggin' zoo, he remembered. They rolled up the sidewalks in Sarasota at dusk, which was fine with him. Unlike New Jersey, he could even see the stars when he puttered out from under these banyan trees. He'd been told his first day on the job that the trees had been gifts to the Ringlings from Thomas Edison. Pretty cool when you thought about it—a genius from New Jersey plants a banyan in Florida and now a regular Joe from Jersey could admire it. With roots coming out of the limbs and anchoring them to the ground, the damn things looked like fortresses. Fat chance someone would try to steal one of them—maybe with a fleet of bulldozers and cranes.

Will belched, tasting a ripe stew of refried beans, raw onions, guacamole, sour cream, salsa, marinated pork, and a hint of tequila and lime. He and his wife always went out to dinner before his night duty, and he took a hearty nap afterward. Today they'd hit their favorite Mexican joint, La Flatulencia, and he was still aglow from the spicy fare. His bowels were humming a tune that only the Roto-Rooter man could love. Will definitely needed some serious toilet time, so he parked in front of the circus museum and hotfooted it toward the john. If some clown wanted to steal a tree while he was taking a shit, so be it.

~

The man in black slunk in the shadows, which were plentiful amidst the night and the trees. The only lighting was directed on the building itself, its coral pink glowing softly in the moist air. He crossed the major walkway, which also served as a tram route, and skirted the right side of the art museum. The building ran east-west, a big rectangle with galleries on three sides and an elevated walkway on the west end. The courtyard in the center was straight from the Italian Renaissance, with marble loggias flanking the galleries, and replicas of ancient Greek, Roman, and Baroque sculpture not only gracing the gardens but also peering down from the roof on all sides.

He climbed a set of stairs shrouded by heavy shrubbery and topped by an iron gate that accessed the west end of the courtyard. After donning his gloves and thrusting his mallet, chisel, and spray paint through openings in the ironwork, he manfully began to struggle around the side of the gate. He scaled the stone banister, grappled a colonnade support, and finally gained a handhold on the crown of the high wall backing the courtyard. Hauling himself up and over, he dropped as gently as he could manage to the marble floor.

He hadn't broken into the galleries and set off alarms, but his heart pounded anyway. A guard could be walking or looking outside—it wouldn't take much—and his ass would be grass. He gathered his tools and slouched Groucholike below the balustrade toward his target. Centered and elevated at the back of the sculpture garden was Ringling's pièce de résistance, a bronze replica of Michelangelo's *David*. The Florentine original stood sixteen feet, five inches; not surprisingly, master showman Ringling's copy exceeded seventeen feet, nearly three times the size of an average man. The front of the nude statue faced the courtyard, while *David*'s massive, athletic buttocks mooned Sarasota Bay.

The man in black knelt below the astounding bronze backside and removed his safety harness. He clambered onto the base of the statue and began the difficult task of looping the harness around the statue's legs. Grappling the colossal appendages as a defense against the precarious footing, he averted his eyes from the precipitous drop to the courtyard below. He finally encircled both legs and cinched himself into the harness, establishing as tight a radius as he thought he could manipulate. Taking a deep breath, he sidestepped to the front of the statue and worked himself up its legs until his face was inches from its groin.

Now that the moment he'd prepared for was imminent, the sweat poured off his brow and into his eyes. He swiped at them with a glove before removing the mallet and chisel from his jacket. He'd practiced carefully on a damaged wildlife sculpture that he'd picked up for a song at Décor Direct, a wholesale warehouse filled with exotica. The bronze penis before him, which was in a flaccid pose, appeared to be somewhat less than twelve inches in length. He placed the chisel where the phallus sprouted from the pubic hair and swung the mallet with all his might. *Sprong!*

"Fuck!" he said between clenched teeth. He might just as well have struck a gong, and the reverberations ran up his arms in spidery aftershocks. He remained motionless for a moment, save for craning his neck to scan the courtyard behind him. Seeing and hearing nothing, he inspected his work—a chip and a crack, he was sure of it. He attacked the big prick with renewed effort on its underside where it reposed on the scrotum. *Sprong! Sprong! Sprong!* Another scrutiny revealed he was definitely making headway, and he began battering the site of his initial blow. *Sprong! Sprong! Sprong!* Two more for good measure—*Sprong! Sprunk!* He stowed the mallet and chisel and grabbed the drooping penis with both hands, wrestling the thing from side to side until it broke free and poked him in the mouth. He spit in disgust, stuffing the penis into his pocket.

He'd meant to assault the scrotum next, but all the racket had unnerved him. Instead, he drew his can of spray paint and whitewashed the statue's crotch. Next, he crabbed his way around the sculpture and coated the imposing butt— which had been part of his original plan. He'd considered leaving graffiti proclaiming the indecency and offensiveness of the statue, but had decided not to overdo it. Finally, he extricated himself from the harness, leapt from base, and fled with his trophy and tools.

An adrenaline rush fueled his escape. No longer could the sculpture provoke his outrage—where Goliath had failed, he had not. He had unmanned the boy and diapered *David*!

~

Will Baker shone his flashlight on his watch after returning to the tram—9:15. He'd spent a good half hour on the pot, but it had been worth it. Nothing like a good crap, he always said. He would've stayed bloated and unsettled all night if he hadn't taken care of business. He was curious about one thing, though. He'd never heard a clock chiming before on his night duty. This one had struck nine, but it seemed to him that the intervals had been irregular. And that last chime was really weird—like the mechanism had broken or something. He put it out of his mind as he eased past the darkened Banyan Café and turned toward the museum.

TWO

November 3, 2002—another day in paradise. Jack Adamson removed his reading glasses, placing them next to the remains of his breakfast and the bottles of glucosamine and ibuprofen on the patio table. He was interrupting his scrutiny of Sunday's Sarasota Herald-Tribune to admire the preserve behind his house.

His gaze shifted with satisfaction across the spacious lanai with its thirty-foot swimming pool and gurgling fountains. Urns filled with brilliantly leafed croton—yellow, orange, and green—lined the back of the pool. He and his wife, Jill, had tried flowering plants, but the blossoms would ultimately fall and then decompose into irritating stains. It was difficult enough to keep the white deck sparkling in the Florida sunshine. Jet fuel leaking from the sky clung to the cage that rose high above the pool and attached to the roof just below the rows of ochre Spanish tiles. A little rain dislodged the inky residue, which would streak the lanai until he or his wife could hose it down.

Some twenty feet beyond the lanai, an unbroken line of saw palmettos filled the first tier of the preserve. Their stiff, fan-shaped leaves appeared to be extending a choice of green stilettos to finicky duelists. These tapered points drew Jack's eye to taller queen palms and live oaks, engaging neighbors whose graceful fronds and sprawling limbs vied respectively for the attentions of the sun. The feathery Spanish moss softly bearding the oaks had earned a foothold even higher, draping the limbs of scrub pines that had surpassed their lowly name.

But beyond the preserve, just visible through the trees, was the hint of a gap. It seemed a mystery, except Jack knew that the Braden River flowed in this breach. That fact explained the other preserve he could also glimpse, actually the far bank of the river. Even though he couldn't see the waterway, Jack could use his imagination. Remembering films that had been shot in Florida, he envisioned Johnny Weissmuller's Tarzan astride a broad-backed manatee, or the Creature from the Black Lagoon snatching an unlucky homeowner.

The realtor for Plumbago Plantation—a little enclave in Manatee County that stubbornly clung to a Sarasota address—had apologized to the Adamsons because this lot lacked a river view. The preserve was an environmental buffer, she warned them, and couldn't be tampered with. So she hustled them back into her golf cart and puttered off to a model home backing up to a "lake." Jack smirked at Jill—they owned a summer home in Maine on a real lake, twelve miles long and three miles wide. No dinky retention pond for them. They wanted a tropical jungle behind them, and that's what they got.

They'd congratulated themselves more than once on their decision, which seemed circumspect with the passage of time. A few days after they bought, a new owner burst into the realtor's office, frantically shouting, "There's an alligator in my pond! What are you going to do about it?" he demanded.

The realtor didn't miss a beat. "Nothing—this is Florida. We share the environment with a number of creatures you won't find up North." The man's countenance sagged like a botched facelift.

Then the dry weather came, from October through May. The ponds shriveled to a stagnant muck, and any emergent vegetation curled up into parched little corpses. When the wind was right, the noxious odor issuing from this salad of mud and decay wafted unerringly toward the houses on the shoreline. To be fair, a splendid array of herons, cranes, egrets, and ibises stalked the lakes in higher water, if you enjoyed watching the birds pick their way through algae and frog scum.

"Jack, what's that noise?"

Jill had been walking their red dachshund, Nefertiti. Jack could just see his wife's sunlit brunette tresses over the hedge of pink hibiscus and the twin pygmy date palms at the left corner of the lanai cage. Although he and his wife were both sixty, her hair had remained dark while his had grayed completely.

There was definitely a rustling coming from the preserve, as if an animal were breaking through the underbrush. Jack stood and walked to the screen door on the left side of the lanai. When he joined his wife outside, the sound grew louder, as whatever beast lurking in the tangle crashed in their direction. Nefertiti's ears arched in alertness, her hackles swelling and a growl rumbling in her throat. Jill locked down on the retractable leash.

A next door neighbor, Connie, bustled from her lanai with Tippy, a beige Chihuahua, in tow. "Dickey, you better get out here!" she pitched back toward her house. Her husband had introduced himself as "Richard" to the Adamsons, and he pouted whenever Connie used the other name.

She was bound tightly in a disturbingly vivid chartreuse bathrobe, neck and waist sashes secured, so that only her hands and feet were exposed; this in spite of the comfortable temperature. Perhaps she meant to be provocative through concealment, Jack thought, knowing that Connie liked to flirt. Or perhaps, due to the early hour, she had little or nothing on under the robe. She possessed a reasonably good figure if one could ignore a few droops and bulges, but he found her hair, dyed red, a bit garish. Clutching Tippy's lead in one hand and a steaming cup of coffee in the other, Connie marched toward them across the dewy St. Augustine grass.

Her glistening black sandals kicked up a little spray as she yelled again, "You're gonna miss whatever it is!"

Nefertiti and Tippy nuzzled each other familiarly, tails wagging, before investigating each other's butt with enthusiastic interest. Jill and Connie yanked the dogs away as if reprimanding a child for a breach of etiquette.

Jack remembered the routine of a comedian whose name escaped him at the moment and said, panting, hands curled next to his face like paws, "It's my job to sniff butt."

"Jack!" his wife admonished, but Connie giggled. Thus rewarded, Jack was disposed to forgive her hair—at least temporarily.

The tardy Richard finally appeared, barefoot, in undershirt and cutoffs, smoothing his thinning hair from the ravages of sleep. As he approached the others, his head leaned forward, seemingly tethered to some invisible chain manipulated by his wife.

"OK," he grumped, rubbing at his pale blue eyes, "what's all the fuss about?" Richard was the same height as Connie, though not when she wore high heels, Jack had noted. At six feet and five nine, both he and Jill outstripped the Lovejoys.

The palmettos to their left parted in answer, as two armadillos scampered into the open, one obviously pursuing the other. They were about the same size as the dogs, even sporting pointy ears and tails of canine proportions. But a long snout and gray carapace further distinguished each creature, making them look less like dogs and more like anteaters from the land that time forgot.

"Aren't they cute?" Jill cooed.

The trailing armadillo promptly mounted the object of his desire and began humping her as if there were no tomorrow. Jack was impressed with the flexibility of their armor. He'd only seen a couple of porno flicks, but the naked actors hadn't demonstrated the level of pliability on display in these shelled critters.

Nefertiti was wowed as well. Sensing that Jill had now relaxed her vigilance, the dachshund dashed forward and mounted the male armadillo. Although female and spayed, she had attempted this maneuver before with other dogs. Jack never discouraged her because—well—he felt sorry for her. She was trying her best to reproduce. He could even visualize the offspring—a "weinerdillo." The thing would have a red shell, a body like a bratwurst, a nose dwarfing Durante's or de Bergerac's, halitosis up the ying-yang, and an insatiable appetite for termite-flavored dog biscuits.

"Nefer!" Jill was not amused—she always shortened the dog's name when angry. She jerked on the leash, but the inflamed dachshund had sunk her nails into the folds of the armadillo's carapace and wouldn't budge. Nefertiti continued to pump energetically, despite much hacking and wheezing interspersed with grunts and snorts. Perhaps out of sympathy with her choking, the armadillos added their own high-pitched squeals to the chorus. The alarming outcry reminded Jack of his own vocalizing in the throes of passion—he and Jill were capable of producing a remarkable medley of groans and moans in the bedroom.

Jill eased off the tension so that Nefertiti could regain her breath. "Jack, I think you're going to have to pull her off with your hands."

Jack rather liked watching the action, but he supposed the time had come. Tippy had other ideas and beat him to the punch. The Chihuahua had been wagging his tail and whining while his owners gaped at the unnatural ménage à trois. Now he could no longer resist Nefertiti's inviting backside. He darted forward, unsheathed his tamale, and began unsuccessfully probing the dachshund's nether regions. Bad luck, Jack thought, Tippy had no chance of siring a Mexican hot dog.

"Don't just stand there, Dickey. Do something for God's sake!" Connie barked.

Before either man could act, Nefertiti yelped—like most women, she didn't like being goosed south of the border. She withdrew her nails from the armadillo's shell and turned on her Latin lover. Instantly the two dogs were rolling on the grass in a frenzied ball of nips, yips, and snarls. Jack and Richard shared a quick look of unspoken communication—no way were they were going to stick their hands into the melee. Instead, Jill and Connie tugged on the leashes and finally dragged the combatants apart. But Nefertiti and Tippy strained to stand upright, gagging and gasping in their efforts to lunge at one another. The armadillos suddenly uncoupled and scuttled back under the banks of palmetto. Whether the creatures had satisfied their lust or simply been scared by the fracas between the dogs was unclear, but they could be heard smashing deeper into the preserve.

"Well, that passed the time," Jack remarked, grinning at the others.

"I would never have thought—" Jill began. She didn't finish her observation. She and Jack had only known the Lovejoys a few months, and she didn't want to offend them.

"I know just what you mean, Jill," Connie said, nodding her head in a calculated manner. "Maybe Dickey could learn something from our little four-legged friends," she added.

"Connie!" Richard snapped peevishly.

She slurped the remainder of her coffee and tossed the dregs toward the preserve. Miraculously the liquid had gone unspilled during the rumpus. Jill raised her eyebrows at Jack, who responded with a bemused expression.

Nefertiti and Tippy had lost interest in each other and were sniffing the ground vacated by the armadillos. Jill and Connie let them roam, but kept a watchful eye lest the dogs' astonishing passions resurface. After a painstaking inspection each animal peed generously on several spots and kicked up sandy soil with hind legs over the anointed earth.

It appeared as if the entire matter had been laid to rest when a bantam armadillo blundered into the open a few feet away. On the trail of his brethren, Jack surmised, probably a juvenile male learning the ropes. The dogs exploded in a fury of barking, straining anew at their leashes as Jill and Connie struggled to rein them in. It was Richard's misfortune to snare his ankle when Tippy began circling. The man hopped on one foot trying to extricate himself while Connie attempted to maneuver the strap, but her husband fell heavily to the ground.

"Shit," he grunted, as he grabbed the leash from Connie and disentangled his foot. The petite armadillo dodged hastily back to the refuge of the palmettos, and the hubbub subsided once again.

"Ow, what's this?" Richard said. He jumped up, dropping the strap so that he could brush frantically at his ankles and feet. Jack looked at the soil where his neighbor had fallen—tiny black specks scurrying in single-minded determination.

"Fire ants," Jack announced. "You'll get pussy bumps all over your feet."

"What kind of bumps?" Connie asked, her brow furrowing.

"Filled with pus," Jack answered. "They'll itch like hell, too."

"That's what you get for not wearing any shoes," Connie said, as if her husband had committed another in a long list of childish infractions.

"I've got some hydrocortisone cream and some Afterbite in the house," Jack offered.

"Will that make the bumps go away?" Richard asked, anxiously inspecting his feet.

"Oh no," Jack said, shaking his head, "but it might help with the itching."

"I hate this place!" Richard said with unexpected bitterness.

Nefertiti and Tippy wagged their tails as they followed the humans into the Adamsons' home. Surely the animals would be rewarded with dog biscuits for chasing away the armored intruders.

THREE

They hadn't seen any armadillos since yesterday, unless you counted the one the turkey buzzards were picking at on the entry road to Plumbago. But Jack and Jill Adamson had seen plenty of the Lovejoys. Connie and Jill were already walking the dogs together, while Richard and Jack were chatting over the newspaper and a cup of coffee. Jill had welcomed the company, and Jack had begun to anticipate the conversation, which the remainder of Sunday had focused on some flaw in the Florida landscape. He relished Richard's compulsive mining of impurities and at the same time delighted in picking apart the nuggets his neighbor had unearthed.

This Monday morning, though, both men were outraged by a headline: *DAVID* DISFIGURED, MASTERPIECE EMASCULATED. There were two photos accompanying the story—a shot of the statue's pubic region, discolored and sans penis, and a close-up of its whitewashed backside.

"This happened Saturday night," Richard said. "I'll bet you money it was one of those goddamn evangelicals," he added, scornfully shaking his head.

"There's a Baptist minister quoted in the article," Jack said, scanning down an inside page where the story was continued. "Says 'no self-respecting Christian should take the law into his own hands, but the statue was offensive to God.' Seems he singled it out along with some other sculptures in a sermon recently."

"I saw that on the news a few days ago—probably one of his faithful did it. All I know is it's another black mark on the area, just like I've been telling you," Richard asserted, returning to his favorite theme.

Jack looked up. "No one's claimed responsibility, and the police don't have a suspect. And Florida doesn't have a corner on zealots—the Attorney General covered the breasts of *Justice*, for God's sake."

Richard scooted away from the table and walked to the edge of the pool, scowling down at the water as if a spy for the Inquisition might be snorkeling for evidence. "Jesus, Jack, have you ever tried finding a decent radio station when you're out driving?"

He turned and plunged onward, not expecting an answer. "Good Lord, all you can find is Christian rock." Richard struck a pose, strumming on an imaginary guitar and singing gutturally,

> *Jeezus, save-uh ma soul,*
> *I got me a cancerous mole,*
> *Livin' in this Florida hole,*
> *This life done taken its toll,*
> *Oh, take me to the Gator Bowl.*

Even though he hated to give Richard points, Jack grinned.

"Christ almighty," Richard continued, obviously warming to the topic, "Orlando is some kind of Christian publishing center, and they trot out Holy Rollers and bomb abortion clinics in Pensacola. Y'all know where that is, don't ya, Jack?

Redneck Riviera. And I saw this building the other day, 'The King's Theater.' Elvis Presley movies, right?"

"I suppose," Jack said, playing along.

Richard made a game-show buzzing sound to demonstrate how pathetically wrong Jack was.

"They were movies about Jesus, Jack. I looked at Connie, and she said 'I'll be goddamned.'" Satisfied that he'd made his case, he plopped down in his chair again and shuffled through his paper for another section.

Richard was somewhat of an expert on radio stations, having owned several in Connecticut before retiring to Florida, but Jack challenged him anyway. "We listen to NPR and a pop station in Tampa, depending on our mood. And Sarasota isn't Orlando or Pensacola, for Christ's sake. As far as that goes, you can find Christian rock anywhere in the U.S., and back in Maryland we had Christian parents trying to ban books and get us to teach creationism."

He and Jill had each taught for thirty years in the public schools outside D.C. They'd been pulling in $120,000 when they retired, and now their pensions totaled $72,000 with a permanent cost-of-living adjustment each year. He didn't volunteer this information to Richard, because local teachers' salaries were poor by comparison.

Richard didn't respond to Jack's arguments, only grunting dismissively while concentrating on some other piece that had captured his attention. Jack returned to his paper, looking up when a squirrel jumped amid the limbs of a live oak. A snowy egret approached from the right, moving with the slow-motion grace of a mime as it inspected the grass for tiny frogs. In the foliage surrounding the pool cage, colorful geckoes—rustling like fallen leaves—tongued insects from the air.

"Ha!" Richard announced, folding his arms in vindication.

"What now?" Jack asked, mildly annoyed.

"It's something every day," he replied, turning melancholy. Richard's face lengthened, his expression suggesting dreadful news, perhaps a death in the family or the delivery of a stillborn child. "Sarasota County is being terrorized by feral hogs."

"Feral hogs?"

Richard pounded with his right index finger on the paper, "2B." Jack located the story and began reading.

"That swine De Soto introduced them when he was mucking around here in the sixteenth century—searching for gold and killing Indians," Richard said savagely.

"This is east of I-75," Jack noted. "You're exaggerating as usual."

"Connie and I looked at homes out there!" Panic registered in his eyes.

Jack shrugged. "So did we."

"You don't think they could find their way to *our* neck of the woods?" Richard said sarcastically, nodding toward the oaks and palms.

Jack considered the question, not unreasonable by Richard's standards. The picture in the newspaper revealed an animal slimmer than your typical farm hog, hairy-faced and beady-eyed, but with an unmistakable porcine malevolence. He remembered the deer in Maryland, who had wreaked havoc even in the dense suburbs. But he couldn't let himself fall prey to Richard's paranoia.

"If they're causing agricultural damage, like it says here, why wouldn't they stay close to farms?" Jack asked, closing the paper.

"I'm sure the farmers would appreciate that observation, Jack. But the article also says that they like moisture and cover."

Richard stood up again and turned toward the preserve, just in case his meaning had escaped Jack. The Braden River nurtured the woods behind them. It would make a perfect habitat, Jack thought. He felt himself wavering, so he decided to make light of the matter.

"They root up golf courses, Richard. I think our tennis courts are safe." They both played at the Plumbago Racquet Club; on the rare occasions that they golfed, it was strictly a lark. In that regard, they were decidedly in the minority in Sarasota. Golfing was like breathing for most in the area. Golf carts were as numerous as cars and perhaps more of a menace, scattering pedestrians in their wake while playing chicken with autos.

"But what about our lawns?" Richard asked, gesturing expansively toward the beds of mulch festooning the landscape. "Hog heaven for them, and nothing but carnage for us."

Both he and Jack had planted extensively. Their houses were lined front and back with flowers and shrubbery—red ixora, blue plumbago, yellow lantana, white star jasmine, watermelon bougainvillea, pink heather, golden and red hibiscus, variegated legustrum, plumed sagos, leafy crotons, and glossy viburnum mingled incestuously in islands of cedar chips. Richard had also nurtured orange and lime trees in spite of warnings not to cultivate them. Only yesterday he'd complained to Jack about the citrus canker and the Florida law that allowed officials to invade private property to cut down infected trees or those in the canker's path.

"These plants are our children, Jack," Richard said melodramatically. "Imagine the massacre—cut down in the prime of life by snout and hoof."

He suddenly placed the index finger of his right hand under the point of his nose and pushed upward. The change in his countenance reminded Jack of the elusive pig man from a hilarious *Seinfeld* episode.

Richard bent low to the lanai deck and mimed a pig with rooting movements of his head and pawing motions of his feet accompanied by feral grunts. "Oink, oink, snort, snort," he said, in case Jack was too dense to catch the other man's drift.

"Would you like some more bacon," Jack offered, gesturing toward the last strip of Jimmy Dean's finest, reposing harmlessly on a paper plate.

Richard ignored the gibe without missing a beat, though he straightened up and shed his pig face. "That isn't the worst of it, Jack. The hogs will shit all over the place, and our dogs will nose around in it. You read the article—parasites, lice, ticks—eight diseases that can infect a human being."

A crash from the preserve arrested his harangue. Richard pivoted in alarm, and Jack popped out of his chair. The last time he'd been startled like that was at the movies years earlier—when Carrie's arm had thrust itself from the grave in vengeance.

Both men held their breath as the underbrush parted and the source of the ruckus slowly emerged—a gopher tortoise about the size of a toilet bowl.

"Attack of the feral turtles," Jack said, smirking.

"Don't laugh," Richard warned, "they eat plants."

Barking to the left caused the terrapin to scramble awkwardly back to cover. Connie and Jill were approaching with Tippy and Nefertiti. Both dogs had spotted the tortoise, and they were straining against their leashes, front feet in the air. The gaunt Chihuahua bolted like a flash of mustard, while the plump, red dachshund quivered like an animated sausage.

"Gotta go," Richard said, opening the screen door. "But mark my words, the moral police are screwing with our statues, and the feral hogs will soon be porking our plumbagos."

"The prigs and the pigs, huh?"

"That's right, man," Richard said, unsmiling, "the prigs and the pigs."

FOUR

Siesta Key, a barrier island some eight miles long, lay off the Sarasota mainland, the two separated by the Intracoastal Waterway. Along its western shoreline, the key faced the Gulf of Mexico, whose waters, though temperate, nevertheless gnawed intemperately at the island's popular beaches. At the south end in particular, houses too close to the jaws of the Gulf had been condemned, and deposits of silt had closed off Midnight Pass.

Kathy Adamson King, thirty-two, worried about the erosion. It nagged at her like so many other issues in her life—the source of her next paycheck, her failed marriage, her inability to satisfy her parents' expectations, her clunker T-bird, and the lumps of cellulite she imagined to be forming, like tumors, in her ass. She fretted about trivial things as well, like changing her last name back to Adamson—her maiden name. Her given middle name had been Kendall, but Kathy Kendall King shrank into an unfortunate set of initials.

She lived in a lime green bungalow just north of Turtle Beach—or what remained of it. There, the Fisherman's Cove condominiums seemed to literally hang over the emerald

Gulf. A trailer park bordered one side of her property and a ritzy hacienda, the other, but her impenetrable surroundings discouraged commerce with either neighbor. Her flat-roofed, two bedroom affair was tucked into an unkempt snarl of necessary mangroves and sea oats, the usual yuccas, coconut palms, gumbo limbos, palmettos, and live oaks, and unwanted Brazilian peppers and Australian pines. There was a beaten path to the water, but she could barely see the Gulf and its spectacular sunsets from her living room, filtered through the tangle of vegetation.

Her parents were fond of reminding her that her grandparents had kept the place trimmed up when they were in residence. After their death, the house had passed on to Kathy's parents, who had recently retired to Sarasota, planning to use the bungalow as a getaway from their more commodious residence in the city. That plan had been altered after she and Brad had divorced.

Having children had always been their intent, but when her biological clock sounded the alarm, she demurred. More than demurred—steadfastly refused. Drawing on her graduate work in criminology and her ability to run a database, she'd established herself in a rewarding career. While Brad completed a three-year fellowship in internal medicine at Johns Hopkins in Baltimore, Kathy joined a rising private investigation firm. Insurance fraud, she learned, was costing the country billions of dollars.

And not just, say, someone without injury suing Amtrack in the aftermath of a wreck. There was also widespread fraud in workman's compensation and long-term disability. At first, her role was limited to convincing businesses that they needed her firm's services. But eventually she participated in investigations, including stakeouts and video surveillance. It was a real rush to tape some guy playing tennis or gyrating with a stripper when he was supposedly laid up with a bad back. And her firm had some cool tools: a cell phone and a brief case, both with hidden cameras.

A baby would've ended her budding investigative career. As a doctor with sometimes impossible hours, Brad was precluded from staying home with a child. And no way would Kathy farm the kid out to a nanny. She would stay at home and do it right or not do it at all. The second option was unacceptable to Brad, so they parted company.

Kathy didn't care for Baltimore with its crime, congestion, expensive housing, faltering Ravens, and failing Orioles. She remembered with nostalgia all those childhood visits to Siesta Key with Nanny and Poppy. Sadly, they were gone, but if she wanted to strike out on her own, her parents would let her live in the beach cottage. Actually, they liked Brad and they wanted grandchildren, but they understood how a young woman with two college degrees might want to pursue a career.

She hadn't deluded herself into thinking that the transition would be easy. She was in the process of introducing herself to businesses around town that might require her assistance. Her old firm had sent her some referrals, Florida being a typical state where workers might relocate while defrauding their employers. She'd filled in the gap by doing background checks on prospective employees for some of these firms. And she'd picked up some overflow cases from the insurer of Tropicana, the big juice maker centered in Bradenton, just north of Sarasota. But the work had nearly evaporated while she waited for some steady customers to develop.

That's why Kathy was so excited about this afternoon's meeting with a prospective client—not only excited, but curious and nervous as well. Curious because Mr. Masterson had been secretive on the phone, saying only that he represented the interests of "influential patrons who preferred to remain anonymous." And she was nervous because he wanted to meet at her office, such as it was, though she practically begged to come to him. She'd converted the second bedroom of her modest dwelling into a workspace, with a teak desk, filing cabinet, and bookcase. The only other piece of furniture was a beige futon with abstract designs in brown and gold. A Dell computer system and a fax machine occupied the desk, but the walls were bare except for her diplomas from Wake Forest—magna cum laude—and North Carolina State.

The rest of the cottage reflected her grandparents' tastes, rattan furniture in subdued prints and artwork depicting local flora and fauna. The décor was not unattractive, but clearly had been locked in place for many years. The choices that she'd made for her office served only to accentuate the time warp.

Kathy had been madly cleaning all day, astonished that she could find so much sand on the tile floors. The other culprit was pet hair, shed by her spirited black dachshund, Captain Kirk, and her inscrutable gray tabby, Mr. Spock. The animals had fled before her vacuum cleaner, but had ventured into her office now that Kathy was sitting quietly at her desk.

She and Brad had agreed that it made sense for her to take Kirk and Spock. Kathy loved them for all the reasons that humans dote on pets, but also held them precious, like treasure salvaged from a sunken ship. They'd been puppy and kitten together and neutered together—though Kirk still had an eye, or a wagging tail, for the ladies. Spock's hooded yellow orbs suggested neither accusation nor acceptance, but appreciation of the logic of his alteration. The two ate, played, and slept together like brothers of the same species; in spite of one's hammy bark and badgering nose and the other's sedate mew and pointy ears.

The doorbell rang, setting off Kirk, but Spock merely turned his head toward the sound.

"Shush, Kirk, don't be so dramatic," she said, finger to her lips. "I expect you guys to behave yourselves." This was intended primarily for Kirk, though Spock was not above using his superior physical prowess to leap atop a kitchen counter and bat food down to his alien brother.

Kathy had slanted the blinds over the glass panel in her front door earlier in the day to deflect the rays of the morning sun. As a result, she could now size up Mr. Masterson before he took her measure. He stood over six feet and was well fleshed, though not stocky. Shifting his weight from one foot to the other, he appeared ill at ease at the moment. Not surprising, she thought, because he was wearing a black suit—something you didn't see much in Sarasota. He was young, perhaps about her age, his brown hair cut above the ears, and he sported a thick mustache. Kathy remembered a course she'd taken on justice in the Old West; if you put a derby on this guy . . .

He triggered the doorbell again.

She opened the door a crack. "Yes?" Kathy queried, as if he might be any one of numerous clients ringing at her door.

"Mr. Masterson," he replied, extending his hand stiffly. She took it, noting that it was firm and warm, but lacking the roughness occasioned by manual labor.

"Kathy King." She ushered him into her office, asking his indulgence for her untidiness and assuring him that the dog and cat were not dangerous. Spock sought out the man's lap after Mr. Masterson sat on the futon, while Kirk stared at him in expectation from an adjacent cushion.

"You must be an animal lover," Kathy said, settling in behind her desk. "Spock and Kirk aren't usually that affectionate with strangers." That was a lie to put the man at ease. The cat was purring audibly, and the dog was now nuzzling Masterson's leg.

The man reddened visibly. "They do seem to like me, don't they?"

His tone suggested both wonder and discomfort, as if he were unaccustomed to such displays. But Kathy noticed he readily began stroking the animals.

"Spock and Kirk, you say?"

"Yes, I'm a Trekkie," Kathy confessed.

"The original crew was the best," he said, scratching Spock's ears.

"Oh, you're a fan?" Kathy said, pleased that they might share some common ground.

His embarrassment returned. "Well, one can't help but notice these things. Of course, I don't have the time—what with my responsibilities..."

"To your employers," Kathy suggested helpfully.

"Exactly," he said, suddenly all business, "which brings me to the point of my visit. You must have heard or read about the atrocity committed at the Ringling Museum recently." He studied her expectantly, then added, "The defacement of *David*?"

Kathy nodded vigorously. "Yes, of course—but 'defacement' isn't the word I would've chosen to describe what happened to the statue." The hint of a sardonic smile played at the corners of her mouth.

He was about to speak, but hesitated a beat, then launched into a coughing fit. Spock sprang from his lap, and Kirk barked in concert with Masterson's hacking.

Kathy rose from her chair. "Can I get you some water?" she asked solicitously.

He waved her back, shaking his head emphatically, although his face was now an alarming shade of scarlet. "Just swallowed the wrong way," he gasped.

A bronze penis is a mouthful, she thought, amused by his reaction. Most men she knew would've responded to her remark differently. Taken it as license for some randy double entendre or a lewd smile at least. She found his primness quaint and more than a little endearing.

Spock was now brushing against Masterson's calves, perhaps imparting some soothing balm from the glands in his cheeks. Misinterpreting the man's gestures, Kirk had leapt from the futon and pressed his nose to the floor in search of some pitched morsel.

Following the animals' movements seemed to calm Masterson, and he cleared his throat. "What I'm about to tell you must remain in the strictest confidence."

Kathy nodded matter-of-factly, as if such a request went without saying.

Without further preamble, he said, "There are a number of men and women who donate generous sums of money to the museum. These patrons want the individual who committed this . . . this sacrilege punished. That is not to say that the police aren't investigating the crime—"

"My background is fraud in the workplace," she interrupted.

Masterson lifted a hand to silence her protestations. "We know. We also know about your studies in college—an excellent record at two fine Southern universities, I might add. You're unencumbered by family and searching for work. And you've acquitted yourself admirably in your efforts thus far."

Kathy wondered darkly how far the tentacles of Masterson's patrons reached. And "unencumbered by family" certainly struck a raw nerve; ironically, they saw her failed marriage as a positive. Nevertheless, she was intrigued.

"But you say the police—"

"They have a full plate." He leaned forward on the futon. "We're prepared to pay twice your normal hourly fee. We know that you have other jobs, but it would please us greatly if you could devote your time to this transgression twenty-four/seven."

How she hated that phrase—they wanted to turn her into a Wal-Mart. "Have the cops made any headway at all?" she asked. No sooner was the question out of her mouth than she realized that she'd accepted his offer.

Masterson tipped his head, then glanced suspiciously at Spock and Kirk, as if they might be spies. "Again, this is strictly confidential. The museum is planning an expansion, and adjacent property owners have been offered generous sums for their land. Unfortunately, these people don't want to leave their homes." He frowned as he contemplated the alternative. "The state doesn't want to force anyone out, but . . ." his voice trailed off.

"You think one of these individuals vandalized the statue to get back at the museum," Kathy surmised quickly.

"The police interrogated them all, and they all had confirmed alibis," he said.

Remembering the press account, Kathy asked, "What about the minister mentioned in the paper?"

Masterson clicked his tongue. "An alibi as well."

"A member of his congregation could've done it," Kathy said, thinking out loud.

He smiled bitterly. "Yes, and that means a lot of legwork." He shook his head in bewilderment. "The museum has an outstanding security system—nothing was stolen, you know. The whole thing seems like a fluke."

"Like a teenage prank that succeeded in spite of the odds against it," she said sympathetically.

"Exactly," he said, pleased that she'd acknowledged luck's collaboration.

After a moment's silence, Kathy said, "I'll want to look at the statue."

He stood, now that their transaction was drawing to a close. "It's been arranged—come to the main entrance just before five this afternoon." He withdrew a check from his inside jacket pocket and handed it to her. "This should cover your expenses for the first week."

Kathy's eyes widened when she saw the amount—*David's* penis was becoming dearer to her by the moment.

"And you can expect a handsome bonus when you expose the vandal. Let's meet here again at the same time next week for a report on your progress," he said. "Here's my card if you need to contact me before then. I can let myself out, Miss King."

Masterson turned abruptly on his heels and was out the front door. Spock and Kirk immediately jumped onto the futon to bask in the warmth left by his body. Kathy looked at the card in disappointment—he was "Brett," not "Bat."

FIVE

"Yes, I was one of the guys on duty when it happened," Will Baker grudgingly admitted. He always tried to spread the blame around when questioned about the crime. Christ, someone in the museum should've heard or seen something. "At least they didn't fire me," he added. But he failed to mention that he no longer drew night duty. He didn't want the pretty young thing walking beside him to think even less of him.

He and Kathy King were making their way through the sculpture garden toward the shrouded statue of *David* at the museum's west end. The sun was almost at eye level as it sank into Sarasota Bay, casting long shadows as its orange brush stroked the canvas of loggias and statuary. Massive urns lining the perimeter were ablaze with red bougainvillea in brazen contempt of the Sun Coast's approaching "winter."

Kathy stopped to observe one of the bronze replicas, *The Rape of a Sabine*. A muscular man straddled the back of his vanquished foe while gripping a woman harshly by the haunches. The woman, soft and feminine compared to the male figures, was elevated and struggling to escape. Not the sort of attention I'm seeking, Kathy thought, turning again to the security man.

"Did you see or hear anything?" she asked, not really expecting a substantive reply. After all, Baker had already been questioned fruitlessly by the police.

Will considered his response. He'd always answered in the negative to make himself seem less culpable, but he didn't feel threatened by the youthful investigator.

"I heard some noises—like a clock chiming nine p.m.," he said, gauging her reaction. When she nodded calmly, he continued, "But the interval between the sounds wasn't the same, and the chiming—if that's what it was—sounded different sometimes, especially at the end."

"You think it could've been someone banging on the statue?" Kathy said, asking the obvious.

"Well, now that you mention it," Will said, as if the possibility had never occurred to him, "it might've been." He neglected to tell her that he'd been on the can, and that someone could have escaped the museum grounds while he was doing his business. "But I drove the tram right over and didn't see anybody."

Two steep flights of stairs flanked either end of the garden, and Kathy chose the right, turned left at the top, and approached the statue. Will untied the bottom of the canvas shroud and eased the covering off, revealing a planked scaffold secured to the bronze replica. Kathy marveled at the unfettered power that seemed to flow up the legs and buttocks to the figure's back.

"The white paint hasn't been cleaned off yet," she observed.

"It's still a crime scene, I guess," Will said. "I know they're gonna crane it outta here to repair the damage."

"Go ahead," he said when he saw Kathy contemplating the ramp that led to the scaffold.

She made her way up carefully and stopped to scrutinize the paint. She wondered if it were from a regular can or a spray dispenser—probably the latter, considering the ease of carrying and application. Could she check stores to see who might have bought a can of white spray paint around the time of the vandalism? Of course, the perpetrator could've bought the paint any time. Kathy extricated a pad and pen from her purse and jotted a note.

She moved around the statue, pausing to gape at the twenty-foot drop to the tiered fountains below. Alfred Hitchcock's *Vertigo* flashed to mind, and she quickly averted her eyes. Surely the vandal hadn't mounted his assault from there, but even if he (or she?)—another note—had taken the more obvious route, it would have required an ungainly balancing act. How had the person done it? Kathy scribbled and underlined the question.

Now she was facing *David*'s groin, and the only thing she could think of was Lorena Bobbit chopping off her husband's penis. She stifled a laugh and composed herself. Then she grasped the legs and leaned in for a closer view of the damage.

"Miss King, is that you?" It was Brett Masterson's voice wafting up from the garden.

Realizing how she must have looked—her head buried in the crotch of the statue—Kathy jerked away and turned. "Um . . . yes . . . I didn't expect to see you for a week." She managed a silly wave, noticing a thin, black film on her palm and fingers where she'd gripped the bronze.

He lifted one hand in response. "I was eager to hear your impressions—but don't let me interrupt. Keep on nosing around and we'll talk in a few minutes."

Kathy cringed at his choice of words, then waited until he began ascending the stairs before returning to her examination. The rendering of the pubic hair and the scrotum impressed her, but the ragged break where the penis should've sprouted inspired no immediate brainstorm. After a few moments of consideration, she formulated a question: what tools were used? The break *was* ragged, not clean, so perhaps at least a pair—something that chipped and something that pounded.

She scrawled this possibility in her notes and stared for several minutes more at the wounded bronze. Think outside the box, she told herself, when nothing suggested itself. Maybe the culprit hadn't held a grudge against the museum, and maybe it hadn't been a member of the moral police. What if there was some other motive for disfiguring the statue? Why was part of the statue maimed and another painted? It seemed to her that there might be some connection between these last two questions, but she couldn't grasp it. Finally, she tucked her notes into her purse and returned to the walkway. Brett Masterson had just dismissed the security man, who smiled at Kathy as he headed toward the interior galleries.

"Well," Masterson said, "what's the verdict?" He seemed less ill at ease than earlier, and he'd removed his jacket in deference to the heat that had built during the day.

Kathy shared her thoughts and questions, such as they were, saving what she thought was her most radical notion for last. "What if the individual who did this wasn't motivated by revenge against the museum or moral distaste?"

Masterson considered the possibility. "Give me an example."

"Well, I'm struggling with that at the moment," she said, glancing off toward the bay, "but let's say some teenager or teenagers on a dare."

He nodded agreeably. "You mentioned that in your office."

"Yeah, just a passing remark—but it occurred to me that some students on a field trip might've hatched the idea. Or it could've been one of those informal student clubs—like a fraternity." She'd hated those cliques in high school and their college counterparts as well.

He brightened. "An iniation rite."

"Exactly," she said, pleased that he followed her line of thinking.

"Any more unusual suspects?" he asked, warming to the prospect.

She consulted her notebook. "That was my best guess, I think, but I also came up with some nut from the women's movement."

"That's feasible," he said, not rejecting it out of hand.

Kathy smiled as she read her notes. "The rest are just jokes—I get that from my father. He was an English teacher, always looking for a humorous twist."

Masterson actually smiled. "I could use a laugh."

Kathy regarded him suspiciously, as if weighing his worthiness to be entrusted with a secret.

He rose to the bait. "As your employer, I demand to know the laughable suspects."

"All right, since you insist." She returned her notes to her purse, then hesitated momentarily to build suspense. "Given the sex of the statue," she said in mock seriousness, "and the body part that was removed—it might've been a Catholic priest."

Masterson chuckled, his mustache curling up into the dimples in each of his cheeks. "I don't think the pope would appreciate that allegation."

"Perhaps his holiness will approve of my final suspect," Kathy said, still overly earnest. "I'm thinking of a Biblical villain—a certain Philistine."

Masterson's face was blank for a moment before he caught her drift. "Of course, David and Goliath—Goliath was a Philistine."

"Very good, sir," Kathy said, bowing slightly in acknowledgment of his powers of deduction. "Goliath would certainly have had a motive for turning David into a eunuch, but there's more to it than that."

Masterson frowned, his smooth brow wrinkling in thought. "Let's see—Philistine, Philistine . . ." He pursed his lips, then raised his eyebrows in triumph. "Ah, I get it. A Philistine is someone with no appreciation of art."

"That's it—I think we'd both agree that whoever vandalized the statue falls into that category." The humor paled as Kathy realized the truth of her observation. Masterson became somber as well.

"So where do you go from here?" he asked, once again her employer.

"I'll be checking the sales of white spray paint, and visiting some local high schools," she replied. She didn't tell him how tedious and fruitless the former task might turn out to be. "I'd also like to come back here at night—the same hour and day of the week that the crime occurred. See what's typically going on. Maybe there's a witness who saw something—or some activity that might be linked to the crime."

"Just let me know, and I'll clear it with security," Masterson offered.

Kathy glanced at her watch. "Well, I'd best be going—having dinner with my parents this evening." She smiled ruefully, "Good way for a working girl to save some money. Did you know that they lived in Sarasota?"

Masterson nodded as they strolled toward the steps that led down into the sculpture garden. "Yes, they just moved here recently, didn't they?"

Kathy shot him a sideways glance. "Is there anything that you *don't* know about me?"

He blushed, his awkwardness returning. "Of course—there are many things I don't know about you, Miss King."

She stopped in front of the bronze fountain—a large Roman male reclining with only a vestige of clothing—and turned toward him. "Kathy . . . please."

He backed up slightly, the way some people do when they feel their personal space has been invaded. The alert penis of the recumbent bronze and its brandished sword framed Masterson's upper torso. "I . . . I'm sorry, formality seems to be part of my nature."

Kathy wondered if that revelation were really true. Perhaps his mysterious employers treated him distantly, and he felt obliged to imitate their behavior.

"Well, is it to be 'Miss King' and 'Mr. Masterson,' then?"

He shook his head. "No . . . Kathy." And then with more conviction, "Please call me Brett."

SIX

Jiggs Landing was a fishing camp tucked away on the backwaters of the Evers Reservoir portion of the Braden River. A rusty overhang protected several small rental boats tethered in their slips, and a modest store sold snacks and fishing lures. The rest of the meager community consisted of shanties and trailer homes, in stark contrast to the upscale communities springing up around it, like a stubborn patch of weeds flanked by freshly planted flowers.

The trim man wearing camouflage fatigues and hat liked the place. The family running the store were down-to-earth locals of long standing, not prissy, transplanted Northerners. Folks sitting in lawn chairs gazed at the promise of the river and guzzled beer in defiance of those sipping wine on wicker settees inside caged lanais. A scruffy parking lot, weathered picnic table, and scarred soft drink machine contributed to the unkempt, but natural look. An article in the local newspaper had offered two views of the camp: those who branded it a "blight" and those who celebrated it as a cheeky vestige of old Florida. He favored the latter.

To put his money where his mind was, he bought a package of ten-inch plastic worms at the store and slipped the owner an extra twenty above the rental fee. These expenditures satisfied other objectives as well. One helped to confirm the camouflaged man's disguise as a fisherman. The second allowed him to keep the boat beyond the normal hours of operation. He still had to relinquish his driver's license as collateral for the boat, with assurances that the document would be kept safely for him until he returned later that evening.

After untying the stays, he stepped off a narrow plank, one of a series corralling the vessels, and balanced himself in the craft. A small horsepower motor powered the sturdy aluminum boat, about sixteen feet in length. He stored his fishing rod and light tackle box along the bottom, sat down on a seat screwed into a cross slat, and pulled the cranking cord of the engine. To his surprise, it started easily, and he backed out of his slip before shifting into forward and maneuvering from the launch site into the reservoir.

The owner had provided him with a duplicate of a hand-drawn map, pointing out several likely fishing spots. He'd listened with great enthusiasm to details that he now ignored completely as he searched for the egress of the river from the basin. He scanned the shoreline to his left, looking for the cut indicated on the map. Not readily locating the passage, he felt the familiar tightening in his stomach now that his mission was underway in earnest. His unfamiliarity with the reservoir and its surrounding terrain contributed to his tension, so he idled the motor and fished a pair of camo field glasses from the tackle box. He sighted what appeared to be more than a cove or simple indentation in the shoreline and steered the boat toward it. His instincts proved correct as a channel opened up before him where the river began its meander through the landscape. From here he planned to follow the Braden to a community of new homes called Plumbago Plantation.

The waterway was broad enough for easy navigation, though it narrowed at bends, only to widen again, sometimes pooling in stagnant backwaters and sloughs. The left bank, sparsely forested, held older homes of quirky character with boat ramps or docks. Most of the dwellings were one story and looked as if they had been fashioned piecemeal, with sections added over time depending on the finances or needs of the owner. He'd heard these houses arrogantly derided as "Bubba" homes in the realtor's office, which said more about the character of the speaker than the homes themselves.

As much as he hated to admit it, it was the other bank, on his right, that unnerved him. The impenetrable jungle there reminded him of another jungle, more than thirty years earlier, where an enemy sniper could fix you in his sights before you knew what hit you. So when a blue heron lifted off from a live oak, the man in camouflage ducked reflexively, and he flinched when a squirrel jumped from limb to limb, rustling the foliage. But he had a battle plan for dealing with his uneasiness, and this evening's reconnaissance was the first phase.

The light was fading now, and he feared that he might not recognize the stretch of shoreline that bordered Plumbago. From examining another map, he knew that the housing development was not far from the reservoir. His anxiety eased as the forest on the right began to thin, revealing the back yards of newer homes—an established section of Plumbago. Carriage lamps supplied welcome illumination, and soon he identified the T-shaped communal pier jutting from the bank on legs like stilts.

So far so good, he thought, but the tricky part came next. The jungle rebounded with a vengeance as he searched the shoreline for a spot to moor his boat. Glimpsing a shoal nestled under overhanging branches, he aimed the boat toward it and killed the engine, tilting the motor as he glided into the shallows. The prow cut softly into the earth and stopped where he could conveniently tie the boat to a respectable limb.

He slung his field glasses around his neck, snapped a flashlight onto his pocket, donned some gloves, and swung one leg out of the boat. *Suck!* The sound of the mire swallowing his boot provided a vaguely obscene commentary on his predicament. His balls pressed uncomfortably against the railing while his other foot wobbled in the boat. He grabbed the limb and heaved himself toward shore, tumbling into the underbrush but freeing his foot in the process. After brushing himself off, he trained his flashlight on the forested embankment sloping upward toward the newest homes. He traced a course he could pick his way through until the ground leveled off. And if he'd chosen correctly, he would then find himself in the preserve bordering the houses he wished to reconnoiter.

He relished the exertion as he climbed, pointing the flashlight, then selecting handholds and footholds with care. Stealth was of the utmost importance because he didn't want to draw attention to his position through some clumsy movement. *Thwack!* A small branch had eluded his grasp and slapped him smartly in the face. Clenching his teeth in anger, he managed to suppress the curse that was forming on his lips. A meddling squirrel chattered noisily somewhere above him, a sentinel signaling that an intruder was skulking in the woods.

Nasty little fuckers, he thought, always giving away your position to the enemy. He reached reflexively for his hip, but no revolver was holstered there. Not thinking clearly, he realized, because a gunshot this close to his objective would unquestionably alert the subjects of his surveillance. He crouched motionless as the sting to his skin and pride abated, only to flare again as sweat pricked his eyes and cheeks.

The rodent finally ceased its shrill warning, and he slunk onward without further incident until he crested the embankment. He switched off the flashlight and stood up, kneading his lower back with both hands, working on kinks that had formed during his ascent. Lights glimmered through the fronds and leaves directly in front of him, beckoning like will-o'-the-wisps. He sneaked cautiously forward, lurked prudently behind a live oak, and trained his glasses through a crotch on the source of the illumination. A set of electrical lights around a lanai cage, he judged, especially with their regular spacing and muted glow. But the foliage was too dense for him to see the house or any people that might be occupying the lanai.

He needed a closer look to determine if this residence was indeed his target, so he inched onward, bringing all his skills to bear on a silent passage. Voices filtered through the tangle, raising his hopes and his heartbeat. It would be a true measure of his expertise if he had boated and trekked to the precise location he'd mapped out earlier in the day. He spied a gap in the mat of vegetation and advanced gingerly toward it, lest his anticipation undermine his prowess. He brought the glasses to his eyes and smiled in gratification: the very man and woman he wanted to catch in an unguarded moment!

They were having dinner with their neighbors, so as a bonus he could observe them as well. A young woman was also present, the daughter of the neighbors by the look of her. To ensure the complete success of his mission, though, he needed to be close enough to hear their conversation; lip reading was not his strong suit. A thick bank of palmettos farther on would conceal him and place him within earshot. He edged in that direction, placing his feet with the utmost care and contorting his body to slip through openings in the underbrush. A few feet away, feeling certain of his goal, he relaxed his vigilance and failed to see a protruding root that had grown into a perfect snare. As he pitched headlong into the palmettos, his face smacked the spiked leaves before he could raise his hands in defense.

SEVEN

"What was that?" Richard Lovejoy said, jumping from his chair as if he'd been goosed with a cattle prod. He and Connie had joined the Adamsons and their daughter, Kathy, for dinner on the Adamsons' lanai. The pool water glowed aquamarine, and the luminaires ringing the cage cast the vegetation in a seductive radiance. Richard scooted around the pool and pressed his face against the screen, scanning the preserve in vain for signs of life.

"Oink, oink," Connie intoned sarcastically. She was wearing purple Capri pants, a matching sleeveless top, and pendant earrings whose purple centers were the size of small boulders.

"Go ahead, mock me all you want," Richard said, turning away from the jungle in obvious disappointment, "but I'll be ready when the time comes."

"So the match was at the Plumbago Racquet Club?" Kathy asked as Richard returned to his seat.

"The finals of the 2002 Thanksgiving Turkey Classic," Jack said proudly. "I used a drop shot on the first point, and you won't believe what my opponent did. First, he put his finger to his nose and blew snot on the court, and then he said, 'Goddam, motherfucking Sarasota!'"

"What does your hitting a drop shot have to do with Sarasota?" Richard wondered.

"Or Oedipus?" Kathy noted. She was rewarded with a blank stare from Connie.

"That's what I couldn't figure out," Jack said. "But I used the drop shot every chance I could, and he went to pieces. His swearing was unbelievable—"

"We get the idea," Jill said, frowning.

"You all know the words," Jack said, gesturing dismissively. "But besides cursing Sarasota, he added Katherine Harris and George Bush. He ran all his words together in a stream-of-consciousness rant—it was almost Joycean."

"What did he say when the match was over?" Kathy asked.

"First, he whined that I'd made him run," Jack said.

Richard was incredulous. "That's like a swimmer after a meet complaining that he'd gotten wet."

"Then he said I'd used an 'underhanded' tactic, just what you'd expect from someone living in a city that elected Katherine Harris."

"There's logic for you," Richard scoffed. "I'd say your opponent was a horse's ass."

"His hair *was* in a pony tail," Jack said.

Everyone laughed but Richard, who preferred to deliver the punch lines himself. "He has a point—the politics are pretty conservative around here."

"Are you adding 'conservatism' to your list of things you don't like about Sarasota?" Jack prompted.

Before Richard could answer, Connie interrupted. "I'm so sick of Dickey's list—I love it here, so don't encourage him."

Richard studied the dregs of his Glen Ellen Chardonnay as if the swallow of pale gold remaining in the plastic wineglass could unravel the mysteries of life.

"You guys were really smart not to use glass out here," he said. Then casting a churlish glance toward his wife, "Don't be surprised if I break something on our deck."

Sensing that Richard was primed for a performance, Jack winked at his daughter. Kathy shook her head almost imperceptibly, but covered her face with her napkin to conceal a grin.

"So, are the natives too conservative?" Jack pressed.

"They helped Bush steal the election," Richard said, downing his wine with a sucking noise that caused Connie to scowl.

Jack attentively filled his neighbor's goblet, and like a priest offering a sacrament, held the bottle up to the others. Connie shook her head vehemently, Jill put her hand over the top of her glass, but Kathy nodded yes.

"Thanks, Jack," Richard said. "But I can talk to most people I've met and have a reasonable exchange of views." He took a hearty gulp before continuing, "A caveat, though. This debate in the U.N. seems to be going nowhere. If Bush takes us to war with Iraq—and I think he will—our fellow Sarasotans may not be so reasonable. Patriotism can turn ugly if you don't agree with the patriots."

"I think we should just go in and blow the s.o.b. out of water," Connie said.

"Sand, dear—out of the sand," Richard said in a supercilious tone, as if correcting an erring student.

"Whatever," Connie responded, fiddling with one of her enormous earrings. If she'd been sitting next to her husband, she might've kicked him under the white, cast aluminum table. The frosted glass top would've concealed the deed, but Jill had insisted on mixing up the seating.

"How can you say that?" Kathy asked, joining the fray. "Iraq hasn't attacked us—I'm not worried about Saddam. Let the inspectors keep the pressure on him, and we don't need to do anything."

Connie smiled condescendingly and began ticking off points with the fingers of her right hand. "Honey, he's got weapons of mass destruction, he's harboring terrorists, he gassed the Kurds, and he probably helped with 9/11."

Kathy shook her head. "The only thing we know for sure is that he's killed his own people. He isn't the first dictator to do that—why should we single him out?"

Jill, ever the good hostess, decided to head off this confrontation before any actual blood was shed. She slid back her chair, revealing its lumbar support and delicately etched pattern of fronds and leaves. "How 'bout some dessert? I've got key lime pie or lemon sorbet."

"Can we have both?" Richard asked greedily "Nothing like a double dose of acid to cleanse the palate and tart up the tongue."

"Sure, have all you want," Jill said agreeably. She took her guests' orders and retreated into the house as Connie and Kathy began clearing off the dinner dishes. Nefertiti and Tippy, both somnolent during the human babble, jumped to their feet at the prospect of food and followed the women inside.

The man impaled on the palmetto took advantage of the bustle and adjusted his position so that he could watch and listen more comfortably. He thought for sure that little asshole had seen him—the one called "Richard." The guy was mouthy and liked his liquor. The others didn't impress the man in camouflage, either. Tennis players and Democrats except for the one that looked like a hooker. The enemy is soft, he thought, but it was best to gather more intelligence; first impressions could turn into Trojan horses.

"I *have* added another item to my list," Richard confided, taking an incautious sip of his chardonnay.

Jack's spirits were buoyed—there was still fun to be had. "I'm all ears."

"Our auto insurance is going to cost us more down here than in Connecticut," Richard announced smugly.

Jack was about to contact his company as well, so he was doubly interested in what Richard had to say on this topic. "How can that be—the traffic's a lot worse up there."

"That's the same thing I thought," Richard said. "The agent told me it's because of the mix down here."

Jack didn't conceal his puzzlement. "What do you mean—'mix'?"

Just then the women reemerged bearing dessert, the dogs hot on their heels. "No one wanted any coffee, right?" Jill confirmed. "There's still plenty of wine," she noted, eyeing the second bottle they'd opened, "although that might be a bit much with pie and sorbet."

"Jill, Richard says their auto insurance is going to be more in Florida," Jack remarked as Kathy handed him his plate.

"Oh no," Kathy groaned, "just what I need."

"Jesus," Connie said, giving her head a rapid little shake, "that's all he's been complaining about the last two days."

"Why's that the case?" Jill asked, genuinely interested.

"It's this mix down here, my agent says," Richard replied. He took another hit of chardonnay to fortify himself and then a bite of both desserts to prolong his audience's suspense. "First, you've got the indigenous population—you know, the crackers."

"What does that mean?" Kathy asked. She didn't care if everyone else knew—she wanted to know the answer.

"The cowboys who drive cattle with whips," Richard explained.

"Ah," Kathy said, her eyebrows raising in enlightenment.

"Anyway," Richard continued, "they and their progeny drive around like NASCAR nincompoops. Imagine that toothless inbred form *Deliverance* coming at you in a truck with mag wheels."

"It's more likely he'd be rear-ending you," Jack quipped wryly as he relished a bite of pie. Kathy giggled, but the frown furrows between Jill's eyes deepened in disapproval.

SIXTY IN SARASOTA

Ignoring the interruption, Richard said, "Then there's the old people—not us—I mean the really old people, who can't see, and drive too slow and leave their turn signal on all day."

"That's an exaggeration," Jill said as she slid some sorbet into her mouth.

Undeterred, Richard didn't miss a beat. "Next we've got foreigners—like the English, who don't know which side of the road to drive on. And the Germans—they know how to drive, but you better damn well drive the same way."

"Don't forget the Canadians," Jack offered, "here for six months minus one day before they hightail it back to Canada to collect their health insurance."

"No, let's forget them," Richard said. "They're not as bad as the hordes of tourists from the North—the snowturds."

"Snow*birds*, Dickey—I'm sick of hearing that shit," Connie said.

Kathy snorted, drawing a daggered glower from Mrs. Lovejoy.

"A quarter of a million of 'em in season," Richard proclaimed. "They don't know where they're going, and they drive as slow as the old farts. They're starting to appear in droves—I'm sure you've noticed how traffic's backing up everywhere."

"We were snowbirds once," Jill said, pointing a fork at Richard.

"Yes, Jill, that's true, and we're only a little more familiar with the roads than they are." He dabbed at he corners of his mouth with his napkin. "And to top it all off," he concluded expansively, "I-75 runs north/south along the city, everybody trying to get someplace or get the hell out of Florida. RV's, boat trailers, eighteen wheelers—all of 'em going at least eighty miles per hour, unless it's an old fart or a snowturd who's lost. No doubt about it, it's more dangerous to drive here than in a big Northern city."

"I guess that means we'll be paying more, too," Jill surmised, looking gloomily at Jack She disliked financial surprises, especially now that they were living on a retirement income.

"It's not so bad for you guys," Kathy complained, "but I really don't need any extra expenses." She decided that she'd kept her big secret long enough and added, "Of course, things are looking up after today."

Jill stared at her daughter. "What do you mean—are you and Brad getting back together?"

"Mom . . . that's not going to happen. No, I have a new client," she said, draining her glass.

Jack leaned forward in his chair. "You mean you've been sitting on this news all evening? Come on—who is it?"

Kathy recounted the events of the day, being careful to identify Masterson only as a representative of the museum. She also avoided mention of possible suspects and how she planned to proceed with her investigation. She held their attention easily, even Mrs. Lovejoy, who softened visibly as Kathy described her intimate examination of the statue.

"Oh, I hope you find out who did it, honey," Connie said. "That was a terrible thing." She batted her eyebrows at no one in particular. "He had the cutest butt and his front—well, who wouldn't be attracted to that?"

"I wouldn't," Richard volunteered.

Jack snickered in mid-swallow, sending a bubble of chardonnay and sorbet up his nose.

Because Connie seemed to be offering an olive branch—or perhaps a fig leaf—Kathy said, "Thanks, Connie, I'll certainly do my best." But she couldn't resist adding, "I know those in the arts community share your sentiment."

"We're all sorry it happened," Richard said. "If you ask me, a religious freak did it—in fact, I'd bet money on it. Do you have any suspects?"

"I have some leads," Kathy answered guardedly, "and some lines of inquiry I plan to pursue."

Sensing immediately that her daughter was reluctant to discuss the specifics of her new case, Jill came to her rescue. "I don't think that Kathy should be sharing any confidential information with us. She wouldn't want to betray her employer's trust or compromise her investigation."

"That's right, Dickey, don't be so nosy," Connie chimed in.

"I was just curious, for Christ's sake. He had such a cute butt, you know," Richard added sarcastically.

The tension in their conversation pained Kathy, reminding her of stabs that she and Brad had taken at each other. "There's really not much to report now because I've barely begun, but I'll give my parents progress reports and they can pass the details on to you."

A resounding crash in the preserve focused their attention beyond the cage—Nefertiti and Tippy rose as one, skirting the pool and barking at the back screen. The humans left their dessert and wine and followed the dogs, straining in the early darkness to see what beast might appear.

"There," Jack intoned in a stage whisper, pointing to their right.

Padding along the edge of the greenbelt, drain plug snout to the ground, tusks curving backward from its mouth, was a hairy-faced feral hog boar. The animal lifted its head, tested the air, and plunged heavily through a cleft in the forest. It was not the barking dogs or gaping people that hastened the creature's departure, however. A knee-high bobcat with tufted ears, tawny coat, and trademark short tail appeared—hot on the trail—and dissolved into the same breach. The cat's stealth was as remarkable as the boar's bullishness.

"Did you see how sleek its fur was?" Jill asked, who agreed with PETA on the issue of fur coats, but had yet to give up meat.

Unimpressed, Richard said prophetically, "I *knew* it would come to this. I've gotta go!" He barged through the group, banged out the screen door, and dashed to the back of his house.

"Oh God," Connie said in disgust, shaking her head.

"What's the matter?" Kathy asked, bewildered by his sense of urgency.

Her father pushed his nose into a piggy shape. "Oink, Oink—attack of the feral hogs."

"I only saw one," Kathy said, sniggering, as she struggled to make out porcine shapes in the darkness, "and the cat was chasing it."

Somewhere Richard threw a switch, illuminating the preserve behind his home in the beams of floodlights. Next he set off the toddler alarm keyed to the sliding door that opened onto his pool from the main house. At the sound of the siren, Tippy and Nefertiti ceased their barking, only to turn their heads to the heavens and burst forth in wolfish ululations.

"What next?" Kathy shouted above the din, not realizing that there would indeed be more.

From stereo speakers mounted on the Lovejoys' lanai, Led Zeppelin exploded into a million decibels of "Whole Lotta Love."

"I would've preferred 'Stairway to Heaven,'" Jack screamed, "but I guess that slow build doesn't work for Richard."

Finally, Richard himself emerged, carrying two large cookie pans. He began banging them together, not at all in time with the music, as he marched back and forth across his lawn like a drum major.

"Is he going to do this every time a hog shows up?" Jill yelled, fingers in both ears.

"You know Dickey," Connie bellowed, "once he gets something in his head—we'll be the laughingstock of the neighborhood."

It was all Jack could do to refrain from screeching "you already are." Besides, he wanted the fun to continue—and it was only fitting. He and Jill had provided the food, and the Lovejoys had provided the entertainment.

The man crouching in the palmetto had been as startled by the appearance of the boar and bobcat as the subjects of his surveillance. The animals had sliced into the preserve only a few feet from him and disappeared rapidly to his right. The opportunity was ripe, he decided, to make his escape without detection. He'd seen and heard enough, though, to determine that these people would be no match for him. They were nothing but a bunch of self-absorbed yuppies, and he'd be able to carry out his plan with little or no opposition. As he began descending the bank to the river, however, he heard a security alarm and the howling of dogs, followed by a male screaming at the top of his lungs. He plunged helter-skelter down the slope, lost his footing, and toppled forward heavily, grabbing at underbrush as he slid out of control toward the water.

PART TWO

EIGHT

Little pins of discouragement had begun to prick Kathy King's resolve. Admittedly, finding a buyer of white spray paint who might've had a motive for defacing the statue was a long shot. She'd planned to limit her inspection of purchase records to those cans bought a few days before the commission of the crime. If the vandal had used a can in his or her possession for a lengthy period of time, Kathy reasoned, she was out of luck. There would simply be too many containers out there. She'd focused on Wal-Mart, Home Depot, and Lowe's—high profile stores with dependable inventories and competitive prices. And she'd struck out.

Not a single store would give her access to its records. She could've lied to management, a tactic permissible for private investigators, though not the police. Invented a crime both bloody and heinous—say, sexual battery with a paint can—but she'd told the truth. Kathy had figured that community outrage at the affront to a Sarasota landmark would carry the day. Boy, had she been naïve. Fear of litigation, bad publicity, accusations of racial profiling (if Kathy glommed onto a minority), yadda, yadda, yadda—the privacy of each store's customers was sacrosanct.

And now she was sitting, as if she'd been a bad girl, in the principal's office at Hernando de Soto High School, a relatively new institution just east of I-75, and one of several schools in Florida and other states based on the Spaniard's name. De Soto had explored the surrounding region in the first half of the 16th century, and legend had it that his daughter Sara was the origin of the city's name. There were alternate theories as well: Sarasota was from the Spanish meaning "a place of dancing," or from a local Indian word denoting "a landfall easily observed."

Shortly after Kathy had arrived in town, the newspaper had been filled with controversy brewing over the school's name. Descendants of native Indians, having stewed over the issue for four years, demanded that it be changed, appalled that a man noted for his brutality to their race could lend his name to a public building. African-Americans were quick to suggest that the school be rechristened Martin Luther King, Jr. High School, but a vocal Hispanic contingent cried "no way, José." In the end, the various strands of political correctness tangled into an insoluble knot and the school's moniker remained, uneasily, the same.

Principal Goren was not in his office at the moment, having left to yank a student from class and escort him to a meeting with Kathy. The room was undistinguished except for two unavoidable objects of interest. Just inside the door was a life-sized, stand-up figure of Steve Spurrier, famous former coach of the University of Florida football team. Emblazoned on the colorless wall behind Goren's desk was a huge orange and blue pennant, proclaiming "Go Gators!" Kathy could only assume that the principal felt uncomfortable promoting his own school's mascots, the Conquistadors, but safe urging on the university's reptiles. Perhaps the image of an armored Spaniard holding aloft the bloody, decapitated head of an Indian was more repugnant than the snapping jaws of an alligator.

Goren, balding, square-jawed, and broad chested—looking from his paunch like a lineman gone to seed—suddenly filled the doorway. Kathy was certain that he was a former physical education teacher and coach. As a matter of fact, her high school principal had taught PE, and her dad had toiled under a former PE teacher. What was the story there?

"Come on in and have a seat, Dan," Goren ordered rather than offered.

A surly teenager with a buzz cut stared suspiciously at Kathy from the hallway and demonstrated no inclination to comply. Goren backed out and placed his hand between the boy's shoulder blades, causing the youth to flinch visibly.

"You're not in any trouble, young man . . . yet," Goren said as he ushered Dan into the office. "In fact, you might be able to help Mrs. King here—a chance to be a team player."

"You mean like look for an opening and run with the ball, Dr. Goren?" Dan said tepidly as he sat next to Kathy.

"That's the spirit, Dan," Goren said, energized. "Gimme five." He slapped at the boy's limply outstretched hand. "I'll leave you two alone—lunch is coming up." He moved nimbly through the doorway in spite of his bulk and closed the door crisply in his wake.

"Sorry to pull you out of what I'm sure was an interesting class," Kathy began.

"Yeah . . . right . . . I wasn't even with my regular teacher," he replied, staring down at the floor.

"Oh?" Kathy said with genuine interest. "Why's that?"

"Remediation—I haven't passed that dumb FCAT yet." He gave her a sideways glance to see the effect of this revelation.

Kathy remembered passing basic skill tests in writing and math before graduating from high school in Maryland. All the time preparing for the tests had been a colossal waste when she could've been learning something really valuable.

"You don't strike me as dumb, Dan. Is the test really difficult?"

He grimaced in contempt. "Only if you're a friggin' moron. I just haven't paid any attention to all the crap in class—all the 'strategies' for passing the test."

Dan's appearance didn't square with his disdain. He was wearing clean khaki pants and a dark green polo with the school's logo in yellow over his left breast—a conquistador's head inside a circle. But Kathy recalled having seen some other students in the same apparel.

"Is that some sort of uniform?" she asked, gesturing toward his attire.

Dan nodded. "We're s'posed to wear it once a week—every Friday. Sorta like a trial run. They may require it every day next year . . . thank God I'm graduating."

He said this as if his completion of high school were a fait accompli, then seemed to recognize the irony of his words. He fidgeted a few seconds before regaining his composure, the false manly confidence affected by so my teenage boys.

"What's the 'yet' s'posed to mean . . . Mrs. King?" Dan asked in mock deference. "Goren . . . Dr. Goren said I wasn't in trouble 'yet.'" The boy even began giving Kathy the once-over, making no effort to conceal his insolence.

She returned his gaze frankly, knowing full well that he was checking out her profile and legs. Guys his age stashed their brains in their dicks, a circumstance she might use to her advantage. To solve an investigation, any tactic was permissible—short of breaking the law. She uncrossed and crossed her legs, giving him a brief flash of thigh.

"You can call me Kathy, Dan. To be honest, anything you say stays between the two of us. I'm not planning to tell Dr. Goren the particulars of our conversation. But he knows that I'm investigating an incident that happened away from school and not during school hours."

Dan's eyes widened, his cockiness ebbing on the heels of her disclosure. "You a policeman . . . er, uh, policewoman?"

Kathy smiled—political correctness could even tyrannize an adolescent male. "Private investigator. I found out from Dr. Goren that there are 'clubs'—for want of a better word—that the school doesn't authorize, but they exist all the same."

"Yeah," Dan said guardedly. He stared at his nails as if some incriminating evidence might be lodged beneath them.

Kathy continued to bait him. "Well, he knows about your group, it's no big secret. What's the name?"

Dan calculated, then grinned with a puff of pride. "Crazy Crackers. You know, party hardy, girls, booze."

"Um," Kathy said, "sounds like fun." She uncrossed and crossed her legs again. "No drugs?"

Dan was offended. "No freaks, losers, or 'heads need apply."

It was such a snappy little slogan that she was sure he'd said it many times before. "So you have some kind of initiation for new members?"

"You like to join?" he leered. He began running a hand along the edge of the Spurrier likeness. Then he stopped abruptly, his expression suggesting he knew why Kathy was interrogating him. "This is about the beer trailer, isn't it? Hey, we can pay for the brew."

She pretended interest, not knowing where this particular fishing expedition might lead. "Why don't you tell me about it?"

"We were lettin' in some new guys—sophomores—freshmen can't hold their liquor, you know." He looked sagely at Kathy and she nodded in agreement.

"The county fair was goin' on, a hot day, and they had this trailer loaded with kegs for backup in a barn. So to get into the Crackers, our new guys had to steal the trailer."

Dan became more animated now as he remembered the event, gesturing with his hands and smiling because he knew he was telling such an entertaining story.

"No one was payin' any attention, and as they pulled it through the crowd, they said they were taking kegs to the beer stands. Well, they hooked the sucker up to a van and drove it outta there, nine bitchin' kegs!"

Here was a real fountain of youth, Kathy determined. "What'd you do with it?" she asked.

"One of our dads has an old garage back in the country. We hid it in there and had brewski up the wazoo." He positively glowed at the memory.

Like mother's milk, Kathy thought, but not the prank she had in mind. "I tell you what, Dan, I'll keep that story under my hat if you fill me in on some other initiations."

"Sure, why not," he said almost too quickly. "We got this one I know you'd like. We have a party and the guy has to stand around naked the whole time. Man, does he take some shit in school the next day."

Dan seemed disappointed when Kathy didn't react with shock to this nugget. "Uh huh, I get the picture. What else?"

Dan pursed his lips in concentration. "There's so many . . . ah, we give a guy a wedgie, pull down his pants, and then make him spell his name on the ground with his butt."

Jim Carrey was alive and well at Hernando de Soto High. Kathy decided to narrow the scope for Dan. "Tell me this, did one of your classes ever go to the Ringling Museum for a field trip?" She already knew the answer; it was the first thing she'd checked with Goren.

Dan was perplexed by this apparent change in direction. "Yeah . . . why? What's that got to do with the Crackers?"

"What do you remember about the day?" Kathy pressed.

He considered a few moments. "Not much . . . it was nice not bein' cooped up in the classroom." Then his eyes brightened. "Wait a minute—there was this statue, a big dude, outside, I think."

"*David?*" Kathy suggested helpfully.

"Yeah, that's it. All the girls thought he had a great bod and were calling him a 'stud muffin.' Geez, he was hung like a horse."

"Do you talk to all the girls this way, Dan?" Kathy said, though it took some effort to suppress a smile.

Dan actually blushed. "I'm sorry, Mrs. King . . . I wasn't thinkin', and it's not like you're a teacher—"

"Never mind, Dan," she said with a dismissive wave of her hand. "What I want to know is this: did your group—the Crackers—dream up some initiation involving the statue?"

He gaped at her as if she were completely mad. "Only a buncha geeks would think of something like that. Why?"

"Well, you know what happened to the statue, don't you?"

His blank stare was too natural to be feigned. "What're you talkin' about?"

She looked him in the eye with as much gravity as she could muster. "You must not read the paper or watch the news—some one broke off the penis and painted the rear end white."

Dan crossed his legs and blanched. "Ooh, that's cold." Then the light bulb clicked on. "You think I had something to do with it?"

"Did you?" she fired back rapidly.

"No," he answered just as quickly.

"And since you didn't even know the statue had been vandalized, I guess you haven't heard about anyone who might've done it?" she said, answering her own question.

"No, when did it happen?" he said, sincerely curious.

"Beginning of November—tell you what Dan, you keep your ear to the ground over the Christmas holidays and then call me if you have some information." She stood up and fished a business card from her purse, handing it to the young man.

He scrutinized it as if it might blow up in his hands. "Is this really your number?"

She nodded.

"And I can call you any time?" he asked incredulously.

"That's right, Dan." She hoped he wouldn't turn into a pest.

"Aren't you going to swab me before you go?" he asked plaintively.

Kathy's eyebrows shot up. "Swab you?"

"You know," he said hopefully, "like they do on CSI. I love it when that hot redhead swabs some guy."

She swallowed a laugh. "I don't think I need your DNA, Dan."

As she turned to leave, he said, "I'll be sure to call you . . . Kathy."

She shot him a warning glance, "You do that, Dan—but don't expect to get swabbed."

NINE

Sarasota was a center of arts and culture, one of the many seductions that Jack and Jill Adamson had surrendered to when choosing the city as their retirement home. Besides the Ringling Museum and the Asolo Theatre Company, the "place of dancing" also boasted the Van Wezel Performing Arts Hall, the Sarasota Opera, the Florida West Coast Symphony, and the Sarasota Ballet.

On this particular evening, the Adamsons weren't attending one of these convenient attractions, but were instead comfortably ensconced in the Burns Court Cinema for a screening of "Lantana," which had already played at the Sarasota Film Festival. Though downtown, Burns Court was paradoxically quaint, with its narrow streets, art galleries, antique and specialty stores, bistros, and brightly painted villas. Tucked inconspicuously into the neighborhood, the cinema was also charming and old fashioned, a cozy playhouse with three screens catering to independent and foreign productions. It didn't have stadium seating nor did it rise obnoxiously—like so many suburban multiplexes—from a strip mall.

The theater was full; the white noise of innocuous chatter, the urgent melodies of cell phones, and the cloying smell of buttered popcorn filled the air. Jack was indulging himself in a plentiful bag of M&Ms, offering them to Jill more to test her resolve than to actually share them. He was intoxicated by chocolate, but she viewed the substance as something the serpent might have offered Eve. Neither Adamson had a weight problem—Jack considered desserts his reward for all his exercise on the tennis court. For Jill, desserts were anathema; sugar and fat were stealthy enemies that conspired to sandbag the hourglass figure she'd maintained since her college days.

During the previews of coming attractions, Jack became somewhat alarmed that the babble of the moviegoers didn't lessen significantly. One couple just behind him seemed driven by a compulsion to share their shallow and obvious reactions to the previews with anyone within hearing range. "Watch, he's going to kiss her," the man predicted. "Wow, that was some kiss," the woman marveled. Just in front of Jill, who was sitting to Jack's right, a woman was working on a box of popcorn the size of Asia. Her thrusting, rustling, and chomping incited Jack to imagine firing an M&M at her defenseless ear. He, of course, was meticulously careful not to crackle his candy wrapper or slurp his goodies.

The shallow couple continued their commentary as the movie began. "Why is it called 'Lantana'?" the woman asked. "I don't know," replied her baffled partner. Why don't you watch the movie and figure it out? Jack thought darkly.

"They're Australian," the man announced, after the actors had spoken a few lines. "I'm going to have trouble understanding them," whined his linguistically challenged seatmate. They're not extraterrestrials, Jack wanted to say.

The married Australian policeman in the film was having an affair with a woman recently separated from her husband, circumstances inducing some discomfort and guilt in the adulterers. Not enough to keep them from screwing each other's brains out, Jack noted, as he admired the actors' technique. The popcorn woman—whether from the passion on the screen or her unbridled appetite—began choking grimly during the scene's climax.

"Gack, gaaaaack, gack, gaaaaaaack," then momentary silence as she desperately stuck a finger down her throat. The digit's insertion prompted an explosion of coughing, deep, chest-rattling hacks that culminated in the expulsion of a brobdingnagian kernel that arced gracefully toward the screen—coincidentally, just as the features of Anthony LaPaglia's cop contorted in orgasm.

"I can't believe what these foreign films get away with," chirped the woman behind Jack. "Wow!" her partner bleated. The popcorn woman fled the theater, ostensibly for water, much to Jack's relief. He was rusty—it had been years since he'd performed the Heimlich maneuver. When she returned, she was still plagued by some anticlimactic coughing, the sort provoked by a maddening tickle.

Finally, both the shallow couple and the popcorn woman lapsed into blessed silence. Jack attributed the cessation of sound to the compelling story on the screen. Four couples' marital lives were linked by a series of coincidences, including the apparent murder of one of the women. The policeman's investigation of the "crime" tightened the chain even further until the screenplay's resolution. What struck Jack as so unusual was the film's focus on the marital relationships rather than the crime. Had the story been given a Hollywood treatment, the emphasis would have been reversed.

As he and Jill were exiting the theater, she asked, "Why do you think it was called 'Lantana'?"

"Well, the thicket of flowers was beautiful, but the woman's body was found underneath." He guided her gently, his hand on her back, as they stepped off the curb and crossed a side street.

"So things that are beautiful on the surface may reveal ugliness if they're examined really closely or deeply," Jill said as they moved away from the other moviegoers.

"Yeah, like the marriages in the story, or any paradise, or even life in general," he reasoned, scanning an intersecting street for traffic. He didn't see any cars, but a solitary man was approaching, his purposeful manner setting off alarms in Jack's brain.

The pedestrian was black, a feature that Jack attempted to ignore, but he couldn't help wondering if a lone Caucasian would have sparked the same concern. As the walker neared, his unkempt hair, ill-fitting shirt, and scruffy jeans inspired further apprehension.

"Let's move quickly," Jack murmured to his wife, nudging her in the back.

"Why, what's the matter?" she said, not sharing his uneasiness.

"I don't like the look of that guy," he replied. Jack spoke quietly out of the side of his mouth, averting his eyes from the man.

Jill glanced in his direction and frowned. "Don't be silly."

Only a few strides away, the man asked, "Hey, friends, can you spare some change for a vet?"

Playing on our guilt and sympathy, Jack thought. He stared ahead toward their car—still a block away—and hustled Jill along, his arm firmly around her back.

"Come on, man, you can look me in the face," the panhandler chided. He was walking next to the Adamsons now in the pinched street, matching their pace.

His tone seemed more disapproval than anger, Jack hoped. But he still feared a physical confrontation. Reconnoitering as nonchalantly as possible, he searched in vain for anyone who might respond to a call for help.

"You don't have to worry about me, man," their stalker said, correctly gauging Jack's state of mind. He rested a hand on Jack's shoulder, which shrank visibly from the touch.

Jack's entire body was now tensed in readiness, as if waiting for an opponent's serve. He was fit, he could put up a fight—didn't muggers usually avoid his type? The man jerked his hand away, and Jack stared hard at him for the first time. Stared at his hands really, scanning them for any sign of a weapon. He would push Jill onward and confront the man if it came to that.

"Maybe you expect *us* to entertain you," the fellow blurted incongruously. He ran a few steps beyond the Adamsons and began to shuffle, his sandpaper thin soles whispering a soft-shoe on the pavement.

Jack was reminded of Lucky's grotesque dance in *Waiting for Godot*, painful movements provoked by an inexplicable existence.

Jill gaped at her husband for the first time during the encounter, "What in God's name . . . ?" They skirted the absurd ballet and made for their car, beckoning like a life raft in an asphalt ocean.

The man left the street and bounded onto the sidewalk. "We can tell jokes, too, you know. How 'bout this one: why did the black man buy twenty boxes of tampons? And it has nothin' to do with his woman."

Jack reached for his keys; the car was only a few yards away. And yet he found himself trying to answer the question in his own mind.

"Not going to play, are we?" their tormentor chastised. "I'll tell you why—because he wanted to put on a menstrual show. Get it? 'Show,' not 'flow.' You know, banjos and black face, Shirley Temple and Mr. Bojangles, yes massah, and all that jazz."

Jack got it, and Jill, too. He thumbed his remote at the same time, lighting the car and opening the locks. "Let's go," he hissed, releasing her. They bolted to the doors, opened them, slid in, and slammed them shut. Jack hit the locks and jammed the key into the ignition in a single, fluid movement.

"Wasn't that performance worth something?" the man shouted. "Hey, I was nice—you don't wanna see me do Denzel's 'Training Day' thing."

Jack rammed the car into gear and screeched the tires. "Stick those tampons up your ass, you fucker," he muttered between clenched teeth as he and Jill fled Burns Court.

"Jack!" Jill scolded as he maneuvered toward Tamiami Trail.

"Well, dammit, the guy had no business accosting us like that," Jack said as he turned north.

"He was aggressive, wasn't he," Jill agreed, softening. "And I thought the panhandlers outside Camden Yards were bad." They both remembered running that gauntlet in Baltimore before the Orioles' games—outstretched hands from the parking garage to Eutaw Street.

"Yeah, but I didn't expect an encounter like that in downtown Sarasota," Jack said, frowning. "I guess some things are the same everywhere."

He could feel the rush of adrenaline subsiding now as he focused on his driving. Traffic was light on the Trail at this time of night, and soon the Adamsons were speeding by such familiar city landmarks as the new Ritz-Carlton and the Van Wezel Performing Arts Hall.

As they approached the customary sign pointing west toward Jungle Gardens, a dark sedan with no lights suddenly turned south onto their northbound lane. Jack honked violently but the other car made no attempt to even move toward the median.

"Jack, look out!" Jill shrieked.

Jack wasn't about to play chicken with an obviously deranged driver. He cut the steering wheel hard to the right, running roughly over the curb and onto a narrow strip of landscaping at a Mobil gas station. The sedan continued onward unfazed—a white head barely at the level of the dash seemed to be in control, so to speak.

"Jesus fucking Christ!" Jill snapped, steadying herself and craning her neck to watch the progress of the other car. It continued on its misguided way, scattering other vehicles in its wake.

"Jill!" Jack scolded as he carefully inched their car back onto the street.

"Well, that old fart just about killed us," she said. "Did you see him—his head was below the wheel."

"It could've been a woman," Jack mused. "It's hard to tell when they get to be that age."

His wife shot him a disapproving look and shook her head. He proceeded to their right turn on University without further incident and soon they were in the safety of their garage. Jill fled the car as if her life depended on it and disappeared into the house without comment. Taking his time, Jack closed the automatic door, unthinkingly reset the security code that his wife had just disarmed seconds earlier, and hung his keys on the lighthouse peg in their laundry room. Jill opened the lanai slider to take Nefertiti for her bedtime walk and shortly the security klaxons bellowed through the neighborhood.

"Shit," Jack cursed, scrambling to turn them off.

Twenty minutes later, they were in the reassuring cocoon of their bed, on the precipice of blissful sleep.

"You know," Jack mumbled, "maybe an early bird matinee would be a good idea in the future."

Jill grunted and pulled her pillow over her head.

TEN

Brett Masterson had surprised Kathy by suggesting a change in their routine. Normally, he met with her each Friday in her office for a progress report, but today he'd proposed lunch at a restaurant not far from her modest cabana on Siesta Key. While elated by this prospect, she was also discouraged that she would have to deliver a lack of progress report. True, she'd been investigating barely more than a month—even less taking into account the Christmas holidays—but she'd hoped to justify the money she was earning with at least some small breakthrough.

The restaurant was located one street south of the Stickney Point drawbridge, the only egress from her end of the key. The bridge was also a source of frustration for Kathy, invariably up whether she was going or coming. She didn't care that it was picturesque. Farther north, the city fathers had come to the same conclusion regarding the Ringling Causeway Bridge, connecting downtown Sarasota to Bird, St. Armands, Lido, and Longboat Keys. A single span bridge, the widest of its kind in the world, would soon replace the current drawbridge, hopefully eliminating the gridlock it produced.

She had no trouble locating Fandango's, a two-tiered affair, its rainbow sign glistening in the warm January sunshine. Masterson was already standing by the front door, and she waved brightly as she drove up, eliciting a small wave and a smile from her employers' representative.

"Didn't this place used to be down in Siesta Village?" she asked after stepping out of her car.

"Yes, I believe you're right," Brett replied. His pulse quickened at the casual tone of her voice. He wished that he could slip as easily into informality—a quality that had attracted him to Kathy. He'd suggested the restaurant setting for that very purpose, hoping that he'd feel less inhibited than he did in her office. As he looked at Kathy now, he could tell there was something different about her hair, but how was he to tell her—without awkwardness—that he found the change attractive?

"But it was really small—I think I ate out front with my grandparents a couple of times."

"I guess the owners saw an opportunity here—anyway, I can vouch for the food, it's fantastic," he said, pushing the door open for her. "I . . . I like your hair."

"Oh," she said eagerly, "better than before?"

What was he supposed to say now? "Well . . . uh . . . I liked it then, too."

"So, you've been observing my hair, have you, Brett? Spying on my follicles?"

He reddened, but managed to laugh. He enjoyed being teased by her, though he was never quite sure how to respond.

"It was nice of you to notice," she said, touching him lightly on the arm. "I had this poofy Farrah Fawcett thing before—a holdover from my adolescence. This is supposed to be sleeker," she said, running her right hand through her hair, "sculpted, sexier."

Their hostess arrived, and Brett was rescued from commenting on Kathy's final adjective. As they were being led to their table, Kathy had a troubling thought: he's going to think I'm spending my paychecks on hairdressers and wasting my time in salons. But it had been a long time since she'd spent some real money on herself, she rationalized. Brett probably had no idea what a cut like hers cost, anyway, or that the stylist had imbued Kathy's brunette tresses with highlights.

The restaurant was filled with natural light from large, tinted windows, revealing a rich, wooden bar at the back and two floors of tables in the front. They were seated on the lower level, which had a bandstand for evening performances in the right corner.

A slim, attractive waitress made the standard offer of drinks, and Kathy was considering her usual selection of diet soda until Brett said, "The margaritas are good."

"Why not," Kathy said, throwing calories to the wind. "On the rocks with salt, please." Then by way of explanation, she added, "The last frozen margarita I drank hit a brain nerve and nearly paralyzed me."

"Don't you hate that?" the waitress said sympathetically.

"I'll have the same," Brett said, pleased that Kathy had accepted his suggestion. He was emboldened even further after their server left. "Don't even bother to study the menu," he said confidentially.

Kathy was non-plussed, but only for a moment. Brett Masterson was actually treating her like a date, she guessed. "The gentleman is going to recommend a certain dish for the lady?" she said, smiling at him.

"They have a grouper sandwich that's to die for," Brett said. Though he'd never said "to die for" before, he knew that people used the phrase in this context. And if he was ever going sound more casual, he had to take some chances—even with words that felt foreign to his tongue.

"Oh, really. I love grouper—not sure I'd drown for one, though." She flipped open her menu. "What's so special about this grouper?" she asked, as if testing his powers of persuasion.

"First, they marinate it, then they wrap it in pita bread, and finally they fill the bread with Greek salad." He surprised himself by gesturing like a chef.

"That *does* sound good," Kathy said enthusiastically. "Yes, I see it on the menu here," she added, reading the description. "Well, you've convinced me, Brett, but it better be good," she warned playfully as she closed the menu.

The waitress arrived with their drinks and left with their order. Kathy took a healthy sip, running her tongue along her lips to capture the salt. Unfortunately, it was time to talk business, but she hoped the alcohol would make it easier.

"I haven't had any more success getting those stores to release their sales records," she began. "Of course, it was a long shot in the first place."

"Perhaps," Brett said thoughtfully, "but any avenue is worth exploring. I might be able to help you with their reluctance."

Kathy stared at him. "What do you mean?"

"My employers have a certain amount of influence— rather far reaching, actually. It's a subject I can broach with them. In the meantime, what about other areas of investigation?"

"I've been to just about every school that's sponsored a field trip to the museum, talked to several students, and turned up nothing. The kids don't even think it's the kind of prank one of them would've pulled off. My little admirer from De Soto High did call the other day, though," she said, smirking.

"Oh?" Brett said, inwardly startled by his annoyance. He remembered her account of flirting with the young man, who she'd hoped would reveal information.

"Yeah, 'just checking in,' he said. I think he wanted to see if it was really my number. Said he'd been asking around, but no one knew anything about the statue. Then he spent the rest of the conversation tying to wangle an invitation to my office."

"Well, if he's got your card, he can find it on his own," Brett said, trying not to show the displeasure he felt.

"I pretty much discouraged him," Kathy said, "but I thought it was kind of cute all the same."

Brett didn't think it was cute at all, but said nothing as the hostess guided some other diners to a nearby table. It bothered him that Kathy seemed to enjoy the crude attentions of the young man, even if he turned out to be an important source.

"I do think that Dan is snooping for me, and he does get around to other schools for sporting events—so I haven't given up on him yet," Kathy concluded.

Hearing her speak the boy's name in such a familiar way irritated Brett further, but he masked his anger by calmly unfolding his silverware and placing his napkin in his lap. His actions took on an air of prescience when the waitress promptly appeared with their sandwiches.

To say that the sight and smell of the food made Kathy's mouth water would be understating the case. The golden brown slab of grouper, marinated and Mediterranean grilled, exuded a faintly spicy aroma as it lay swathed in Greek salad—olive oil and feta cheese oozing lasciviously around the edges of the pita bread.

"Can I bring you anything else—another round of margaritas?" the waitress asked.

"I'd like some water," Kathy said, eyeing the sandwich as she mapped out a preliminary plan of attack.

"The same," Brett said.

"Here goes," Kathy said, taking a cautious bite from one end of the succulent concoction. She managed to savor some of all the ingredients, but spilled food onto her plate in the process. The grouper didn't taste like fish at all, more like an imagined meat, impossibly soft and intoxicatingly seasoned.

"Umm, that's unbelievably good," Kathy moaned.

"It's ruined me for any other grouper," Brett said. "This is the only place where I'll order it."

Kathy grinned wickedly as he attacked his sandwich. "Do you remember the eating scene from the movie *Tom Jones?*" Brett could only shake his head as he worked on his mouthful. "Never saw it," he finally said.

"Well, this man and woman are gorging themselves at a big table—a feast—and the way they eat each type of food . . ." Describing the sexual symbolism of gnawing on a chicken leg or sucking on a clam suddenly seemed inappropriate for a business lunch; she decided not to go any further. "It's hard to explain, you have to see it for yourself."

He nodded agreeably, though he had no clue what she was talking about. He was delighted, however, with the way she was relishing the entrée he'd recommended. They ate in silence for several minutes, so engrossed in feeding themselves that they barely acknowledged the waitress when she returned with their water.

Kathy polished off her margarita and started on the tall glass of water garnished with a lemon. "Something disturbing happened to my parents the other night," she said. "I've been thinking about it, and the incident might have some relevance to our case."

Alarmed, Brett said, "What happened? Are they all right?"

"Oh, they're fine, just a bit unsettled, that's all. They were accosted by a homeless man down at Burns Court." Kathy proceeded to recount the details of the incident, though she omitted the outlandish joke the man had told.

Brett shook his head disapprovingly. "I can see where they thought they might be in danger. Pretty bad when you can't go to a movie downtown without something like that happening. You know the police swept the homeless camps recently—vacant lots, woods—they didn't find that many. But when it starts to get cold up North, we get more of them, just like the snowbirds."

Kathy carefully wiped the last vestiges of her sandwich from her lips. "Yeah, well, what I was thinking is that a homeless person might've vandalized the statue."

Brett sipped thoughtfully on the remainder of his margarita. "What would be the motive?"

She placed her napkin on her plate and fiddled briefly with her silverware. "Let's say a guy gets rousted from the grounds of the museum, then sneaks back in on the night in question to exact his revenge."

"Hmm," Brett said. "You could check with security to see if they've kicked any vagrants off the grounds." As an afterthought, he added, "Mondays are free days at the museum. I could see a homeless person taking advantage of the air conditioning and even the art."

"And maybe falling asleep on a bench or creating a stink," Kathy said, wrinkling her nose.

Brett chuckled. "Always with the joke."

"It's genetic," Kathy said. "My father does it all the time—you'll have to meet him, and my mother."

"I'd like that," Brett said, and he genuinely meant it.

ELEVEN

The joke in Sarasota is that winter lasts about two days, usually some time in January. But even the average temperature for that month reaches into the low seventies. Jack figured that those two days had just passed—one day had only crawled to the upper fifties, and one night had plunged to thirty-four degrees. He and Richard had covered their plants, his neighbor going to such excessive lengths that he might as well have invested in a tarp cut to the dimensions of the yard. Richard had cursed the weather, adding it to his list of Sarasota's defects just below the dangers posed by homeless people. He had nodded as if to say "I told you so" when Jack had colorfully narrated the Burns Court adventure; even Connie had been shaken by the account.

This morning the sun had rediscovered its strength, though, and Jack and Richard were relaxing on the Adamsons' lanai. Jill was at Selby Botanical Gardens in downtown Sarasota, where she volunteered her time to teach visiting classes from the local schools. Connie had rushed off to Bealls department store for a senior days sale.

"How's your new neighbor?" Jack asked. "I heard he's a widower."

"Yeah, that's a little odd, don't you think?" Richard replied. "It's usually the man who croaks as soon as a couple retires here. I think he's about our age, but there's something else peculiar about the guy."

Overly familiar by now with Richard's tendency to exaggerate, Jack was skeptical. "What do you mean?"

"He spends all his time staring at the preserve—just stands in his yard looking. Sometimes he walks right up to the edge and gawks for ten or fifteen minutes," Richard said, as if such behavior verged on madness.

The pot calling the kettle black, Jack thought. Wasn't Richard spending a lot of time staring at his neighbor? "What's wrong with that? It's beautiful, and there are always animals and birds to watch."

"It's a gut feeling, that's all I can say," Richard said dismissively. "It's like he was plotting something . . . devising a grand plan for the woods." He stretched out his arms in an expansive gesture.

Richard had his back to his own house, and Jack caught a flash of movement over his neighbor's shoulders. He stood up for a better view and smiled in spite of himself.

"Looks like your friend is back."

In his back yard Richard had mulched an island filled with variegated legustrum, red ixora, India hawthorn, a twin pygmy date palm, and a king sago. At the base of the sago, an enterprising armadillo had burrowed a nasty hole. Much like Sisyphus and his rock, Richard had filled the hole day after day only to find it tunneled anew morning after morning.

"I'm gonna get the little bastard this time," Richard vowed, jumping to his feet. He dashed to a storage closet on Jack's lanai, opened the door, and grabbed the metal utility pole that could be attached to the pool's skimmer, brush, or vac. He galloped through the cage door and charged—Don Quixote jousting with an armadillo.

The armored creature was taken by surprise and instead of heading for the jungle began circling the island with Richard in hot pursuit. Jack wondered how a feral boar hog might have countered such an assault—standing its ground probably and opposing metal with tusk. A conflict of more epic proportions, Jack mused, but man versus armadillo would have to do for this morning's entertainment. Richard jabbed with the pole, goosing a squeal from the animal as it scrambled under the fronds of the pygmy date palm.

"Ha! Think you're safe, do you?" Richard chortled. He whacked its carapace, and the armadillo squirted forth again into the field, where Richard alternately poked and pounded with his lance. Most of these thrusts missed as the creature performed an admirable imitation of a broken field runner, feinting and darting with reckless abandon.

On the second circumnavigation of the island, the armadillo tucked itself into the hedge of hawthorn, thick and low to the ground. Richard beat the bushes, so to speak, but failed to dislodge his antagonist. But necessity being the mother of invention, he shrewdly conceived a new function for the simple pool tool. Richard dropped to his knees and slid the pole flat to the ground into the hedge and underneath the armadillo.

"All right, mister armadillo, I'm gonna jack your ass right outta there," he hissed fiendishly, gripping the pole with both hands. Richard jerked upward vigorously and then sideways, parting the hedge and catapulting his stunned adversary back onto the battleground with a thud. Disoriented, the animal lay on its side for a few seconds before regaining its wits and just dodging another blow. Richard toppled forward after the miss, righted himself, and scrambled to his feet to continue the campaign.

On this go-round Richard's belated start spared the armadillo a beating. Instead of escaping, however, the dim-witted beast dove snout first into its hole. The burrow was deep enough to house the bulk of the animal, but its charming little butt was invitingly exposed.

"Playing the ostrich, are we?" Richard sniggered. "We'll see about that." He assumed a batting stance and swung mightily, delivering a resounding thwack to the armadillo's backside. The creature wriggled uncomfortably in the hole but remained an easy target. Man walloped beast again, and this time the armadillo backed out and made a beeline for the preserve as Richard was readying another swing.

"Gotcha on the run!" Richard shouted mercilessly. Blood in his eyes, weapon at the ready, he lurched toward the greenbelt, but the armadillo plunged headlong into the palmetto and disappeared. Richard smashed at the nearest plant and readied the pole for another blow, but arrested his swing, listening like a tracker instead. The sounds of the armadillo in flight were intensely audible—crashing, crackling, and crunching as the harried creature barged through the undergrowth. The alarming noises suggested a much larger animal, but Jack had noticed that even a squirrel thrashing in the limbs could sound like a small army. Gradually the clatter of the armadillo's escape faded and then subsided entirely.

Richard dropped his makeshift lance, turned his head to the heavens and shouted, "'Vengeance is mine, saith the Lord'!"

Jack joined his neighbor at the edge of the preserve and said, "I thought you didn't hold with that superstitious nonsense."

"It fits the occasion," Richard grunted.

Jack retrieved his blue aluminum pole and turned it over in his hands. "Hmm . . . no worse for wear."

Suddenly anxious, Richard asked, "How much memory do you think it has?"

"This pole?" Jack said, feigning ignorance.

"No, you idiot, the armadillo," Richard retorted.

"Oh, the armadillo . . . well, my Dell hard drive has eighty gigabytes, but I'm not sure about the armadillo."

"Fuck your hard drive, you know what I'm talking about."

Jack decided that there was no more fun to be had, so he answered reassuringly, "I think that you've probably seen the last of that armadillo. And I wouldn't be surprised if the smell of fear lingers in its spoor—a warning to other armadillos not to mess with Richard the Conqueror."

"'The smell of fear,' I like that," Richard said, smiling.

"Nice battle plan, Richard," called an approaching voice.

Both men turned as a trim man with a military haircut strode in their direction. He was wearing cut-offs, a T-shirt stained yellow at the armpits, and work gloves.

"I sure wouldn't want to cross bayonets with you," the man added, punctuating his admiration with a pair of plant clippers.

Richard basked in the glow of his accomplishment—he was indeed the guardian of his garden, the spanker of armadillos. "Thanks, Tim." Gesturing to Jack, he said, "This is my neighbor on the other side, John Adamson."

Jack extended his hand. "Call me Jack."

"Tim Butcher, nice to meet you," he said, enclosing Jack's hand in a work glove. "Thought I'd do some work back here, hopefully not as strenuous as what you just went through," Tim said, smiling at Richard.

Richard glanced slyly at Jack. "What kind of work?"

"Oh, clear out some of the dead stuff—you know, like those brown palmetto fronds there," he said, gesturing to his left. "Fallen branches, leaves, trash that's blown in from the neighborhood . . . anything that doesn't belong. They'll pick the clippings up, won't they?"

"You can put them out Saturday morning," Jack said, nodding. "Be sure to bundle them up, though."

"Would you like some help?" Richard offered. "Jack and I aren't doing anything."

Jack knew that Richard wasn't simply being neighborly; he wanted to keep an eye on Tim. "Richard's always offering my services without asking me," Jack said, "but I know how important male bonding is to him, so count me in."

"Up yours," Richard countered.

"Hey," Tim said, laughing, "three pairs of hands are better than one. I'll take any help I can get."

Jack and Richard retreated to their homes briefly to sheathe their hands against the palmetto spikes and retrieve clippers. Jack also donned a pair of rubber knee-high boots that he'd purchased at Wal-Mart for $14.99.

"Planning to wade in the river?" Richard asked, eyebrows raised in derision.

"My granny put boots likes these on me so that I could walk the creeks and hills of the Ozarks," Jack said with a hillbilly twang. "I weren't never scratched nor snakebit."

"Snakes?" Tim said uncertainly, pulling his hands away from a palmetto.

"Oh, yeah," Jack said, "especially pygmy rattlers. I don't think their bite would kill an adult, but you don't want to find out. Just make a lot of noise and watch where you put your hands and feet."

The men worked boisterously for a while along the edges of the greenbelt, pulling at the stubborn fronds and cutting their stems. Soon the effort had yielded a satisfying pile of dead vegetation, endowing the preserve with a cleaner, greener aspect.

Richard stepped back and admired the men's handiwork. "That certainly looks better," he said.

Tim was pleased that the men had helped, but could he co-opt them even further? Don't push, he decided. "Thanks, guys, I think I'll do a little more."

Richard stared at Jack in puzzlement. "Did we miss some?"

"No, no . . . I'm just going to work a few feet further in," Tim said, pointing with his clippers. "Some of that palmetto back there and some of those branches on that small oak."

"You can hardly see the brown there," Richard protested, "and it'll drop off on its own soon enough."

"Those branches might bear leaves," Jack suggested. "You've got a nice natural look now."

"Oh, I'm not going to cut much," Tim assured them, "just a tad here and there."

Richard couldn't contain himself. "You know you could pay a fine if you cut down any of the preserve. I don't think anyone is going to object to our cleaning out this stuff," he said, gesturing to the pile, "but you don't want to go too far."

"Not to worry," Tim said with his habitual smile.

Richard stared again at Jack, who shrugged in response, and both men retuned to their houses to clean up. Jack was certain that Richard would probably stand behind the slanted verticals of his bedroom slider, where he had an unobstructed view of Tim, who continued to toil in the bushes.

TWELVE

Marie Selby Botanical Gardens flourished on a mangrove-lined point of land that looked across Sarasota Bay at the sparkling city and its adjacent keys. Jill Adamson had fallen in love with the tropical enclave and its famous orchid and bromeliad collections when she and Jack were exploring the city as a prospective retirement spot. Having been a volunteer at Washington National Cathedral while they were still living in Maryland, she'd brightened at the prospect of serving in Selby's volunteer program.

The personnel at the Gardens immediately saw Jill as someone who could instruct visiting classes from local schools. She'd never been a science or botany teacher, but both she and Jack felt that an experienced teacher, given the proper training, could teach almost anything. Their belief had proven true as Jill was now working with seventh graders twice a week on a palm unit she had created herself.

The inspiration for the unit had been ancient Egypt, a subject Jill had taught with great enthusiasm for many years in Maryland. For the classes at the Gardens, she'd captured their interest with the palm's significance in Egyptian religious ceremonies. The more mundane instruction in how a palm is not a tree, but a treelike plant, and in the different types of palms had gone reasonably well. This morning's classes had moved outside in pairs to adopt a palm, which included noting its features, health, and changes with the passage of time.

Jill had been pleased as she circulated from pair to pair that the students were on task and sharing their respective talents. There had seemed to be at least one child in each twosome who could draw the palm and another who could record observations. The students' regular teachers had been impressed as well, complimenting Jill before they returned to their home school. Now she had an hour for lunch before the two afternoon groups arrived.

She claimed her bag lunch and diet soda from the refrigerator in the Activities Center and then sought out a shaded bench along one of the walkways. From where she was sitting her view of the bay was not obstructed by the thickets of mangroves, which began just below the north end of the Gardens. A number of small boats, some rather derelict in condition, were moored within walking or wading distance, depending on the tide. One such boat cleverly captured this phenomenon, its side emblazoned with the name "Row v. Wade."

Jill watched as closer in, a motor boat with a laughing young couple ran aground in the shallow waters. A barefoot man hopped over the side and shoved the craft to a more manageable depth before climbing back in and starting the motor. A lone fisherman—sometimes there were several—was standing in water up to mid-calf and manipulating his rod and reel. And on the shoreline a blue heron balanced on one leg, the other crooked at the joint, as the sharp-eyed bird scanned for unsuspecting marine morsels.

Jill rummaged in her bag for her half sandwich and cup of yogurt. She had barely removed the top of her yogurt when two women she judged to be older than she approached nervously. They were both wearing flamingo pink stretch pants and long-sleeved blouses and carrying light sweaters in spite of the warmth of the day. The taller of the two, her bluish white hair tightly coiffed, stared bug-eyed at Jill's identification badge through thick lenses set in spangled frames.

"Do you work here, honey?" she asked, her tone fairly pregnant with indignation.

"Yes, I'm a volunteer—" were the only words Jill managed to speak.

The taller woman's water burst. "There's a man," she gushed, jabbing vaguely with her right index finger, "sleeping under one of those trees with the funny roots."

"A *black* man," her companion warbled like an elderly Greek chorus.

"We thought he might be dead at first," the taller one said, as if such an outcome were desirable.

"But he was breathing," chimed the chorine.

"He didn't have his smiley face," the first lady said, referring to the orange sticker that visitors had to display after purchasing a ticket to the Gardens. To prove that she was a paying customer, she proudly thrust her stickered left breast in Jill's face.

"And he smelled," the second one said, pinching her nose in reproach.

"I think he's one of those bag men 'cause he had a sack lying next to him," the tall one recalled, nodding her head knowingly.

"And his hair and clothes were a mess," her cohort sniffed, patting her own hair, although it was as unlikely to blow out of place as the strands of a Brillo pad.

"I think I get the picture," Jill said, sliding off her bench and standing—more to escape the smiley face bobbing in front of her nose than anything else. "Selby appreciates your reporting this matter, and I promise you that I'll take care of it," she assured them. "Now you be sure and enjoy the rest of your day."

"We'll try," the taller one said, though she seemed mollified by Jill's praise and pledge.

Jill smiled and waved them on as she turned in the direction they'd indicated. Before she alerted any of the paid staff, she wanted to check the situation out for herself. The walkway led her into the denser groves of the Gardens—oaks draped with epiphytes and a bamboo garden—and alongside a koi pond. She soon discovered the man, much as the women had described him, lying at the base of a massive banyan tree. How had he slipped in? She couldn't imagine this fellow scaling the fence or sneaking by an attendant without being noticed.

He opened one eye and squinted at Jill. "Waded in, done it before," he said, reading her mind.

She gave a little start and then regarded his face warily. Suddenly she experienced a jolt of recognition. "I know you," she said accusingly. "You tried to bum money from me and my husband at Burns Court."

He opened both eyes and appraised her briefly. "Could be."

"You don't recognize me?" she said incredulously.

"It's kinda hard seeing as how you all look alike," he said. That set him laughing so hard that he experienced a coughing fit.

Jill actually began to feel sorry for him, fearing the paroxysms wouldn't stop. Rather than immediately demanding that he leave, she asked, "What are you doing here?"

"I'm the orchid thief," he said when the coughing finally stopped. He sat up so that his back was up against the banyan. "You know, the snaggle-toothed guy Chris Cooper played in 'Adaptation.' He even got to screw Meryl Streep." He flashed a smile, showing a ragged row of teeth.

"Yeah, I saw it," Jill said, frowning. She wondered what this bozo was doing at a movie like that. "Security will have to look in your bag."

"Oh, I haven't taken anything . . . yet. I'm after that big slipper orchid you got stashed here."

Not that again, Jill thought. "That orchid was not brought here at Selby's request. All the scientists did was name it and send it back to Peru." Why was she defending the Gardens to this street person?

"So you say, so you say. Well, are you gonna kick me outta here? Or you could keep me in, play games with my head—your chance to be Big Nurse." His tone wasn't challenging, more playful than anything else.

"Did you really wade in, or did you pay?" Jill asked uncertainly.

The man snorted. "What do you think, lady, I got a smiley face tattooed on my butt?"

"I'll go get someone from security," Jill said.

"OK, OK, I can take a hint," he said with resignation. He pulled himself up slowly, grimacing from the effort and bracing himself against the banyan's formidable trunk.

Jill couldn't refrain from studying his physical aspect: he was only slightly taller than she and frailer than he'd looked in repose. After steadying himself, he reached down into a large plastic bag, whose faded lettering read "Wal-Mart, Another Roll Back." The second "O" was in the shape of a big smiley face, which caught both their eyes.

"Hey, here's my sticker," he smirked, waving the bag aloft.

"I don't think so," Jill said, barely suppressing a grin.

He extracted a grubby southwester and jammed the canvas hat onto his unruly salt-and-pepper curls, finally stepping away from the tree. Jill accompanied him toward the main entrance at what she thought was a safe distance, although she didn't feel particularly threatened.

There were several things about the man that perplexed Jill. He had alluded to race more than once, and he knew about the orchid scandal; clearly he possessed political awareness and intellectual curiosity. He had an offbeat sense of humor—with a crude streak—and more than a passing interest in films. Most significantly, he didn't speak "black English," the street tongue that she was reasonably familiar with from her years of living in the D.C. area. Was he suppressing it or had he been reared in an educated environment? And if that were the case, what had brought him so low?

On their way to the entrance, Jill and the man approached some cheerful sightseers, two couples who looked to be in their sixties.

He hung his head, moaning, "Dead man walking." The smiles on the visitors' faces froze, and the foursome gave him a wide berth as they hurried by.

"For God's sake," Jill complained, "you're not about to be executed."

"Might as well be, I get kicked out of all the good places," he griped, self-pity permeating his tone.

He said this with such conviction that Jill sensed he was speaking the truth. And then she experienced a tingling sensation as her mind began to make connections. When she'd told Kathy about the incident at Burns Court, her daughter had formulated a theory about a homeless person vandalizing *David*. Well, here was a chance for Jill to play detective.

"You know, the Ringling Museum has free days on Mondays. Why don't you go there?" she asked.

"Oh, they booted my ass outta there, too. And off the grounds—I had a real nice tree near the Ca d'Zan," he said nostalgically. "I guess I just wasn't artsy-fartsy enough," he added sarcastically.

Jill couldn't believe it—here was a homeless person with a motive for defacing the statue: revenge. She would try to pry some more information out of him and pass it on to Kathy.

"You said the other night that you were a vet. Is that true?" Jill asked.

"Oh yeah, me and Robin Williams served together. Good morning, Vietnam!" he unexpectedly howled. Heads turned at the entrance as Jill tried to conceal her embarrassment. "I did my time, so you won't be seeing me in Iraq. He's gonna send the troops in the there, the U.N. be damned, mark my word."

Jill didn't comment because that's what everyone was saying—the war had become a foregone conclusion. There was an awkward silence; she had to get back to her lunch, and he had to return to the streets

"So . . . where do you stay?" she finally asked, as if concerned for his welfare.

He eyed her cagily. "I hang around the downtown here doin' the best that I can. There used to be a little café over on Main where I was welcome, but that just went out of business. Sometimes I sleep on the pier," he added, nodding in the direction of the bay. "How 'bout giving me a little donation?"

"You've got to be kidding," Jill answered quickly. Then, after some reflection, she said, "What would you do with it?"

"Go to the movies," he answered candidly. "Burns Court and Hollywood 20 usually. There's that discount theater on University, but that's a hike. I buy some food *before* I go in, 'cause they charge more for the damn candy than the film. Put it in my bag," he said, shaking his Wal-Mart carryall. "If they don't tell me I can't take it in, that is, and then I sit as far away as possible from the other folks. Don't want any complaints messin' with my movie-going experience."

Jill wished that she could get a look inside his bag, but that was Kathy's province. Was there a bronze penis in there?

Jill reached into her purse, but didn't withdraw her hand. "What's your name?"

He drew himself into a stylish pose, knuckles under his chin. "Movie Man," he said proudly.

"Do you expect me to believe that?" Jill said, hand still inside her purse.

A flash of pain crossed his face. "There may have been another name in another life, but now it's Movie Man." When Jill still didn't withdraw her hand, he added, "If you went to any police station, they'd know me by that name."

Jill extracted a ten dollar bill and handed it to him. "OK, Movie Man, catch a flick on me."

THIRTEEN

Richard Lovejoy couldn't believe his eyes. It was bad enough that Tim Butcher had pushed the boundaries when pruning dead vegetation from the preserve behind his house. Perhaps no one else had noticed, but Richard had kept a close watch on his neighbor. Tim hadn't stopped at brown palmetto fronds and dead branches—no, a little clip here and a little chop there. Nothing big, mind you, but the effect of removing small pieces of live growth was noticeable all the same. The greenbelt was thinner; there were no two ways about it. What was he up to? It seemed to Richard that the section of forest closest to Tim's' house had received the most attention. Perhaps the man was trying to make his back yard appear larger, Richard surmised.

But this morning's activity was setting that theory on its ear. Tim had leaned an extension ladder against one of the live oaks, climbed the rungs, and grabbed a handful of Spanish moss. When he'd draped as much over one arm as he could manage, he descended the ladder and dumped the moss into a tall garbage bag.

Both fascinated and appalled, Richard continued to watch as Tim pursued an obviously premeditated course of action. He would remove the moss from as high as he dared go on the ladder, then commence stripping the lower branches until he reached the bottom of the steps. The only variation in this routine was when Tim simply chose to throw the moss to the ground, which he did when the graceful strands had a clear path to earth. These he eventually gathered and stuffed into bags as well, which were beginning to multiply at an alarming rate.

Richard had to shake himself, so mesmerized was he by the implausible scene unfolding next door. What to do, he thought as he left the window. Connie was engaged, as usual, in her obsessive and expensive pursuit of new clothes, so he decided to call Jack.

"Hello," his neighbor answered.

"You won't believe what Tim's doing now," Richard said, urgency in his voice.

"Oh, what's that?" Jack said through a drone in the background.

"He's taking the Spanish moss off the trees," Richard said, hoping his indignation would be matched by Jack's.

"He's what? I couldn't hear that—the dishwasher's running."

"The Spanish moss . . . Tim's carrying armloads down and bagging it," Richard said irritably.

"Spanish moths? He's spraying them?"

"He's taking the fucking Spanish moss off the goddamn trees!" Richard screamed into the receiver.

"Jesus, Richard, no need to yell like that. I heard you . . . why's he doing that?" Jack asked.

"How the fuck should I know," Richard seethed. "Why don't you come over and we'll ask him."

"Oh, you want moral support," Jack said, finally grasping the situation.

"That's the idea," Richard said. "Meet me out back." He hung up without waiting for Jack's answer.

"You weren't kidding," Jack said as they stood just outside Richard's lanai observing Tim fill up his bags with moss.

Affronted, Richard said, "Would I make something like that up?"

Jack was about to say "yes," but decided that his neighbor was in no mood to be trifled with. "Well, let's find out what he's up to."

As they approached Tim from behind, Jack could see what was troubling Richard. The preserve seemed to be losing its density; it was more porous than before, with gaps and openings where the vegetation had previously presented a solid front. Tim had been careful not to stray across what would've been Richard's imaginary property line, but the view had been compromised nonetheless. The forest behind the house on Tim's other side had also been left untouched, although this home was a rental property—at least it was until the Plumbago HOA could eliminate a loophole in the community's by-laws.

"I guess no one could compare you to a rolling stone," Jack called out with a little chuckle.

From one of the middle rungs Tim glanced over his left shoulder with his trademark, vacant smile. "Hi, guys . . . you'd be right on that score. I'm definitely gathering my moss."

"So we see," Richard said impatiently. "The question is *why?*"

"Oh, I don't want this stuff killing the trees," Tim said matter-of-factly. "Look at that dead limb," he said, pointing to the ground just below him.

Jack located the branch, which was about seven feet long and the thickness of an oar handle. He grabbed one end and dragged it easily from the underbrush out onto the grass at the edge of the preserve.

"Hmm," Jack said as he and Richard examined it. The larger strands of moss had sent out runners along the limb, culminating in little nests of moss at irregular intervals.

"Just because this branch fell doesn't mean the tree's in danger," Richard said without conviction. He had to admit the limb looked diseased, as if it were under attack from some parasite.

"You know, Jill's familiar with all these plants now that she teaches at the Gardens," Jack said. "I'll go get her and we'll see what she has to say."

"Seeing is believing," Tim said, his back toward the men on the ground.

Jack didn't like the implication, but he hurried back to his house, where he resisted the urge to taint Jill's assessment of the situation. "I want you to see something" was all he said. She put down the novel she was reading, *The Girl with the Pearl Earring*, and followed him outside.

"What on earth . . ." Jill said, as she gaped at Tim's handiwork.

"Claims the moss is killing the trees," Richard said, unable to contain his displeasure.

"It's not even moss, really," Jill said. "It's an epiphyte—an air plant. It's just using the tree for support and elevation. It takes its food from the air, not the tree."

"There!" Richard said triumphantly. "I'll help you put the moss back on, Tim," he offered, although it was unclear whether he was merely being facetious.

Jack said nothing, and he shook his head negatively at Jill; the affair of the Spanish moss was not *their* affair.

"That's not the only branch I found," Tim said stubbornly. "There won't be anything left standing unless I remove the moss."

Jill refused to bite her tongue. "Branches fall all the time. The forest wouldn't be here if the moss was killing the trees."

Tim said nothing in response and continued his methodical removal of the impugned Spanish moss. Richard, dark of countenance, turned and marched toward his home. He disappeared inside, but emerged almost immediately gripping a video camera; crouching in the shadow of a potted palm, he aimed his weapon at the massacre of the innocent epiphytes.

~

Kathy had been cruising downtown Sarasota for about an hour, circling from the bay front through Burns Court to the Hollywood 20 cineplex and back again. Her mother's two encounters with "Movie Man" had encouraged her to pursue the eccentric homeless person as a lead in her investigation. So far, though, she hadn't seen anyone fitting his description or even any of the city's homeless. As she was idling alongside a vacant lot on Orange Avenue, a police car pulled alongside her T-bird. The passenger side window eased down and a uniformed officer gestured for Kathy to reciprocate.

"Good morning, ma'am, do you need some assistance?"

Kathy decided that she would refrain from revealing her objective if possible. "No thanks, officer, no problems," she said through her open window.

The man, who appeared to be about her age, considered her response while checking his rearview mirror. "It's just that I've monitored your movements for almost an hour, ma'am, and you seem to be driving more or less in the same circle." It wasn't a question, but he seemed to be requesting an explanation.

Best to be truthful at this point, Kathy concluded. "I'm a private detective, officer—I'm looking for someone."

His eyebrows lifted slightly at this response. "I'm going to park, ma'am, and if you'd like do the same, then maybe I could help you out."

Though she didn't feel intimidated, Kathy had every intention of taking him up on his offer. She knew that the police sometimes harbored resentment against PIs, though she had no reason to believe that to be the case with this particular officer. He probably just wanted to be helpful.

Kathy exited her car and met him on the sidewalk. Slightly taller than she, he had close-cropped hair, almost a buzz cut, and a good physique. She gave him her business card, and he introduced himself as Lieutenant Daniel Crouse.

"If I might ask, Mrs. King," he said after the introductions, "who are you looking for?"

Kathy knew she didn't have to answer, but she'd experienced no success up to this point. Perhaps the man could help her out.

"It's 'Miss' King, Lieutenant Crouse. A homeless person—goes by the name of 'Movie Man.'"

The policeman chuckled, revealing dimples in otherwise unlined cheeks. "What's he up to this time?"

Kathy couldn't believe her luck. "You know him?"

"I've rousted him, even put him in jail, but he just keeps coming back for more," Crouse said with what seemed like begrudging admiration. "We recently swept him and some others out of here for violating a no-camping ordinance. We don't have it in for these people, but we can't have them hanging around the downtown area. They pester people for money, and our citizens and tourists don't like that."

"Sort of like a black eye for Sarasota," Kathy said, using an image she thought he'd appreciate.

"That's it exactly, Miss King . . . but you haven't said why you're interested in him."

"I want to talk to him about the vandalism of the statue of *David* at the Ringling," Kathy said, watching closely for Crouse's reaction.

He ruminated a bit, flicking at a fly that suddenly had taken an interest in his scalp. "We've had complaints about homeless at the museum . . . I don't know if the department has investigated that angle. Who are you working for?"

Kathy had anticipated this question. "They prefer to remain anonymous," she said, as though it weren't in her power to disclose the information. "I don't think they've lost faith in the police—"

"But we've got a full plate," he said, finishing her thought.

Kathy nodded. "So . . . do you have any idea where I might find 'Movie Man'?"

"Well, he might be up in Bradenton waiting for things to cool off here. But if he's returned to our business district, I'd stake out the movie houses—you might spot him at any of the bargain matinees this afternoon. If you don't see him there, you could check out the Saprito Pier. He and some of his buddies like to sleep out on the end at night."

"Thanks, Lieutenant, that's very helpful," Kathy said, pleased by his cooperation.

"Dan, Miss King, glad to be of assistance," he said, extending his hand.

"Kathy," she said, accepting the handshake.

"One thing, Kathy," he said. "If you go down to that pier at night, I'd be careful, especially . . . ." He stopped abruptly, looking slightly embarrassed.

"Since I'm a woman?" Kathy said, amused by his discomfort.

"I'm sorry, Kathy. We take those PC workshops all the time, but some of us are slow learners."

"I'm not offended," she said, shaking her head. She'd never linked gallantry with sexism.

"If I were married, I'm sure my wife would straighten me out," Dan said pointedly. "Anyway, if you'd like any more information, you know where to find me."

And you know where to find me, Kathy thought as she climbed back into the T-bird. Dan had made more moves in a few minutes than Brett had attempted in a few months.

FOURTEEN

January had bled seamlessly into February, bearing the mild, dry weather that beckoned legions of snowbirds to flock to Sarasota and the Sun Coast. Instead of cursing this congestion, instead of likening it to some Biblical plague, Richard Lovejoy had ignored it so that he could marshal all his energy and resources in the defense of a helpless patch of tropical forest. Jack had never witnessed such focused behavior on the part of his neighbor, who typically saw threats to his happiness poised to attack from every direction—like vultures hovering over a festering armadillo. For the moment there was only one source of his happiness: the view of paradise from the windows of his home. And the threat to that vista of bliss was a single entity: the aptly named Tim Butcher.

Since the purgation of the Spanish moss, Richard had not spoken to Tim about his assault on the preserve. "It won't make any difference," Richard said. Jack agreed, and as the days fell one by one, so did the forest. Initially, Tim's back yard appeared to expand as low plants bordering his property bit the dust. But a more sinister plan of destruction began to emerge with the passage of time.

Tim began pruning all branches at the height of his head or below. He didn't confine this truncating to the edges of the greenbelt, eventually shifting his efforts by feet and then by yards into the woodland. A day or two might go by when Eden was unmolested, as if Tim were evaluating his progress, followed by more deforestation. Any sapling or low shrub, even robust saw palmettos, fell to his axe or machete, the pruning shears now sidelined in favor of weapons of mass destruction. As he gained access to more trees, Tim trotted out his extension ladder and gathered more moss, plumping his garbage bags with the carcasses of epiphytes.

But Richard didn't run screaming from his house with a cry of "¡*no más, no más!*" In fact, his self-control in the face of such ruthless carnage was remarkable in the extreme. Calmly he videotaped one day at a time, and with steely nerves he snapped before-and-after photographs with his digital camera. Whether Tim knew that his activities were being recorded, Jack couldn't tell. Richard was always stealthy in his shoots, lurking in windows and shadows, camouflaged by foliage, as though reconnaissance and espionage had been his true callings.

Uncharacteristically, Richard had said little to Jack in the weeks of surveillance that had followed Tim's opening salvo on the preserve. When Jack asked if Richard was still capturing the botanical mayhem on film and tape, his neighbor responded with a grunt or a curt nod of the head, nothing more. Until today.

"I want to show you something," Richard said on the phone. It was clear that he expected an immediate reply and that rejection was not an option.

"I'll be right over," Jack said.

Richard ushered him into his study, and pointed proudly to a tack board nearly half the size of the wall on which it was temporarily mounted. The board was crammed with photos, with the earliest at the top and the most recent at the bottom.

A day was represented by two pictures: the preserve before Tim laid hands on it and the preserve after his amputations. Jack was stunned. Had the greenbelt really looked as lush and abundant as it did in the earliest photos? The transformation, almost imperceptible at first, was devastating by the final snapshot.

"Wow!" summed up Jack's reaction.

"And the back of each print is dated," Richard said, as if he were a lawyer entering exhibits into evidence.

"Of course," Jack said in admiration. "But Tim isn't in any of the pictures."

"Wouldn't prove anything without continuity," Richard said sagely. Then he aimed two remotes at the opposite side of the room, energizing a VCR and a plasma television. "Reality TV sinks to a new low," he said, sounding like an anchor for tabloid news, "as your local butcher rapes the environment."

The effect of the video was even more compelling than the array of photographs. Tim was in every frame, here bagging moss, there dismembering healthy branches, and everywhere whittling down the preserve; there would be no doubt in anyone's mind when it came to who had committed these crimes against nature. Tim could also be seen each day enlarging the scope of his atrocities, so that an impartial viewer could not help but recognize a plan and its execution. Richard had even zoomed in on Tim's sweaty face to capture the rapture in his expression as he savaged the scenery.

Jack could restrain himself no longer. "What are you going to do with all this evidence?"

"Taking it to the DEP in Tampa. They'll make him replant the entire locale and supervise his efforts for three years to ensure that the new vegetation is flourishing. It will be costly and time consuming for Mr. Butcher."

"So you're ready to lodge a complaint?" Jack said, which is the course he would have followed.

"No," Richard replied smugly. "I'm going to wait until he finishes the job . . . until he's done all the damage he can do."

Jack was speechless. "Why on earth would you do that?" he finally asked.

"I want that asshole to pay through the nose, to replant the whole goddamn preserve if necessary," Richard said, a look of Old Testament vengeance in his eyes.

"In other words, you want to teach him a lesson," Jack said.

"You got it," Richard said, clicking the video into rewind mode.

Jack walked to a window where he could see the greenbelt and stared thoughtfully. "How far do you think he's going?"

"All the way to the river," Richard answered without hesitation.

"Oh, for Christ's sake," Jack said, horrified at the prospect.

"He doesn't give a shit about the woods, about us, about anything else. It's all about him and a clear shot to the water. The erosion buffer, the habitat . . . fuck it, says Tim." Richard ejected the video and cradled it lovingly in both hands.

Jack nodded his head. "The evidence you'll have will be overwhelming."

"Like our President says about Iraq," Richard said, smiling wanly, "when I decide to wage the war, it'll be over like that." He snapped his fingers.

"He's going to know who turned him in," Jack said, worrying.

"So?"

Jack glanced back out the window. "So . . . will you be able to win the peace?"

~

Kathy King watched the orange sun as it sank into Sarasota Bay. She shaded her eyes and stared intently, hoping to see the green flash in the water that others had described to her. When the elusive phenomenon failed to materialize, she wondered if it occurred only in the Gulf and not in the Bay. She was standing on the first few feet of the Tony Saprito Pier, which stretched northwest from the footing of the Ringling Causeway Bridge. Above her and to her left rose two impressive piers and segments of the replacement bridge that was due to be completed by August of the current year. Barges carrying segments and cranes to lift them into place had been working busily on the project for several months. At the end of the pier several fisherman were trying their luck.

In the two weeks that had passed, Kathy had almost given up hope that she would find Movie Man. She had searched for him in Bradenton without any success, but in recent days more homeless people had begun drifting back into downtown Sarasota. Apparently, the cycle consisted of crackdowns by the police, dispersal or arrest of the homeless, reappearance of the homeless, and then more crackdowns. She had talked to a few of the individuals—they all knew Movie Man and indicated that it was just a matter of time before he returned to his familiar haunts. Kathy had already staked out the movie theaters at the bargain matinees that afternoon, but the object of her search had been a no-show.

She turned away from the water and directed her gaze toward the bustle of the city behind her. In the last couple of days, one homeless man had camped on the end of the pier, which was shaped like a capital T, and spent the night. "You can hear people coming," he'd said. "Can't sneak up on a man out here." Kathy wondered if it were possible to get a good night's sleep without deadbolts and security systems in place—or a gun next to the bed. She noted the weight of her purse, where her handgun lay concealed; she hadn't dismissed Officer Crouse's warning. She'd seen Dan twice since their first meeting, friendly chats about her progress with the investigation. She sensed that he might be close to asking her out on a date.

Imagining that pleasant prospect was interrupted by the approach of a man that set Kathy's heart pounding in anticipation. He was black—wearing tattered jeans and shirt, a southwester crammed onto his head—and he was toting a blue Wal-Mart bag imprinted with the trademark smiley face. He fit her mother's description to a T.

"How's it going, Movie Man?" she said.

"Whoa," he said, perusing her suspiciously. "Do I know you?" He stopped short of the pier. "Damn, you got me to answer."

Kathy had already decided to be honest. "My mother told me what you looked like."

He peered at her, trying to make out her features, which were in shadow. "Yeah, that lady at Selby—you'd be her daughter by the look of you. Man, are you with the police?" The frustration he projected was palpable.

"Private investigator," Kathy said. "Like to ask you some questions."

He relaxed visibly. "You guys usually pay for information, don't you?" he asked cagily.

Kathy was willing to play along. "That depends on its quality."

He was staring at her quizzically. "You know who you look like?" He took a few steps closer. "Yeah."

Kathy had lightened her hair further since Brett's tongue-tied reaction, and she was curious. "OK, I give up . . . who?"

"Sally Kellerman—she played Hot Lips in 'M*A*S*H*.'"

"Yeah, I know who she is." Kathy agreed with her father about the film. It had been overpraised—the TV show was better, and still superior in reruns to most of what passed for entertainment on the tube.

"Well, fire away, Hot Lips, I'm ready," he said, giving her a toothy grin.

"Miss King is my name."

"Oh," he said, bowing with an exaggerated flourish, "*excuse me*, Miss King."

Getting right down to business, Kathy said, "I understand that you used to hang around the Ringling Museum."

He walked onto the pier, dropped his bag in front of him, and leaned against the railing opposite her. "As long as they'd let me," he acknowledged.

"But that wasn't very long, was it?" she said, hoping that her mother had been accurate in assigning him a motive.

"No, they didn't like the 'aura' I projected in the galleries," he said, sniffing loudly. "And they didn't like me napping under their damn trees." He removed his cap and stuffed it into the bag. "Wait a second," he said, scratching his unkempt curls, "I told your mother all this. What's the big deal?"

"I expect you wanted to get even with them for kicking you out," Kathy prodded.

"I've been kicked out of lots of places," he said, sighing heavily. "It's goes with the territory."

"Yeah, but you *really* liked the museum, Movie Man, because you're no ordinary bum, so you slipped over that little wall one night—"

"What the hell are you talkin' about, lady?" he interrupted, his voice pitching higher. "I didn't slip over any wall . . . 'no ordinary bum.' What the fuck do you know about anything?" He turned his back on her and stared out across the Bay.

"Then you sneaked around the back of the museum, climbed into the courtyard, and vandalized the statue," she said, surprising herself with her own intensity.

Movie Man began to laugh, convulse actually, turning around and collapsing on the deck in a heap. A coughing attack followed, and when he could finally get his breathing under control, he pounded his fist next to him and said, "Is that what this is all about?"

Kathy had knelt down to his level, fearful that he might require some assistance. "Do you know something?" she said keenly. "I'll pay you good money."

His expression was almost sympathetic when he answered. "Being no ordinary bum, I read about it in the paper. I can scrape one up just about any day. But I'm sorry to tell you that I had nothing to do with it, and I don't know of anyone who did. And if you think some homeless person ran off with that bronze prick, you don't know much about us."

Kathy's heart sank, but she wasn't ready to give up. "How can you be so sure?"

"Lady, you got three kinds of homeless," he began, almost as if he were lecturing a student. "The first type is on the street not by choice, but because of some financial catastrophe. This person will always be looking for employment, for some way to jump back into the mainstream. He got better things to do than screw around with a statue, right?"

Kathy sensed that she was being browbeaten, but she nodded begrudgingly.

"Then you got your mentals," he said, ticking off the second finger of his left hand. "They're messed up in the head, can't hold down a job, and got no one to take care of them. No way one of these guys could plan and carry out your museum caper."

Kathy had to admit he was making sense. "And the third kind?" she asked, suddenly more interested than probing.

"Guys like me," he said, unsmiling. "We dropped out 'cause we don't give a fuck any more. We don't want to be tied down and we don't want to work." Then the corners of his mouth turned up sardonically. "We con bleeding hearts into giving us money so that we can pursue this leisurely lifestyle."

"And someone like you wouldn't want to mutilate the statue?" Kathy said, sensing what his response would be.

"What's in it for me?" he asked rhetorically, extending his arms, palms up. "There's no money in it, it's gonna be hard work, and it could land me in a shitload of trouble."

She knew he was right, but she'd come too far to just walk away. "Where were you at nine p.m. on Saturday, November second, of last year?"

"Jesus," he said, snorting. "Let me consult my appointment book." After a few seconds of thought, he said, "OK, there used to be a café on Main where bums like me were welcome. It's closed now, but I was probably there."

Kathy persisted. "May I look inside your bag?"

He shook his head in disbelief. "You're something else, lady. Go ahead, 'be my guest, be my guest,'" he sang in a remarkably good voice. "That's my best Jerry Orbach," he said proudly.

He's just full of surprises, Kathy reminded herself. Keeping her eye on him, she picked up the bag. She could tell immediately by the heft of it that *David*'s penis wasn't likely to be lurking behind the smiley face. She removed his hat and placed it carefully on the pier. The first thing she saw was a ticket stub, scads of them actually, and almost as many candy wrappers smelling of chocolate and sugar. There was also a section of the newspaper that prominently displayed movie times. She dug down deeper, as if she were on a treasure hunt, and came up with more of the same—until something of a different texture caught her eye.

It was a photo, a picture of a younger, more civilized Movie Man, an attractive woman, and two school age children. Kathy looked inquiringly at the homeless man.

"Don't ask me to go there," he begged, a look of such sorrow in his face that she thought he might cry.

Kathy returned the picture to the bag along with the rest of his possessions. She stood up and scanned the lights glittering from the luxurious homes on the keys across the Bay.

"Why do you go to the movies so much?" she asked finally.

He rose stiffly, stretched, and then held out his arms as if he were trying to encompass the universe in his grasp. "Is *this* world enough for you?"

Kathy considered this, pondering silently all the unresolved issues in her life. After some moments had passed, she said, "I guess that was some useful information, Movie Man."

She opened her purse and withdrew a twenty dollar bill that had been lying next to her gun. She extended him the money, which he accepted wordlessly before looking away.

"Enjoy the show," Kathy said.

PART III

FIFTEEN

Connie Lovejoy was pacing her great room, flashing her magenta toenails as the heels of her gold sandals tapped an agitated tattoo on the eighteen inch terra cotta tiles. Occasionally, she would stop behind one of the pieces of furniture—ponderous sofas and chairs in African and tropical motifs purchased at Sarasota Kanes—and scratch her manicured, magenta fingernails along the rich upholstery. She stared up at the twelve foot tray ceiling where an antique bronze Palm Bay fan whirred, its frond-like blades assisting the air conditioning in the unexpected late March heat. When she could no longer endure her break from the two issues captivating her attention, she returned to the aquarium glass window at the back of the room.

That was the signal for her husband to leave his sentry post and retreat into the heart of the house. As Richard passed his wife, he betrayed no emotion, though he couldn't avoid noticing the nasty curl of her glossy magenta lips. It occurred to him that Connie was the only woman he knew who made a fashion statement in the privacy of her own home. She was wearing leopard print Capri pants that extended to mid-calf and a matching top that exposed her tumescent midriff, where a topaz stud pierced her navel. Her earrings matched the gem in her belly button, drops of dark honey against the unnatural red of her hair. She might've sprung from one of the jungle prints on the furniture's upholstery if she'd only been more lithesome or a little less inelastic.

Instead of gazing at the ceiling fan, Richard directed his attention to the Sony forty-two inch plasma TV on the far wall. The unthinkable had become the inevitable—U.S. missiles were lighting up the skyline of Baghdad, and in an ironic coincidence, it was the first day of spring. War fever was running high, and the Bush administration was predicting a rapid progress for the conflict. CNN was reporting rumors that Saddam Hussein himself might have been killed in the shelling. Contrary to his wife, Richard didn't think his country had any business attacking Iraq—since when did America launch preemptive wars? But if it was going to happen, he prayed fervently that it would be over quickly. His greatest fear was that Iraq would use its weapons of mass destruction—possibly deadly chemicals—on U.S. soldiers. Why wouldn't a country so obviously overmatched go out with a bang?

"When is this guy supposed to show up?" Connie asked with growing impatience.

The mundane is always with us, even in the midst of death, Richard thought, though he was rarely disposed to consider such things. He was even more obsessed than his wife with the punishment of Tim Butcher.

"He said today, that's all I know," Richard answered, recalling the conversation. After Tim had carved his passage to the Braden River, Richard had finally taken his video and photographs to the DEP in Tampa. There a Mr. Palmer had thanked him after viewing the materials and shaken his head. "I guess I just don't understand people," he said. "It would've been so simple to leave the preserve alone." Palmer indicated that he'd have to see the "crime scene" for himself, then told Richard when he would drop in on Tim Butcher. Maybe, Richard thought, Palmer was watching television like everyone else at the moment.

"Dickey, if you'd had the balls to stop the jerk at the beginning, we wouldn't be looking at this mess now," Connie charged, snapping her head toward the gaping hole in the forest. Tippy, who sensed the tension between his owners, began to whine from where he lay on a sofa. He was silhouetted against the body of an elephant on the fabric, giving the Chihuahua comical girth and bestowing pointy ears on the pachyderm.

"Shush," Richard said, who didn't welcome the addition of the dog's voice to the angry chorus of wife and TV.

"Shush yourself," Connie said, her face contorting in spite of the rigidity imposed by her make-up.

"I was talking to the dog, dammit," Richard said. "And you know that I confronted Tim the very first day—the Adamsons can vouch for that."

Connie shook her head. "That's not what I'm talking about and you know it. After a few days you had enough evidence to go to this Mr. Palmer. That would've been the end of it." She turned to the window again. "Jesus, you could drive a goddamn truck through there."

"If you remember, I took the issue to the HOA early on—Chester Marquardt asked Butcher nicely to stop and was totally ignored," Richard said. He wasn't about to let her blame him for Butcher's actions.

"That old coot can barely walk a straight line," she scoffed.

"Well, at least he had the balls to call the DEP and identify me as the community's representative," Richard countered.

"Yeah," Connie smirked, "and look how long it took. If he tried to hit on a woman, he'd be charged with assault with a dead weapon."

"Look," Richard said with exaggerated patience, "I accumulated incontrovertible evidence with my approach. If I'd jumped the gun, Butcher could've said he was lawfully removing nuisance exotics like Brazilian peppers or Australian pines. It would've been hard to prove otherwise. But he cut down so many native plants, and I have so many before-and-after pictures that the DEP will have *him* by the balls."

"All I know is the preserve looks like shit," Connie said, growing bored with the argument now that she'd succeeded in putting her husband on the defensive. She continued her vigil at the window, and he returned to the images of war on the tube. Tippy ceased whining and rested his head between his paws.

A few minutes later, Connie startled both her husband and the dog with a sudden clap of her hands. "Hot dog! Butcher's out back and there's a man with him."

Richard, with several weeks' worth of anticipation ready to overflow, scurried over to the window. "That's Palmer," he said in triumph. "Those must be my photos he's holding."

Like peeping Toms peering out instead of in, the Lovejoys pressed close to the glass so as not to miss any of the long awaited confrontation. Mr. Palmer, a robust man in his forties, was more physically imposing than the shorter, slighter Tim Butcher. The DEP official held pictures out for Butcher's perusal, then gestured to bare sections of the preserve. This process went on for several minutes as the two men shifted ground, eventually standing where the land sloped down to the river. The Lovejoys couldn't see the water from their vantage point, only a gap and then the unspoiled foliage on the opposite bank.

It seemed to them as though Palmer had become more animated as he pointed toward the water and then back toward the flora left untouched by Butcher. Richard could imagine a lecture on the importance of the greenbelt as a buffer, its implications for erosion, chemical runoff from lawns, and wildlife. He could see his ensnared neighbor visibly cringe and shrink from what now must have been a tongue lashing. When the two men turned and headed back toward the house, Butcher stared down at the ground, his head hanging like a dog beaten by an angry master. He did lift his eyes once, to glare with what appeared to be malevolence in the direction of the Lovejoys. Richard and Connie recoiled sharply from the window, as if dodging an irate wasp.

"I don't think he saw us," Richard said, "especially with the tinted glass."

"Palmer didn't tell him who turned him in?" Connie asked, apprehension in her voice.

"He assured me he wouldn't," Jack said, "but I imagine Tim will figure it out—if he hasn't already. The beauty of it, though, is that there's not a damn thing he can do about it."

And as the Lovejoys continued to spy on the drama unfolding in their neighbor's back yard, the coverage of the war continued behind them—where the might of the United States of America was pitted against the seemingly defenseless Iraqis.

~

"I've got good news, Kathy," Brett Masterson said as she sat down behind her desk. He was sitting on the futon in her office scratching Kirk's ears while Spock rubbed repeatedly against the man's shins.

"Let me guess," Kathy said. "Someone confessed." If asked, she'd say it was fine with her. Her teenage prank theory had come to nothing, and although she'd interrogated additional homeless besides Movie Man, that avenue was also proving to be a dead end. She was getting nowhere and feeling increasingly guilty about the money she was earning.

"We wish," Brett said with a rueful smile. "I decided to talk to my employers because you weren't making any progress—in spite of the tremendous effort on your part," he quickly added.

It hurt to hear the truth, but Kathy managed a weak "thank-you" for his praise.

"As I've said before, I work for some extremely influential people. To make a long story short, I think that you'll find that you now have access to the sales records at Wal-Mart, Home Depot, and Lowe's."

Kathy felt a surge of optimism, hoping the culprit had purchased the white spray paint very close to the time of the crime. If not, she'd be looking for a needle in a haystack. She left her chair and came around to where Brett was sitting.

"Thanks, big guy," she said affectionately, planting a kiss on his left cheek. Kirk wagged his tail and received a smooch on the top of his head from his mistress. Kathy reached down and stroked Spock's back, which arched at her touch, and the cat began kneading Brett's pant leg. For his part, Brett turned an unnatural shade of purple.

"Ow," he said, as Spock's claws found flesh.

"I'm sorry," Kathy said. "I didn't mean to hurt you."

Brett wriggled uncomfortably. "Not you, it's the cat."

Kathy bent down and grabbed Spock by the waist. "Naughty," she scolded, "you always underestimate your own strength." When she lifted the animal, Brett's pant leg was still attached to one paw, and Kathy had to squat with her skirt hiked up and work a few seconds to disengage the two.

"There," she said, rising from her kneeling position. Her ministrations had made Brett even more uncomfortable, she noticed with amusement, so she hurried back to her chair with the purring feline.

"I really don't deserve any credit," Brett said, more as a statement of fact than an attempt to appear humble. "I just described the problem and they took care of it." He was no longer flushed and appeared to be in control of his emotions.

"Well, you get kissed for being the messenger, then," Kathy said flirtatiously. She wondered how much more encouragement he needed to ask her out. There had been more business lunches, but still not a real date. She didn't think he was gay—not that there was anything wrong with that—because his reactions to anything remotely sexual suggested that women were the objects of his desire.

"Kathy . . . I . . . well . . . I was thinking . . ." Kirk nuzzled the man's hand because the heavenly scratching of the dog's ears had stopped.

"Kirk, don't be such a nuisance," Kathy chided. "He always has to be the center of attention."

"Would you like go out Saturday next week—dinner and a movie?" The words burst forth from Brett as if they had been bottled up under great pressure. And the expression of relief on his face matched that of one who'd just been released from a lengthy constipation.

"Why, Brett, it's so sweet of you to ask. Let me just check my calendar." Kathy wasn't toying with him; in fact, she was experiencing a moment of panic because she was almost certain that she was going out with Dan that night. Officer Crouse had moved quickly—they'd already been out on one date, dinner at a local comedy club. He'd said that people in their business really needed to laugh, and she'd appreciated his thoughtfulness. She hadn't asked him in when he brought her home—she didn't want to appear too eager—but there had been a chaste kiss at the door. She sensed that the action would move inside this time because her hormones were raging. Yes, March 29, there it was in her date book.

"Brett, as luck would have it, I'm tied up that night. I'd love to do it some other time." She smiled at him expectantly. Kirk nudged the man again, and Spock stopped his purring as if he were hanging on Brett's response.

His head drooped along with his shoulders, and his complexion colored. "It . . . well . . . uh, it was just a thought," he finally said, almost straining to say the words. The constipation had returned in full force. Brett extricated himself from the dog and stood to leave.

"I'll get on those sales records right away," Kathy said, standing as well.

"What . . . oh yes, the records . . . good luck."

He was out the door before Kathy could even clear her desk. "Well, guys," she said, scratching Spock's chin, "'faint heart never won fair lady.'"

SIXTEEN

For the Lovejoys and the Adamsons, the first week of spring had been gloriously sunny as well as fraught with anticipation. Since Mr. Palmer's momentous visit, there had been little activity at the home of Tim Butcher; in fact, no one had even seen him in his back yard. Richard and Connie were chafing at what seemed to be their neighbor's lack of compliance. Jack and Jill weren't as exasperated as they, but even from their vantage point, the scar in the preserve was an eyesore. The foursome was sitting on the Adamsons' lanai with the dogs, where presumably Tim Butcher couldn't hear the abuse hurled at him.

"Mr. Palmer said on the phone that Butcher had agreed to be cooperative," Richard said. "He wouldn't discuss the particulars, but he predicted we'd see some action soon."

"When the hell is 'soon'?" Connie griped. "We've had to stare at that goddamn hole in the jungle for weeks now."

She bent forward in the lounge chair where she was working on her tan. Her lime green bikini revealed titillating cleavage, and although Jack wasn't attracted to Connie, he could admire the show with impunity behind his Bollé sunglasses.

"What I still don't understand," Jill said, shaking her head, "is why he thought he could get away with it. We told him it was wrong—we warned him."

"You know my theory," Jack said, ignoring his wife's frown. "Some people are just natural assholes. I'm working on an invention called the asshole gun—you aim it at a person's forehead and a laser beam leaves an imprint of an asshole. Then everyone knows what to expect."

Connie giggled, imparting a jiggle to her breasts. "I like that, Jack. Put me down for one."

I might be aiming it at you instead, Jack thought.

"How much do you think it's going to cost him," Richard said, ignoring as he usually did Jack's attempts at humor.

"Well, let's see," Jill calculated. "We added another two thousand dollars in landscaping to the builder's package—some trees, a couple of berms, and the hibiscus, pygmy date palms, and ornamental grass around the cage. He has to fill in a much larger area, and the vegetation has to be denser. That should be multiple times what we spent."

"Exactly what I was thinking," Richard said with satisfaction.

Without warning, Nefer and Tippy leapt from their somnolent state at the feet of their owners and dashed to the side of the cage, barking madly in the direction of the Lovejoys' house. Like a fish out of water, the nose of a truck appeared on the lawn between Richard's home and Tim Butcher's. Then the entire vehicle slowly emerged as if it had been birthed by the two residences. "Tropical Paradise Nursery" was emblazoned on its door and several Hispanic men in overalls, long-sleeved shirts, and hats with ear flaps were attending to its progress.

"Jesus Christ!" Richard sputtered, alarmed by the prospect of tire tracks on his yard.

"Is today Palm Sunday?" Jack asked, noting several of the trees in the back of the truck, their root balls wrapped in burlap.

Richard ran wildly from the cage, waving his hands for them to stop, although his frenzied gestures could just as easily have been interpreted as an ecstatic greeting.

"Go around the other way," he screamed, when the truck continued to inch forward.

"Yeah, that owner won't care," Connie said, jumping from the lounge chair. "He's never there 'cause he rents it out." She went no further than the door of the cage, waiting to see how the situation played out.

Probably doesn't want to display her body to *those* men, Jack thought. Unfortunately *he* was treated to a generous view of her backside, which from his perspective could have benefited from some judicious liposuction.

"Jack, you know enough Spanish to talk to them," Jill said. "I don't think they understand Richard."

Jill was prescient when it came to ruining a potentially hilarious confrontation, Jack thought. He would have to help Richard now instead of reveling in the breakdown in communication. He rose with a sigh and ambled past Connie, where the smell of sunscreen and baking flesh invaded his nostrils.

"Don't let the dogs out," Jill warned.

He slammed the screen door just in time—the dogs yelped as their snouts were briefly pinched and the mesh brushed against Connie's ample breasts.

"Sorry," Jack said.

"It's all right—most excitement I've had this week," Connie said.

Jack hastened on to his assignment, happy to let the comment go answered. As Jill had predicted, Richard and the men from the nursery were speaking gibberish to each other's ears. The driver had left the cab, and he and Richard were babbling incoherently while the other workers, confounded by the mad gringo standing in front of their truck, had gone to inspect the preserve.

"They don't know what the hell I'm talking about!" Richard complained in frustration.

¿Como estás? Jack said to the driver.

The man's scowl changed to a smile. *"Muy bien. ¿Y tú?"*

"Muy bien, tambien. "Uh . . . *el otro lado de la casa, por favor,"* Jack said, tapping first the hood of the truck and then pointing at the yard between Tim Butcher's and the rental.

The driver's eyes widened in understanding. *"Ah . . . el otro lado . . . comprendo."*

"Muchas gracias," Jack said.

"De nada, jefe," the man answered, giving Jack a little salute. The driver shouted to his men and then reentered the truck. While he was backing up, some of them came to give him signals while the others awaited the delivery of the trees.

"What the fuck do you think you're doing?" It was Tim Butcher; he'd emerged from his house and was now clanking through the screen door of his lanai cage.

Richard, to his credit, took the heat away from Jack. "I just asked them to drive the truck through the other side."

"Oh, I see, you don't want anything to happen to your precious yard," Butcher snarled sarcastically.

"That's right," Richard said coolly. "The guy next to you doesn't care."

"There wouldn't be a truck driving through here in the first place if you hadn't tattled to the enemy," Butcher charged.

"Tattled?" Richard said, feigning ignorance.

"Don't play innocent," Butcher said in disgust. "I know it was you. You'd think a grown man would have better things to do than spy on his own ranks . . . sneaking around, shooting pictures and video."

"I don't know what the fuck you're talking about," Richard said, growing testy.

"I'm talking about this goddamn preserve," Butcher said, gesturing toward the forest. "It doesn't belong to you—you should mind your goddamn, fucking business."

"It doesn't belong to you, either, asshole," Richard countered.

"Fuck you," Butcher spat, taking a step toward his neighbor.

"Oh, is that what you're into?" Richard said in a mincing voice. He turned and pointed his butt toward Butcher. "Kiss that or whatever turns you on." He followed his exhortation with an enticing little waggle of his posterior.

It was obvious to Jack that the testosterone levels had reached a critical mass, and he snatched Richard by the arm just as Butcher was aiming a violent kick at his antagonist's nether regions. Butcher missed awkwardly—like Charlie Brown attempting to boot the ball held by Lucy—and fell to the ground with a thud. On Jack's entertainment scale, this morning was definitely a "ten," but he didn't want either man to come to serious bodily harm, so he continued to tug Richard away.

"Where's an asshole gun when you need it?" Richard taunted, but he allowed himself to be dragged toward the safety of Jack's lanai.

Butcher was silent at first, checking himself gingerly before rising with exaggerated care from the indifferent grass. "Meddling prick!" he finally said, loud enough for the others to hear. He dusted himself off and then marched, blood in his eyes, in the direction of his opponent. In the meantime, Jill throttled the dogs while Connie held the door open for Jack and Richard.

"Dickey, that was stupid thing to do," Connie said. "He's mad enough having to pay for all the planting."

"He deserves all the abuse he can get," Richard said, red-faced, as he plopped into a lounge chair.

"Lock the screen, Jack," his wife urged, reacting to the menace in Butcher's demeanor.

Jack clicked the lock and waited for the show to continue. Nefer and Tippy were beside themselves at the man's threatening approach. The hackles rose on both their backs until the two canines were puffed up like blowfish. To say that they were barking would be understating the case; a vet might have diagnosed rabies, such was the fusillade of growls and snarls, complete with foam and drool, which erupted from their volcanic throats.

Butcher didn't try the door—he pressed his face against the cage, the screen distorting his hateful features like a nylon stocking masking a thief. The dogs tried in vain to rip his ankles and shins to shreds, but the barrier of the screen only deepened their frustration.

"Good morning," Butcher said wickedly over the din.

"Tim, my man, how's it goin'?" Jack said cheerfully, as if deforestation, trying to dropkick your neighbor's ass, and rapacious dogs were routine events in Plumbago Plantation.

"Jesus, Jack," Jill said, giving her husband an exasperated look.

Butcher ignored them and stared homicidally at Richard. Even Connie was taken aback by his malevolence, retreating to a chair behind her husband.

"You couldn't just leave it alone, could you, Lovejoy?" Butcher said.

Richard stared straight ahead, according Tim no more regard than a turd in a toilet bowl.

"Well, I've got news for you, Dickey boy," Butcher said, his teeth bared. "You're going to pay for sticking your nose where it doesn't belong."

Richard flinched in spite of himself. He hated that name—it made him feel small and unmanly. He'd told Connie not to call him that, especially in front of others. Now Butcher had somehow picked up on the humiliating moniker.

"You won't know how and you won't know when—but you'll pay," Butcher continued, drawing out the words with relish. And don't say that I threatened you, or I'll tell how you stuck your ass in my face and then sicked your dog on me."

He bent below the cage's support bar and growled at the dogs, which were beyond hysterical by now. They hurled their bodies at the screen, bounced off, and hurled themselves again. Tippy began to wheeze as if he were in the throes of an asthma attack. Connie vaulted from her chair and scooped the distressed animal into her arms.

"Nice tits," Butcher said, licking his lips. "Too bad your husband's such a pussy, but that's why he'll be so easy to handle. And your little dog, too," he cackled. He stood up, pirouetted, and stomped off.

"Dickey, did you hear what he said," Connie whined. "Aren't you going to do something about it?"

"You told me I'd said enough already, goddammit! And don't call me that name."

"But what are you going to do?" Connie persisted.

"Watch the workers do their job," he said, fatigue in his voice.

The others turned toward the preserve, where the brown men from Tropical Paradise were already dragging trees to their appointed plots.

SEVENTEEN

Kathy King was parked in the shade afforded by a sprawling live oak on a residential street in Bradenton. Every few minutes she would steal a glance at the house she was staking out, then return to her scrutiny of the reams of computer printout piled next to her on the seat. Even with the help of Brett's powerful employers, she'd practically had to sign an oath in blood to obtain the sales records. Of course, an unscrupulous woman could sell the personal account numbers on the receipts or even engage in identity theft herself.

Her eyes were growing weary of the continual shifting from long-range to close-up inspection. She'd been surprised by the all the brands and shades of white spray paint, each with its own description and code. She was still working her way through purchases on the day of the crime, wondering if it was all worthless effort and calculating how many days prior to the crime merited a reasonable examination.

It always amused her how film and television rarely showed the donkey work of a private investigator, preferring instead to focus on the glamorous or the dangerous. She'd been sitting for two hours working the two jobs. An insurance company for a major employer in Sarasota, Lennar Homes, had hired her to videotape an employee who was drawing workman's comp for a back injury. So far there'd been no activity at the man's residence, so she'd been able to fill the down time with record checking. She had a phone book handy to locate the address of anyone who'd bought a can of white spray paint, but her efforts had yet to uncover any suspects.

She took off her reading glasses and closed her eyes, then reached for a bottle of Zephyrhills spring water. A blue Dodge pick-up entered her field of vision from the right and turned into the driveway of the house in question. Kathy could see large plastic bags of some sort nestled in the truck's bed, so she grabbed her binoculars. Some of the bags contained mulch and others contained gravel; she trained the instrument on the driver as he stepped out of the cab.

That's my guy, Kathy thought, but she double-checked the photo sitting on the dash just to be sure. No doubt about it, so she aimed her video cam at the subject as he began to unload the contents of the truck. She played with the zoom function, making sure that his face and the bags would loom large in the finished tape.

Two hours later her man had unloaded and dumped forty bags of cypress mulch and ten, fifty pound bags of landscaping gravel. True, there had been a break while the subject had guzzled two bottles of Miller Genuine Draft, but Kathy was absolutely certain that the insurance company would be pleased with the footage. And she was pleased with herself—it was nice to have success, to see a concrete result for a change. She didn't know how much longer she could continue accepting checks from Brett in good conscience.

After tucking the camera in its carrying case, she decided to devote a few more minutes to the sales records before heading home. Once there she intended to pamper herself before her evening date with Dan. Just thinking about it gave her a tingling sensation that moved from her breasts down to her loins.

Kathy willed the delicious arousal away and started on another computer printout. Nothing. She scanned a second page and did a double take. A man named Samuel Sweeny had purchased a can of white spray paint the day of the crime. She let her fingers do the walking through the pages of the phone book, where she discovered "Rev" attached to his name. Her pulse quickening, she leafed through her notes on the case. Yes, there he was, the minister who'd spoken out against the statue in a sermon. The police had verified his alibi, but they hadn't known about the paint.

~

"Did you notice that a few people walked out?" Kathy asked.

"Yeah, what was that all about?" Dan wondered.

"I overheard somebody in the lobby say his jokes about suicide were offensive," Kathy offered as a possible explanation.

"He was making fun of reality TV . . . saying why not show someone committing suicide every week," Dan remembered.

"Some of those suicides he described were hilarious," Kathy said. "But this person said what if someone in the audience had lost a loved one to suicide."

"That's ridiculous," Dan said. "If a comedian had to worry about offending his audience, he'd never tell a joke."

"And you know what to expect when you go see George Carlin," Kathy reasoned. "So why buy a ticket if you're worried about being offended?"

"Lots of old timers in Sarasota," Dan conjectured. "Maybe they only remember him from his 'Wonderful WINO' days. My parents still have those records."

"Mine, too, but I don't think they have a record player," Kathy said, chuckling.

The topic exhausted, they stood silently for a few seconds in front of Kathy's bungalow—that awkward end-of date moment.

"Would you like to come in?" Kathy asked. She had no doubt about Dan's answer. All through Carlin's performance at the Van Wezel Performing Arts Center, they'd been stealing glances at one another. They were both laughing or groaning at the same jokes, catching the flash of emotion in each other's eyes. She'd complimented him on his choice of entertainment, which pleased him, because Carlin wasn't everybody's cup of tea.

"I was hoping you'd ask," he replied.

"This is Captain Kirk and Mr. Spock," she said, indicating the dog and cat, who were all over her when she opened the door. Dan bent to scratch Kirk's ears and ran a hand along Spock's arching back. The dog licked his hand for a treat, and the cat swished his body across Dan's leg.

"You've passed the test—they like you," Kathy said. She didn't tell him that the two animals were affectionate with nearly everyone.

"I like your living room," he said after straightening up.

"Well, this is all my grandparents' stuff," she explained apologetically. "I haven't really had the time or the money to change anything yet."

Dan made a gesture with his right hand encompassing the rattan furniture and the tropical art. "You'd be surprised how much of this I see in local homes—it never really goes out of style."

"Do you mind if I check on the war?" Kathy asked as she clicked on the television. She wasn't really asking for his approval.

"No, let's see what's happening." He sat down on a love seat featuring red and blue parrots perched on green foliage.

His choice of furniture wasn't lost on Kathy—there was a larger sofa in the room. She sat down beside him as the

CNN reporter, supported by a banner of "BREAKING NEWS," summarized the day's action. 800 bombing sorties, sixty percent of which had been aimed at Baghdad, had flown as the last day of March approached.

"They're softening the city up," Kathy observed. "My God, the troops are almost there," she said, reacting to graphics displayed by the network.

"Let's hope it's over quickly," Dan said, "with as few deaths as possible."

"Amen to that," Kathy agreed. She didn't want to get into a discussion with him about the morality of the war, which she opposed. She knew that policemen could be a conservative lot, but the fact that he'd chosen the Carlin concert was an encouraging sign. Dan had grown up right in Sarasota County, graduated from Sarasota County High School (a building that she loved, turning back the clock as it did in the midst of more contemporary buildings), and attended four years at USF, where he'd earned a B.A. in Criminology before joining the police department. At the moment he was working on his master's at the same school. He had a good head on his shoulders, no doubt about that, but she preferred to postpone discussion of weighty subjects till later. They could both agree on a speedy conclusion to the war without putting a damper on the evening.

Kathy switched off the TV and stood up. "Are you game for a walk? Kirk needs to do his business."

"Sure, we've been sitting for a long time."

She retrieved Kirk's leash from her tiny laundry room and a plastic bag for disposing of the dog's waste. Kirk was beside her in a flash when he heard the jingle of his collar, which was attached to the leash.

"This way," she said. "Want some mosquito repellent?"

"I'll brave it—they prefer sweet Northerners to tough locals," he said, his tone teasing with a touch of male bravado.

"Hey, I told you about my family's place in Maine—up there they call the mosquito the state bird."

He laughed as they exited through the laundry onto the soft sand of Siesta Key. They had worn slacks and short-sleeved tops to the concert, more than adequate for the temperature, which was still in the mid 70's at ten thirty at night. An egg-shaped moon illuminated the narrow path, catching the sand's crystals and tracing a white rivulet as it snaked through untended tropical banks.

"I need to trim back some of this growth," Kathy said after they'd been brushed by some palmetto spikes.

"I don't know," Dan responded, "it's beautiful . . . unspoiled, I'd say."

Kirk kept his nose to the ground and moved rapidly toward the water, as if he were on a mission to go where no other dog had gone before. Soon they broke clear of the undergrowth and stepped onto a narrow strip of beach lapped by the thirsty waters of the Gulf. A heady perfume of brine and organic matter flared their nostrils.

"This is nice," Dan said with obvious sincerity. "Beachfront is hard to come by."

"There was more of it when I was a kid—I guess it's just going to keep moving inland. I worry about storms eating it up, too."

"You shouldn't worry about things you can't control," Dan said.

"I think I've heard that advice before," Kathy said, mocking him. "Let's see, was it Oprah or Dr. Phil?" She grabbed at his side, giving him a little pinch.

"OK, OK," he said holding up his hands. "But it's true."

"Easier said than done . . . wanna sit?" She plopped down on the sand, making sure there was play in Kirk's retractable leash. Dan joined her without hesitation and they sat silently for a few minutes, absorbing the fleeting caresses of a fitful breeze and the patchy ebb and flow of irresolute waves.

"You can see a lot more stars down here than in Baltimore," Kathy said, breaking the silence.

"Why is that?" he wondered, staring up at the sky—a ceiling faux painted with whorls of gold specks over deep black.

"The heat and light coming off the city create a haze," she explained, "and of course, Baltimore is much bigger than Sarasota. Maine is even better because it's so rural. I saw Saturn on my telescope one night."

"Maine must be important to you," Dan observed. "You've mentioned it several times."

Kathy appreciated a man who paid attention to her comments, however banal they might be. "Yeah, I grew up there in the summers, saw the same friends year after year... had my first boyfriend." A remarkably vivid image of Bobby Grimes—dark hair and brown eyes—materialized in her thoughts. They were swimming in shallow water off one of the many islands in the lake. He kissed her and reached for the strap of her bikini top.

"Oh... what happened?"

"What happened... we tried to stay in touch when school resumed. He lived in Massachusetts, but when he came to visit me in Maryland at Thanksgiving, it wasn't the same. And I wanted to see other boys at my school."

"Sounds like you're a real heartbreaker," Dan said, teasing once again.

Kathy kicked some sand on his right loafer. "Ever had a long-distance romance?"

"No, I've only dated girls from around here," he confessed.

"Oh, I hope that isn't going to make you a dull boy," she said, taunting him back. "Anyway, they don't work."

Kirk wandered back from the edges of the sea grass and settled down between them. This involved circling over the ground for a few seconds and finally kicking up some sand with his paws.

"Good boy," Kathy said affectionately, scratching his back. Although she'd vowed not to, Kathy couldn't resist bringing up her case. "The minister who criticized the statue bought white spray paint the day of the crime," she said abruptly. Dan had likewise avoided the topic, but now it was fair game. "But he had an alibi—I've looked at the file."

"I know—he was working on his sermon, as he usually does on a Saturday night."

"Yeah, his wife verified it."

"Maybe she was lying," Kathy said. "Or maybe he sneaked out of the house, did the deed, and sneaked back home."

"How are you going to prove that?"

"I don't know, but I'm going to ask him about the paint," she said stubbornly.

"You're really a bull dog, you know that?' he said with admiration. "I was impressed with the way you went after Movie Man."

That was the nicest thing anyone had said to her in a long time. She bent over and gave him a light kiss on the cheek. Encouraged, he turned and found her lips, slightly parted and accepting. He leaned toward her and she let herself lie back on the sand, anticipating the weight of his muscular upper body. It had been a long time since she'd felt the touch of a man, so long that like the characters of *Seinfeld*, she hadn't been master of her domain. Unfortunately, Dan's elbow found Kirk's tail, and the dog yelped out of all proportion to his injury.

"Geez, I'm sorry," Dan said, as he tried to extricate himself from the dog's leash.

I guess I'm going to have to wait a little longer, Kathy thought. "It's OK, I step on him all the time." She took Dan's hand. "Let's go inside, we'll be more comfortable there."

She untangled man from dog, and the trio made their way back to the house, Kirk running ahead to avoid the clumsy appendages of humans. Later in her bedroom, Kirk jumped on the bed and licked Dan's ear as he was attempting once again to kiss his target.

He started giggling uncontrollably. "That tickles."

"Kirk," Kathy scolded. "Are you jealous?" She moved the dog to a far corner of the bed where he circled and settled. "All right, let's try again."

From his vantage point on the flat top of the headboard, Spock switched his tail and studied the changing geometry of the human figures. Kirk stayed on his corner of the bed, dreaming of dachshund bitches with ripe buttocks . . . and of a bare-bottomed poodle in Baltimore who'd squatted at his favorite tree.

EIGHTEEN

"April showers bring May flowers" may have been the rule for springs in the Northeast, but not in Sarasota. Great globs of rain fell from June through September, but the other months were generally dry, even drought prone. Jack and Jill had been ambushed by this feast or famine character to the local climate, a feature they'd failed to uncover while they were considering the city as a potential retirement site. Watering was even restricted during the dry periods to once a week with fines charged to anyone caught exceeding this limit.

Today was the Adamsons' turn to water according to the staggered schedule published by the county. Jack was outside checking each zone in his yard to ensure that the pop-up sprinkler heads were working. Sometimes they became covered with mulch or sand, settled, or sustained damage from mowing; and occasionally they needed adjusting so that they sprayed water on the appropriate patch of lawn. The sprinklers in the first two zones had passed muster, their little erections and ejaculations neither premature nor overextended. Jack was standing just out of range, mildly entertained by the waterworks and amused at himself for deriving any sort of pleasure from a spectacle only one level removed from watching grass grow.

The heads rose on cue in zone three, which bordered the Lovejoys' lawn, and spurted eagerly—little fountains of fertility. While making his rounds, Jack hadn't seen Richard and Connie; he suspected they were watching the war or waiting for the men from Tropical Paradise to show.

"Jack?"

Speak of the devil. It was Richard's familiar voice wafting from the Lovejoys' lanai. "Yeah?"

"Is your TV on?"

"No, Jill's at Selby, and I'm irrigating."

"Irritating? What have you done to be irritating?"

"IrriGATing. I'm irrigating . . . watering the lawn."

"Oh, why didn't you say so? Go turn on your TV."

"Why?"

"Just do it."

Jack heard the sound of Richard's slider closing—he never saw him, and no further explanation was forthcoming. He checked out all the sprinklers to his satisfaction and ducked inside. The television was tuned to CNN, as it had been since the beginning of the war. A crowd of Iraqis had draped a rope around a giant bronze of Saddam Hussein atop a concrete pedestal. While Jack watched, the citizens had no success dislodging the statue, but one frustrated man banged away at the base with a sledgehammer. Eventually, some marines attached a cable to Saddam's neck and draped a U.S. flag over his face.

Uh-oh, Jack reflected, that doesn't look good.

After some jeering from the crowd, the first flag was replaced by an Iraqi one, which met with general approval. The cable was attached to a tank or a truck—Jack wasn't sure which—and the vehicle began a tug of war with the bronze. When it finally budged, the statue drooped, much like a hard-on softening toward flaccid impotence. No more fucking over your people, Jack concluded, as Saddam finally toppled. The crowd leaped on the statue to deliver the ultimate insult in Islamic society, stomping on his likeness with their feet.

That was definitely more entertaining than checking the sprinkler heads, Jack thought as he clicked off the tube. He still had time, though, to do just that, because the final zone had five minutes left on its cycle. On inspection they were all working, and Jack realized that it was indeed a fine April day—God was in His heaven and all was right with the world.

Richard must have thought so, too, because he was uncharacteristically jaunty and jolly as he strode toward Jack in flip-flops and a T-shirt that proclaimed "Fish fear me, women want me." "What'd you think of that, neighbor?"

"Pretty impressive—thanks for alerting me. You can bet that'll be on the front page of just about every paper in the world tomorrow," Jack said, pushing the bridge of his sunglasses up his nose.

"Yeah, I can't believe how fast everything's happened. Maybe it's going to turn out for the best, after all."

This was quite an admission from Richard, who had almost as many complaints about the Bush administration as he did about Sarasota. Jack had been more ambivalent about the war, hoping that it was the right thing to do.

"That's not all, Richard. Have you noticed something missing this morning?"

Richard was speechless for a few seconds, not expecting a quiz. Then he turned toward the preserve.

"The men from Tropical Paradise—they're not here!"

It appeared as though nearly three weeks of planting had finally ended. Of course, the forest wasn't bursting at the seams like before—a prosperous child growing too big for its britches. Butcher's savage handiwork was still evident in spite of the palms, oaks, palmettos, and pines now bandaging the wounds he'd inflicted. The new trees were smaller, more sparsely foliaged, and farther apart; they had to be allowed time and space to grow and spread.

"It doesn't look half bad," Richard observed. He was feeling especially generous today.

"After the summer rains, I bet it'll really take off," Jack predicted.

"Yes, but until then, Butcher will have to keep on top of the watering, and that will cost him more money," Richard said, his vengeful self returning.

"Still," Jack said, waxing poetic, "Nature has been restored to her former state, and Butcher has accepted his proper fate."

"Cute," Richard acknowledged. "He hasn't made good on any of his threats. I think he spoke in the heat of the moment . . . all's well that ends well. This is the way it was for me in the radio business," he continued smugly. "Advertising campaigns, ratings wars—all it takes is aggressive planning and perseverance."

"And you win in the end," Jack said, nodding affirmatively.

"Speaking of which," Richard said, scanning his yard, "I've got to water again."

"You already watered on the alternate day," Jack pointed out. "You're not supposed to do it twice in the same week."

Richard shrugged, making a dismissive noise. "No one pays any attention to that. I've worked hard on this yard, and I don't intend to lose a single plant."

He strode off and disappeared into his garage, where the controls for the watering system were located. Jack returned to his home to change for a tennis game with one of his regular partners at the racquet club. He was just lacing his shoes when a hideous, unearthly shriek made his flesh crawl, arresting his hands. It sounded like Richard, so Jack bolted from the bedroom onto the lanai and out the screen door. His one unlaced shoe flopped awkwardly, imparting a hobble to his stride. Normally graceful, he now looked like a man possessed of one leg shorter than the other.

Richard crouched at the side of his house, his head in his hands. "Oh God," he moaned. The sprinklers in the first zone were squirting straight up in a solid stream—without the spray, there was virtually no ground coverage.

"Jesus Christ," Jack said, "I thought someone had been injured." He knelt down to tie his shoe, now that CPR wasn't required.

"I have been," Richard snapped, pouting like a troubled child.

"Are they all that way?" Jack asked, straightening up.

"I don't know," Richard answered, a flicker of hope in his expression. "I'll advance the zones manually, while you check."

He dashed back into his garage and activated the next zone. Jack frowned as each sprinkler geysered identically.

"Well?" Richard screamed.

"The same," Jack yelled back.

The two men repeated the process with the remaining zones, but the results didn't change. After Richard had turned the system off, Jack bent down to examine one of the heads.

"Huh, well that explains that."

"What?" Richard said, coming around the corner of his house. "Explains what?"

"Look for yourself," Jack said, gesturing toward the ground.

Richard eyeballed the head at close range, like a pathologist at his microscope. "The thingy . . . the part . . ." Richard said, groping for the right words.

"Yeah," Jack confirmed, "the piece that channels the water and adjusts for watering radius—it's gone."

"Fuck . . . fuck," Richard muttered as he went from head to head confirming the catastrophe.

Jack knew exactly what his neighbor was thinking. One missing thingy could be written off as a defect or an accident, but every thingy gone missing had to be part of some sinister plot.

Richard thrust his eye over the next-to-last sprinkler in the first zone when the system sputtered and suddenly sprang to life. His neck twisted in an evasive maneuver, but not before the pop-up head delivered a glancing blow and a jet of water for good measure.

"Fucking sonofabitch!" Richard cried, holding his right eye. He rolled and writhed blindly on the ground, nearly bowling Jack over before coming to rest face down a safe distance from the water. "Jesus, I can't see," he moaned. "I can't see." Jack knelt to comfort him as Connie, barefoot and wearing matching fuchsia shorts and a halter top, walked around from the garage.

"What's all the commotion? What's he doing on the ground? What's the matter with the sprinklers?" she asked with mounting alarm.

"They came on while he was checking the system and caught him in the eye," Jack explained. "Richard," he said, focusing his attention on his fallen neighbor, "roll over and let me look at your eye."

"Well, I turned it on," she said. "We talked about watering, and I thought he'd forgotten—I'm always having to remind him about something."

"You stupid bitch!" Richard spluttered. "Someone took all the thingies out of the sprinklers."

"Shut your mouth . . . the thingies?" Connie was both infuriated and dumbfounded, a rare condition for a woman accustomed to wielding the upper hand.

"The system's been sabotaged, Connie," Jack said, cutting to the chase. "It won't spray."

"Butcher," she said ominously.

"That'd be my guess," Jack said.

Connie joined Jack in ministering to her husband. "Come on, Dickey, let us look at your eye."

"Don't fucking call me that!" Richard wailed, still inconsolable.

Jack, tiring of his neighbor's performance, said, "For Christ's sake, Richard, be a man. Let us look at the goddamn thing." That seemed to shame him, and he rolled over slowly.

"Take your hand away," Connie said, touching him gently on the wrist. He obeyed, squinting badly, though his wife and Jack could now see the eye.

"What do you think?" she asked cautiously.

"It just looks a little red to me," Jack replied. "Can you see?"

"Everything's double," Richard said, peering narrowly at his wife. "I see four breasts."

"That's more than an eyeful—that's a handful and a mouthful," Jack quipped.

"Boy, you've got a nasty mouth," Connie said, smirking. Richard started giggling.

"That's a good sign, Jack said. "I think the patient will survive. I had a tennis ball fly off the side of my racquet once and smack me in the eye. I saw double for a few hours, but it cleared up. Why don't you take him inside and let him rest," he continued, taking command of the situation.

Jack and Connie helped Richard to his feet, where he managed to steady himself, though barely opening his right eye. He took a few tentative steps, and Connie moved to support him, but he shooed her away.

"I'll be OK if I hold a hand over one eye. Let's go inside, and I'll lie down for a while."

"Richard, I can pick up the parts you need while I'm out," Jack offered. "I'll put them in if you like—it's no big deal."

"Would you, Jack? That'd be great," Richard said, relief evident in his left eye.

"Thanks, Jack," Connie said as she and her Cyclops gave the cold-blooded sprinklers a wide berth.

"Do you want me to turn those off?" Jack asked.

"No thanks," Connie replied, "I'll get them."

~

Three hours later, while he was still in a sweat from his game, Jack fitted the pieces he'd picked up at Home Depot onto the Lovejoys' sprinkler heads. Lest they spring to life and smite him, he refrained from placing his face too near their insidious reach. Mission accomplished, he thought, when the last thingy was in place. He had to admit to both pleasure and satisfaction in completing the task and helping his neighbors. Calling them and receiving his well-earned thanks was the next step.

"Hello," Connie's voice answered in Jack's ear.

"How's the patient?" Jack said.

"Hi, Jack. He's definitely better—he says he's sees less of me now." She laughed suggestively.

"I guess that's an improvement," he answered in kind. "Anyway, I fixed the sprinklers if you want to try them."

"That's wonderful, Jack. We really appreciate it."

As Jack luxuriated in his heated pool, perfect therapy for post-tennis muscles, the Lovejoys' watering system gurgled into action. With a sense of fulfillment, he noted that the heads were spraying normally. I am a man who can fix things, he thought happily. A man who wins tennis matches. A man who lives in a country that pounds the shit out of its enemies. But a nagging voice intruded on his reverie: someone removed the thingies, and that may just be the beginning of the mischief.

Late in the day, after Jill had returned and told him of her adventures at Selby Gardens, Jack related the saga of the sprinklers. While they were enjoying golden glasses of Glen Ellen Chardonnay, Jack noticed a county government car in the Lovejoys' driveway. Shortly afterward, a man entered the car and drove off. As if on cue, the Adamsons' phone rang.

"Jack, did you see that car?" Richard asked, barely contained fury sharpening his voice.

"Yes," Jack replied, his stomach tightening.

"They fined me for overwatering!"

NINETEEN

Kathy King had not set foot inside a church in years. Her parents, according to their own account, had once been Protestants—he a Methodist, she an Episcopalian—who drifted toward agnosticism as teens. They had neither encouraged nor discouraged their daughter in the pursuit of religion; in fact, little had been spoken on the subject of theology in the Adamson household. Occasionally, some catastrophe in the news would provoke her father to lament "the millions killed in the name of God." Or he would happily shout "hypocrite" when some evangelical was caught with his pants down or his hand in the till. Her mother would not contest these pronouncements, though she would gently suggest that some people derive comfort from their faith.

Out of curiosity, Kathy had attended the churches and synagogues of some of her friends, but these inoculations, rather than cure her faithlessness, had infected her further with skepticism. Her studies in college had led her to conclude that no sect had a corner on the truth, no matter how deafening the shouts of its adherents. More damning were the mythologies offered and the holy books followed. Examples of the former were as transparent as Santa Claus and the Tooth Fairy, lies held true only by children; and the words of the latter were too often relevant only to distant times, peoples, and places.

Why, then, did she feel a quaking in her stomach as she stood before the My Redeemer Liveth Church, where she was to interview the Reverend Samuel Sweeny? The façade of the church faced east, allowing the sun on this April morning to bathe the white exterior in light. In fact, the building struck Kathy as one of the whitest she'd ever seen—the doors, the trim, and the window frames were all the same dazzling color as the stucco walls. A set of whitewashed stone stairs led to the prim entrance, which was topped by an unadorned wooden cross fixed to the base of a spare, yet impressive steeple. Joined to the square, symmetrical front was the longest section of the church, a two-story chapel with tall, stained glass windows recessed at regular intervals and a pitched roof of white tiles. The chapel was intersected at the back by equal segments that probably housed offices and classrooms, and another straight section extended from the center of this wing, completing the cruciform shape. The total effect was one of neatness, order, and purity.

As Kathy approached the church, she noticed that its lawn was immaculately groomed and none of the trees—mostly queen palms and live oaks—was immediately adjacent to the building. Curiously, there was no Spanish moss on any of the oaks. A sign board at the bottom of the stairs read "God bless our troops." She ascended, opened one of the double doors, and was met with another set of doors leading into the rear of the chapel. Pushing through these, Kathy gasped. White walls, white pews, white carpet—all drawing attention to the kaleidoscope of the windows. Even an unbeliever such as herself recognized the scenes depicted in the stained glass: moments from Christ's life, death, and resurrection. In the white setting, the colors, especially nimbus yellow, thorn green, and blood red, lured and held the eye. Though deliberate, the end result was mesmerizing all the same, capturing her attention like clusters of flowers gilding a field of bleached bones.

Kathy succumbed to it for several minutes before continuing on the path outlined to her on the phone by Reverend Sweeny. At the front of the chapel, there was a door on either side where the pews ended and before the raised sanctuary began with its little railing, two pulpits, and choir. She opened the door on the right and immediately heard the buzz of human activity, the first sounds she'd encountered in the preternaturally quiet church.

She passed classrooms where adults were engaged in lively discussion and a larger day care chamber where lurching toddlers played under close supervision. Finally, she arrived at the innermost recess of the church, where the word "Ministry" was emblazoned on an ordinary (again) white door. She'd been told not to knock, so she lightly turned the handle and entered.

The tall man who rose from behind a simple office desk was dressed entirely in black—slacks, belt, and light cotton turtleneck. He looked to be about her parents' age, trim, with a full head of salt and pepper hair. The penetrating blue eyes, sharp nose, and full, sensuous mouth of his face would have been attractive, except for what seemed to be well-worn lines of disapproval. A younger woman dressed in a black blouse and skirt stood at an open filing cabinet in one corner of the room, her ensemble, though modest, revealing a shapely figure. Immediately behind Sweeny was an oil portrait of a blond, blue-eyed Christ. Another wall was hung with a reproduction of Da Vinci's *Last Supper*, and another held what Kathy guessed to be maps and photos of the Holy Land.

"Mrs. King, I presume?" He possessed a resonant basso profundo.

"'Miss,' Reverend Sweeny," Kathy said, advancing into the room and extending her hand.

He took it firmly, but frowned as he appraised her. "You are nubile and therefore should be married—promiscuity is rampant these days. The Devil sees to that."

"I was, but I'm divorced," Kathy said, regretting her words almost immediately. Why should she let him put her on the defensive? And now his frown lines had deepened in reaction to the dissolution of her marriage. She also noticed a door leading to the outside—the bastard had made her run the gauntlet of his faith before meeting him.

"Have a seat," he said, more as an order than an offer, "and let us begin your inquisition."

She took a chair in front of his desk, withdrew a notebook from her purse, but glanced uncertainly at the voluptuous woman in mourning attire.

"I have no secrets from my wife," he said, noting Kathy's hesitation. Mrs. Sweeny favored Kathy with a curt, condescending smile before returning to her filing.

"As I said over the phone," Kathy began, "I'm investigating the desecration of the Ringling *David*—"

"Miss King," he interrupted, "one cannot 'desecrate' something that wasn't sacred or holy to begin with. That statue was already profane, a lewd embarrassment to the community, so what was done to it actually rendered the statue more acceptable—the opposite of what you're suggesting." He licked his lips in satisfaction, having taken the bite from Kathy's sentence, while leaving her to eat her own words.

"Some would argue that art is holy—the product of a woman's or man's inspiration," Kathy countered. She was not about to be browbeaten, and she calculated that the politically correct language would nettle Sweeny as well.

The minister pursed his lips into a bloodless line. "It is abundantly clear in *Genesis* that nudity is evil. When Adam and Eve saw their own nakedness, they clothed themselves."

"So what was done to the statue pleased you," Kathy said, purposely avoiding the interrogative. If he was going to be so damned self-righteous, she'd use it against him.

"It's no secret," he said, smiling malignantly. "What you refer to as 'art' has no place in a Christian country. Fortunately, we now have leaders who are working to stem the flow of filth from your so-called 'artists.'"

"And if that means vandalizing private property, you would support such actions."

"Ah, Miss King, I didn't say that." He regarded her as if she were a pitiable schoolgirl, and he a sagacious teacher. "Christians are law-abiding citizens; we will work to alter offensive statutes (here he paused to observe the effect of his pun on the young woman), but we will not break them."

Kathy grimaced, though she was surprised that anyone so sanctimonious would possess a sense of humor. "And if members of your congregation took the law into their own hands?"

"We must all submit to a final reckoning," he said inscrutably.

"Reverend Sweeny, where were you at nine p.m. on Saturday, November second, of last year?"

He stared at her in genuine puzzlement. "As I told the police—and I'm sure you must know—I was in my study polishing my sermon. It's what I do every Saturday evening," he added.

"And who can confirm your whereabouts?" Kathy asked skeptically, as if men of the cloth were untrustworthy sorts.

"I can," Mrs. Sweeny interjected. She turned from the filing cabinet and threw back her shoulders, her impressive breasts pointing like twin torpedoes at her husband's interrogator.

She speaks, Kathy thought. "Is there anyone other than a family member who can verify that?" she asked, daring the wrath of the black bosoms. If looks could kill, Mrs. Sweeny's malevolent glower would have sent Kathy directly to the morgue.

The minister laughed arrogantly at the implications of her question. "Let me see if I've caught your drift, Miss King. Are you insinuating that I wasn't at home and that my wife is covering for me—as you dreadful people put it? Or are you suggesting that I opened the window of the study, popped out the screen, drove to the museum, did violence to that disgusting statue, and sneaked back into my house?"

"Whichever fits," Kathy said tersely.

"Oh," Mrs. Sweeny said in revulsion, wrinkling her nose as if Kathy had passed gas in the church.

Sweeny stood, glaring down at Kathy the way he might have reproached a sinful congregant. "Your questions have degenerated into rudeness, so I think it's time to end this interview."

"But you haven't explained what you were doing with the white spray paint," Kathy said, unmoving. "I have a record of your purchase right here." She reached into her purse again and withdrew the printout, snapping it like a whip to open the folds. "You bought it the day of the crime."

For the first time during the interrogation, surprise flickered in Sweeny's eyes. He and his wife exchanged furtive glances before an expression of relief softened the lines of his face. Kathy couldn't tell whether the minister had adroitly concocted an alibi or if he'd remembered a legitimate reason for buying the paint.

"You're quite the Jesuit, Miss King," Sweeny said with begrudging admiration. "The paint must have seemed suspicious to you, and frankly, I'd forgotten about it. If you'll come out back, I'll show you something."

He strode from behind the barrier of his desk as Kathy rose from her seat. Sweeny placed his hand heavily on her right shoulder and gestured toward the exit door. She felt the urge to recoil from his touch, but controlled it, unlike the buxom Mrs. Sweeny, who did a poor job of concealing the jealous glint in her eyes. The door led to a short set of steps that descended into the church's ample back yard, where picnic tables, a children's playground, and a little amphitheater prospered in the shade of some live oaks. Sweeny escorted her to the latter, which contained a few rows of stone benches surrounding a statue of the crucified Jesus.

"*Here* is a work of art," the minister announced proudly.

"Hmm," Kathy intoned. She detected nothing extraordinary about this Christ—the icon looked like numerous others that she'd seen. But she refrained from offering her opinion.

"Do you see how white it is?" he asked fervently.

"Yes, like the rest of the church," she said, unable to restrain herself.

He smiled beatifically, as if might bestow upon her one of the sacraments. "It's impossible not to notice, isn't it?" he said, pleased. "The whiteness represents the purity of the ideal Christian soul. Christ lived his life in this impure world, which is why we have the color in the stained glass."

"Then why do you and your wife wear black?" Kathy asked, a paradox that had been baffling her since she'd met them.

"All my sermons, all the communications that my wife and I have with the congregation concern the wiles of the Devil," Sweeny explained, bringing his face closer to Kathy's, his eyes zealously studying her. "He puts blackness in our hearts, Miss King, and we must be constantly striving for the white—the purity we enjoyed before the Fall."

She backed away, discomfited by his intense scrutiny, which possessed more than a hint of carnality. "Why do the trees have no moss in them?" she asked abruptly, shifting the focus away from herself.

"Every week," he replied, turning away from her, "volunteers remove it." He gazed up at the limbs. "The tree is a perfect thing God has given us; impurities that attach themselves must be removed." He faced her again, remarking almost offhandedly, "It's like removing sin from a soul. Our country," he continued musingly, "would benefit from removing the impurities that attach themselves to our soil."

Kathy felt a brief wave of nausea pass over her. Here was a fanaticism not unlike other forms of extremism bedeviling the world. And Sweeny still hadn't accounted for his purchase of the spray paint. She held up the printout again. "I'm still waiting for an explanation."

The minister shook his head. "I was about to give you one, but you have led me astray. That's the meaning of 'seduce,' did you know that?"

Kathy stared at him in reproach, but said nothing.

"All right, then, every few months I buy a can of spray paint to whiten Jesus. The elements of this world, especially in Florida, conspire to sully what is beautiful and without corruption."

Kathy walked over to the icon and gave it a cursory examination. She had to admit that it appeared whiter than normal for statuary that had been left outside. For a brief moment, she harbored a disgusting fantasy: why not spit on the thing or lift her skirt and rub her crotch in its face. She suppressed these urges but not a coarse peal of laughter. Sweeny was taken aback, she noted with satisfaction, and she strode away from his company without uttering another sound. He might have been telling her the truth, but he could just as easily have been lying. Fanatics were capable of anything.

TWENTY

"There's dog shit all over my yard!" Richard Lovejoy screamed into the receiver.

Jack Adamson recoiled from the phone in pain, the distorted voice of his neighbor still ringing in his ear. "There's a dachshund in your yard?" he said tentatively, thinking that Nefertiti might somehow be running loose.

"DOG SHIT!"

This time Jack had the foresight to hold the receiver a safe distance from his ear. "Oh, well, somebody didn't pick up," he reasoned, wondering what all the fuss was about.

"You don't understand me," Richard said, enunciating ever so slowly, the way one might speak to a simpleton. "It's everywhere—in the entry, the driveway, the grass, the flowers, even on the lanai screen. Come see for yourself."

The line went dead, leaving Jack to ponder this new development. It had taken all his powers of persuasion to stop Richard from retaliating after the sabotage to his sprinklers and the fine for excessive watering. There was no doubt that Butcher had masterminded the former and reported Richard for the latter. Jack's argument had been that Butcher had exacted his revenge, so Richard shouldn't attempt to even the score. Any escalation on his part would lead to a response from Butcher, and who knew where it would end? To Jack's surprise, Richard had agreed—perhaps the injury to his eye had subdued his volatile nature. He'd been wearing a patch for three weeks, and the doctor was hoping to remove it tomorrow.

Now it appeared that Butcher might be continuing his assault, and Jack feared he would not be able to restrain Richard a second time. The first day of May had begun in such a promising fashion, Jack lamented. President Bush had just appeared of the deck of the USS Abraham Lincoln and declared that major combat operations in Iraq had ended. A dramatic banner in the background proclaimed "Mission Accomplished." What if that boast were as premature as Jack's advice to his neighbor?

As he walked out the front door, he wished that Jill were home and not at Selby Gardens already. He liked to have moral support when facing Richard in one of his irrational states. As he approached the Lovejoys' driveway, Jack grimaced—little piles of poo festooned the brick pavers. How long had Butcher been stockpiling the crap? He walked his dog, a Llewellyn spaniel named Odie, regularly and picked up the poop in plastic bags. Apparently, though, he'd been hoarding Odie's dumps as if they were black gold.

Richard and Connie were in the exterior entry, bending to the pavers with hands gloved in plastic bags, picking up the waste and dumping it into a white garbage bag.

"Ahoy, mates," Jack said, saluting Richard's piratical countenance.

"That really is getting tiresome," Richard said, squinting through his uncovered eye.

"Just trying to bring some levity to the proceedings," Jack said. "Did you guys just discover this? It's pretty late in the morning."

"We saw *West Side Story* last night," Connie said, dropping another turd into the bag.

"At the Van Wezel," Richard added.

"That's WAYsel, not weasel," Jack corrected.

"I don't give a goddamn if it's Van Ferret," Richard snapped.

"Yeah," Connie agreed, "can you believe this shit?"

"I was willing to take your advice, Jack, but no more," Richard said, blood in his one eye. "From now on it's total war—I'll make Butcher wish he'd never bought a house in Plumbago Plantation."

"I think we should call the police," Connie said. "Who knows what he might do next."

Richard shook his head. "We don't have any proof he did it."

"We all heard him threaten you," Connie countered, looking at Jack for support.

Jack decided he wanted no part of this argument, nor did he wish to be privy to whatever Richard's plan for revenge might be. Nothing was going to jolly up this pair, so he took another approach. "Would you like some help?"

Connie looked relieved and Richard actually smiled. "That's the nicest thing anyone's said all morning. There are more bags inside the door."

Jack bagged his hands and took a fresh garbage container to the driveway, where he began cleaning up the mess. Thank God the stuff was dry, he thought, though he was sure that Richard would want to hose down everything when they were done. The Lovejoys advanced from their entry to the walk and soon joined forces with him until shortly they were ready to tackle the rest of the property.

"We'll cover the side next to Butcher, if you'll do your side," Richard suggested. "Any stuff on the flowers, might as well just knock it to the ground and leave it as fertilizer."

"Aye, aye, Captain," Jack said cheerfully, as if picking up dog feces were a delightful activity for a fine May morning.

Richard frowned and awkwardly blotted a line of sweat forming above his eye patch with his forearm. "What do you think, honey, should we make Jack walk the plank or give him a good flogging?"

"Oh, I'd like to whip him," she said throatily, bags on hips in the pose of a dominatrix. "Shit," she said, lifting her sheathed hands and checking her jean shorts.

Fifteen minutes later they met at the lanai, where Odie's deposits had somehow been scattered across the top of the cage.

"Pretty good throwing arm," Jack mused, reflecting on the lightness of the missile and the height of the cage.

Richard ignored him as he considered the problem of removal. "Any ideas?" he said finally.

"Get your extension ladder and your armadillo lance," Jack replied, sizing up the situation. "Attach your net to it . . . we should be able to reach most of it."

Jack steadied the ladder as Richard jousted with the excrement, thrusting, sweeping, and withdrawing in an attempt to dislodge the canine caca. Connie gathered the fruits of the labor as they came tumbling to earth until only a small number of hard-to-reach pieces remained.

"I don't care where we put the ladder," Richard concluded, "I won't be able to get to those."

"Hose," Jack suggested.

"Ah," Richard said, his one eye widening in comprehension. He unrolled the hose stored on his lanai and blasted away. That did the trick except for a few nuggets that rolled down to where the screen attached to the roof. Richard stared at these in frustration.

"Hey," Jack said, "they'll disintegrate eventually."

"I'm done," Connie announced. "I'm going to clean up and head for the club—got a massage scheduled. Boy, is that going to feel good." She straightened and groaned as she stretched her back. "You guys'll have to go to Publix to get the barbeque stuff."

That hadn't been on Jack's schedule, but he was resting today between tennis matches. And it was probably better not to leave Richard to his own devices.

~

The store had more shoppers than Jack had expected, especially since most of the snowbirds had returned to the moderating North. Richard had been sullen on the drive over, the latest wound festering as he contemplated a suitably nasty revenge.

"Who does he think he is?" Richard finally said as they turned down an aisle of breakfast cereal. "I nearly lost an eye, and now he's rubbed shit in it."

A woman pushing a blonde, blue-eyed girl in a grocery cart looked askance at Richard as she squeezed hurriedly past the two men.

"Geez, watch the language, Richard." Jack glanced over his shoulder at the woman, who was reaching for a box of Froot Loops.

"That man said a bad word, Mommy," the little girl complained. Her mother, who was wearing tight jeans and a form-fitting top, scowled at Jack.

"I'll say whatever I fucking want to," Richard insisted petulantly, raising his voice. He turned toward the mother and child and made a face, sticking out his tongue and hooking his thumbs in his ears while his fingers wiggled.

The toddler laughed musically. "The funny man looks like Cap'n Crunch, Mommy."

Jack couldn't resist. "See, you do resemble a seafaring soul."

"Yeah, I'm a flaming Errol Flynn thanks to Butcher. He called me a pussy and that's what I've become."

He turned carelessly and caught his foot at the end of the aisle, struggled to right himself, but pitched sideways into a free-standing display of Corbett Canyon wines. Jack grabbed at him, keeping him upright, but not before Richard's right elbow and hip had toppled several bottles onto the hard floor.

The crash arrested all movement in the store. The mother and child froze with their mouths open. An elderly man strapped with a breathing tube and snailing along with a walker clung like death to a counter of Krispy Kreme doughnuts as a river of wine and glass surged toward him. The reverberations transformed shoppers into statues along the entire back length of the Publix. That wine really does echo, Jack thought, always impressed by truth in advertising.

"Fuck!" Richard said, surveying the damage. His face was livid, and a vein began to bulge in his forehead.

"They'll take care of it—just stay calm," Jack urged.

"FUCK!" Richard screamed, lifting his head toward the ceiling, his hands outstretched in supplication.

Jack shook his head. "God won't hear you in Publix."

"CLEAN-UP, AISLE THIRTEEN," the pubic address system boomed.

"On second thought . . ."

Richard squinched his one eye, bent at the waist, and gave it all he had. "FUCK! FUCK! FUCK!"

"Somebody help me, please," the man with the breathing tube pleaded. The doughnut counter was now an island in a sea of wine.

The mother and child, who lacked only badges to identify themselves as language police, pushed toward Jack and Richard. The girl had her eyes closed and her hands over her ears. The woman, filled with righteousness and accusation, thrust her breasts at Jack.

"Can't you control your friend? When I come to the grocery store with my daughter, we don't expect to hear words like that."

Jack shrugged and stared at her breasts. Richard tucked his thumbs under his armpits and began flapping like a chicken.

"Fuck, fuck, fuck, fuck, fuck," he clucked. Then he squatted above the floor and grimaced, as if he were straining to lay an egg. "Fuuuuuuck, Fuuuuuuuck, Fuuuuuuck."

A man with a comb-over and an unsightly growth on his forehead turned the corner of aisle twelve. He was wearing a shirt and tie and a nameplate identifying him as "Ass. Manager Bruce Bean."

"We'll have this cleaned up in a jiffy," he said cheerfully.

"This man," the busty mother began, wagging her finger at Richard, who had risen from his ovulation, "is a very bad man. He's been shouting filthy language, and my daughter is terrified." Here the little girl shrank into a fetal ball as if she wanted to return to the silence of the womb.

"Oh . . ." Bean fumbled. "What did he say?"

"FUCK!" Richard shrieked, returning to his former cadence.

"Sir, please," Bean implored. "This is a public place, and we can't have language like that.

"Why don't you go manage some ass . . . Mr. Bean," Richard said, peering at the nameplate, madness in his visible eye. "FUCK!"

"Help, please, for God's sake," implored the man at Krispy Kreme Island. "I'll be late for my dialysis appointment."

"Someone will be with you in a second, sir," Bean assured him. He rushed off as a teenager pushing a mop and bucket on wheels rolled up from aisle fourteen.

"Hey, dudes, like this really sucks, you know," he said, calculating the clean-up effort.

"Tell me about it," Jack said, tugging on Richard's arm. "Come on, let's get out of here."

"FUCK!" Richard responded.

"SECURITY, AISLE THIRTEEN," blasted the public address system. "ASSISTANCE REQUIRED WITH MAN IN A PIRATE COSTUME."

"They're talking about Cap'n Crunch, Mommy," the little girl said, opening her eyes.

Richard went limp, his entire body slumping in abject defeat. "Fuck," he mumbled.

Seizing the opportunity, Jack hustled Richard up the aisle, caroming off the shopping cart and brushing against the woman's breasts. She recoiled from the contact as if the men had cooties, or perhaps Ebola. Richard allowed himself to be tugged and finally shrugged Jack off, walking of his own volition. Once outside, both men began swiping at small black flies with red thoraxes. Pairs of the insects, locked in a mating embrace, filled the air and flew without regard into any object in their path.

"Lovebugs, lovebugs!" Richard shrieked. He waved his arms wildly and weaved erratically through the storm of bugs toward the car. Jack followed and when they were both safely inside the vehicle, Richard calmed himself for a second time. Guilt tortured his face, though, as the two men stared at the insects littering the windshield.

"What about that guy?" Richard asked in anguished tones.

"The one with the tube?" Jack asked.

"Yeah."

"Last I saw he was eating a doughnut."

TWENTY-ONE

Kathy King had identified everyone who had purchased white spray paint the day of the crime and checked each person's alibi. Everyone except Reverend Sweeny had bought paint for some typical home project, and no one other than Sweeny had any motive for doing harm to the statue. On this warm, mid-May evening, she was sitting in her T-bird in the parking lot that served both the Ringling Museum and the Asolo Theatre. While she studied receipts of paint purchases the day prior to the crime, she was also scanning Bay Shore Road for pedestrian traffic.

There was method to her madness. Although Sweeny was a likely candidate, he could very well have been telling the truth. So, she needed more suspects. And this wasn't the first time she'd staked out Bay Shore. There was a chance that someone had seen the vandal the night of the crime, and Kathy had come on different days of the week over the last five months, hoping to find such a witness. Thus far, she'd been batting zero; there had been plenty of theatergoers, but no foot traffic on Bay Shore.

It seemed to her that there was not much point in interviewing those who had attended a play the evening in question. After all, they'd been inside watching the show, except during intermissions, and even then, probably just a few had ventured outside the theatre. Of those few, how many would've actually been in a position to notice someone leaving the museum grounds at the critical moment of the criminal's departure?

If she grew desperate, which was entirely possible, she'd pursue that line of investigation.

On the other hand, if someone had been walking along Bay Shore that night, he or she might've passed right by the person who vandalized the statue. Kathy could only arrive at one explanation for the absence of pedestrians on the stretch of road that she was staking out. The museum grounds covered a large expanse of property, and perhaps walkers didn't stray that far from their neighborhoods, which were situated on either side of Ringling. The kind of pedestrian she'd expected at this time of night was a pet owner. The older population of Sarasota loved dogs, but again, someone walking a dog might stay closer to home.

As she continued her drudge work, thoughts of Dan and Brett insinuated themselves, helping to alleviate the monotony. The mysteries of the former were becoming increasingly few, while the latter had distanced himself even further from Kathy, like a planet retreating to the extremities of its orbit.

Both she and Dan shared the field of law enforcement, a love of Sarasota, a ready sense of humor—and the hots for each other—she smiled at the tingling in her breasts and loins. Nothing like a good roll in the hay to improve one's mood and relax the tensions of investigative work. But how ready was she to dive into another relationship?

She sensed that Dan might quickly become serious, though he'd tactfully avoided asking her about the failure of her marriage. Kathy wondered how he'd react to her disclosure that career was more important to her at the moment than children.

Brett, in contrast, was even more of a mystery than when they'd first met. There had been no more business lunches, or even office visits, for that matter. Instead, he called for weekly updates, maintaining a distant, professional tone in their conversations. Oddly, this change in his behavior piqued Kathy's curiosity. Why had he become so easily discouraged by her refusal, especially since she'd left the door wide open for another date? What would cause an attractive, well-connected young man to be so timid with regard to women in the first place? She knew nothing of his childhood or education; and who were his mysterious patrons—her employers—who obviously possessed reserves of wealth and power? Whoever they were, she feared that they wouldn't support her investigation much longer if she failed to produce any results.

She glanced up from the figures, which were beginning to swim on the paper, and shook her head in disbelief. Refocusing, Kathy confirmed that what she saw was no mirage: a man was walking a dog along Bay Shore. She dropped the receipts on the seat, scooted out of the low-slung T-bird, and practically power walked in his direction.

The man's dog, a pert little Scottie, was investigating a light pole next to the wall bordering the Ringling grounds as Kathy approached. The owner had his back to her, and she called out in the friendliest tone she could manage so as not to startle him.

"Sir, I don't mean to alarm you, but I was wondering if I might ask you a few questions."

He turned at her voice, surprise registering on his face at the apparition before him. He inspected her through wire-rimmed spectacles, while she considered his appearance: wispy white hair, a T-shirt that proclaimed "Seniors do it slowly," and baggy walking shorts that fell just short of knobby knees.

"The only thing alarming is that you're so much younger than me," he said in a sure voice.

Kathy smiled hopefully; the guy's brain seemed to be functioning normally. After introducing themselves—his name was Harry MacDonald—she said, "I'm a private investigator looking into the vandalism of the statue of *David*."

"You mean they still don't know who did that? That was a while ago, wasn't it?" He waited for her to supply a date, as if to confirm his own memory.

"November of last year," Kathy answered.

He nodded his head. "That's what I thought. I was out here that night, you know."

Kathy tried to stay calm—she had to be certain before going to the heart of the matter. She extracted her notebook and pen from her purse. "I wonder why I haven't seen you here before," she said.

"Oh, Bernice usually walks Haggis, and she wouldn't come down here. Now tonight, she and her gourmet club are having a do, so I've got the job. I believe in giving the little fellow a proper walk—keeps me in shape, too."

He puffed out his chest, and Kathy struggled to suppress a grin. "How do you know you were here the night of the crime?"

"It was a Saturday, and the story appeared in the Monday paper. I remember telling Bernice that me and Haggis could've been suspects ourselves. 'Course we had nothing to do with it, you understand," he said, winking at her.

"About what time did you walk the dog?" Kathy asked, her pen poised.

"Around nine—it's always the same every night," he responded.

Kathy could restrain herself no longer. "Did you see anyone that night?"

"As a matter of fact, I did. You see that clump of trees yonder?" he asked, pointing south along the wall.

Kathy noted the location, especially all the shadows generated by the thick foliage. "Yeah."

"Well, this guy suddenly appears—it was like no one was there and then he pops out of the shadows. He crosses the street there," he said, gesturing, "and then walks on over to the parking lot—where I guess you came from."

Kathy held her breath. "Did you get a good look at him?"

The man nodded emphatically. "When he came into the light."

"Was he carrying anything?"

"Not that I could see, but he was wearing a jacket... might've had something on him," the old man conjectured.

"I'm going to show you some pictures," Kathy said, reaching into her purse. "Tell me if you recognize the man you saw." She first handed him a photo of Movie Man.

"Oh, he wasn't colored," he said with assurance. "But I remember now he was dressed completely in black—jacket, shirt, pants."

Kathy felt a surge of vindication as she handed him a photo of the satanic Sweeny.

"This fellow has way too much hair. The age may be about right, but the man I saw had thinning hair. And the face isn't the same at all," he added. "I guess you'd say this man is good-looking, and my guy was just average." He handed the two pictures back to Kathy. "Who's next?"

"I don't have any more suspects... at the moment," she replied, barely able to conceal her disappointment. "So you'd say he was about sixty," she said, noting the information.

"Close enough."

"How tall, what sort of build?"

"My height, five nine. I'm seventy-five and haven't shrunk an inch," he added proudly, straightening his posture, which caused Haggis' leash to stretch taut. "Nothing has shrunk, and all the parts are still working," he confided, waggling his eyebrows suggestively.

"I'm happy for you, sir," Kathy said, wondering if her witness would next extol the virtues of Viagra. "And his build?" she pressed.

"Oh, he wasn't heavy or particularly thin . . . pretty average, I'd say."

Kathy thanked Mr. MacDonald and took his address and telephone number. She brightened his evening with assurances that she would be talking to him again. Now all she had to do was place someone matching the witness' description at the time and place of the crime.

~

"Are you guys really going to be gone the entire summer?" Richard asked, his displeasure evident.

The Lovejoys and the Adamsons were lounging under the latter's overhang, the afternoon sun having forced them out of the heat.

"Only an act of God would keep us away from Maine," Jack assured him. While Jill was looking the other way, he tossed a cheddar-flavored goldfish to Nefertiti and one to Tippy as well. One of his wife's ambitions was to keep everyone as slim as she, even the pets.

"Why don't you and Connie come up for a week?" Jill offered. Her invitation was sincere, but she'd carefully proscribed a lengthy stay. "Kathy's going to break away for a visit—don't know when—but we've got three bedrooms."

"That would be fun, don't you think so, Dickey?" Connie said, warming to the idea.

Richard winced at the hated name, but he nodded his head. "If we can plan it when Butcher's away."

"Oh, would you stop obsessing about that man," Connie said, obviously weary of the topic.

"It's been, what now, three weeks since the big dump?" Jack said.

"Yeah," Jill said, picking up on her husband's implication. "Maybe that was Butcher's coup de grâce, his pièce de résistance," she said in reasonably good French.

"His piece of shit, you mean," Richard growled. "I listened to that argument once before, and you see where it got me. No, I don't believe he's finished, and I haven't even begun. When I finally figure out how to get back at him, he's the one who's going to be sorry."

Jack was doubly happy that he and his wife were about to depart for the North and their beloved cabin on the lake. Not only would they be escaping the intolerable heat and humidity of Sarasota's summer, but the Plumbago wars as well. Richard had been concocting scenarios of revenge and running them by Jack ever since his neighbor's meltdown in Publix. Jack didn't really want to be a party to Richard's plans, but he had managed to dissuade each scheme so far as unimaginative, inappropriate, or self-defeating. Now he and Jill could flee to their other paradise and leave Richard to his own devices. Perhaps over the summer the whole thing would disappear, or at least not involve the Adamsons.

After a few moments of quiet in which Richard fidgeted while the others lounged blissfully as only retirees can, he said, "I've got another idea I've been kicking around."

"Jesus," Connie said, shaking her head.

Nefertiti and Tippy moaned in low, sepulchral tones, as if providing a chorus of disapproval.

"Have you been feeding them again?" Jill asked accusingly.

Jack held out his empty hands and shrugged innocently, but the dogs rose to their feet in expectation.

"What if I killed all the plants?" Richard said, more loudly than necessary.

"In his yard?" Jack asked incredulously, deftly shifting away from Jill's scrutiny.

"No, in the preserve," Richard answered impatiently, the way one might respond to a dim-witted fellow. "I've been talking to the nursery . . . there are ways. I could call DEP and complain that Butcher is letting his obligation slide. Or I could just wait till Palmer makes one of his visits."

"But Butcher will see something's wrong," Jack pointed out.

"He won't be able to do anything about it once I've done the deed in the dead of night," Richard said, wide-eyed and melodramatic.

"That just punishes us," Connie said, breaking her silence. "We'd have to wait even longer for the preserve to come back like it was."

"You don't want to start breaking the law," Jill admonished.

"What's *he* been doing?" Richard said defiantly.

"Human behavior is a wonderful thing, isn't it?" Jack said. "We finally punished the Iraqis for years of misbehavior, some of which we apparently condoned, but we have yet to find any evidence of weapons of mass destruction. Their country is in chaos—looting and lawlessness everywhere—and how many American boys have died since the war was declared over?"

"We're averaging one death a day," Connie said tonelessly. "But I'm sure they'll find the weapons," she added with false optimism.

Silence hung over the group like a shroud. Shamed by the others, Richard sat expressionless, staring off into vivid green of the forest. Finally, he stood up and walked wordlessly out of the lanai toward his house.

"This isn't over by a long shot," Connie predicted.

Jack and Jill exchanged apprehensive glances. Maine was looking better all the time.

PART IV

TWENTY-TWO

Leaving the asphalt for the bumpy, pitted side road always signaled an escape from civilization for Jack. This illusion had become harder to maintain in recent years with the appearance of Wal-Mart, Home Depot, and a movie multiplex only fifteen minutes away. Too, homes now dotted most of the shoreline, but the woods were still thick around the lake, he noted with satisfaction. He crested a hill and maneuvered carefully down the last stretch of road, avoiding ruts etched by the runoff from the spring's vanished snow.

Jack could sense his wife's anticipation, a match for his own, and even Nerfertiti began whining as he edged onto the long oval around which the log cabins were situated. All were A frames, either single or two stories, circling an area of common ground the size of a football field that opened at one end onto the lake.

Lake Longawonga, which meant "stiff branch" in the Kennebec tongue, lay between the cities of Augusta and Waterville in central Maine. The body of water had earned its name by being straight and narrow, running ten miles from north to south, while averaging only two miles in width. The Adamsons had chosen to visit Longawonga their first year of marriage after receiving information on lakefront, housekeeping cabins from the state of Maine.

It turned out that the cabins, twelve in all, had been built in the forties by a mill, eventually defunct, as weekend getaways for its managers and their families. The property was then bought and turned into a fishing camp in the late fifties, whose picturesque name—Loon Lodges—attracted the Adamsons with its promise of unspoiled northern scenery and wildlife. The fishing camp began to lose money in the seventies, and the owner reluctantly elected to sell off the individual cabins, which incorporated into a homeowner's association. Jack and Jill bought the first cabin to go up for sale in 1982, and several of their summer friends soon followed, and the rest, as they say, was history.

"It's so rustic compared to Sarasota," Jill observed, delighted by the contrast.

They had been commenting on the differences between Florida and Maine all morning. Where one was flat and tropical, the other was hilly and northern. Palms flourishing in porous, sandy soil had been replaced by seventy foot pines that somehow thrived in the hard, rocky dirt like immigrants succeeding in a hostile country. Instead of live oaks garnished with Spanish moss, the eye was treated to stands of birch trees with their reedy, ringed trunks of mottled white. Beds of plumbago and bougainvillea had given way to meadows ablaze with orange tiger lilies, blue lupine, and pink spirea, their colors urgently intense in a growing season that began late and ended too early. And most refreshingly, the sauna of Sarasota had cooled to a salubrious seventy degrees.

"I don't see Rudy's truck," Jack commented as they drove toward the lakefront. Rudy Hamilton lived in the only year-round cabin and served as the community's caretaker, maintaining the grounds, septic system, well water, and docks during the summer. He also supervised distribution of the local newspaper, plowed roads, constructed additions to homes, and who knew what else. The Adamsons had long ago given up trying to keep track of all his enterprises.

"I'm sure he's around somewhere," Jill said. "Looks like we may be the only ones here." That wasn't unusual—it was early in the season, the first week of June, and a Monday. Many of the homeowners lived in nearby states and came up for weekends, while others, who weren't retired like the Adamsons, would arrive around Independence Day for extended stays.

They held their breath as they stepped out of the car and surveyed their cabin. The horizontal, bark brown logs were unscathed, the boards were still in place on the screen windows of the porch, the roof had gathered a few patches of pine needles but no heavy branches, and the chimney was in one piece.

Satisfied that there was no emergency, they released Nefertiti and walked the mere twenty feet to the water's edge. Their cabin was tucked into the corner of a cove shaped like the curve of a J. A long point ran several hundred feet to the right, blocking their view of the south end of the lake. To the left of the point and in front of their cove were two islands of rugged boulders and sentinel pines—where herons and ospreys nested—peeking like turtles from the clear, faintly green water. And far to their left in the north end of the lake sat Longawonga Light, the only freshwater lighthouse in Maine.

"God we were lucky to find this place," Jill said in a husky voice.

"I know," Jack said.

They kissed like newlyweds while the dog lapped greedily from the shallow water, flinching when a little wave surprised her.

"Well, shall we get at it?" Jack said, releasing his wife.

Removing the boards from the porch windows was always the first task, and Jack pried out the nails so that they could carry the four pieces behind the cabin. Each was about the size of a ping-pong table, but much thinner and not nearly so heavy. The boards were cumbersome, though, and had to be hauled down the steep porch steps with Jack backing blindly and Jill unable to see where she was putting her feet.

"Not so damn fast," Jill complained, struggling to keep her balance. "We're not trying to set a record."

"Well, we've got a lot to do," Jack countered.

"What you mean is you want to go pick up the boat," Jill said dryly.

That was true, and he resented the fact that she was right, so he stopped dead in his tracks.

"Shit, what are you doing. I scraped my nose on the board," Jill said, glaring around its edge.

"Well, you told me to slow down . . . and you just poked me in the chest."

They finally achieved a rhythm and a satisfying result: there was light on the porch and an expansive view of Longwonga filling their vision. Then Jill turned to the front door, peeking through a small picture window set in the logs.

"Looks dusty," she said, knowing full well that it was because no one had set foot inside in nine months.

They entered and immediately began carrying porch furniture out of the living room—a faux marble dinette set, wicker chairs, a lobster trap coffee table and a rocker. Back inside they surveyed the dark hardwood floors, the pine paneling, and the two-story stone fireplace that led their eyes to the second level. A set of stairs to the left climbed to the upper bedrooms, which were connected by a footbridge that spanned the width of the living room and arced over the heads of anyone on the first floor. Behind the living room were two bathrooms, another bedroom, and the kitchen.

Jill sighed. "It's going to take a while." She was referring to dusting, making the beds, and sorting out the rugs, pillows, artworks, and knick-knacks that they'd stored at the end of the previous summer.

"We don't have to do it all in one day," Jack reminded her.

They spent the next half hour unloading the car and checking periodically on Nefertiti. She was running the circle of cabins, stopping at each, and waiting expectantly for someone to give her a treat.

"Before we go for the boat, can we get the big stuff from under the cabin?" Jill said.

"I was planning to," Jack replied, although if she'd said nothing, he'd happily have waited until later.

The first item was a replica of Longawonga Light, five feet in height, sitting just inside the swinging door that opened to the storage area. They managed it without much difficulty, clambering over the embedded boulders next to the cabin before depositing the lighthouse on a bank gently sloping to the water. Jack reconnected the buried wires and then plugged the other end into the timer under the cabin.

Next was a black and yellow paddle boat, a two-seater, which Jill pedaled around the cove and islands, accompanied by the dog or any willing guests. Heavier and bulkier, it was the item they least enjoyed moving about. Complicating their effort was the height of the storage area—five and a half feet. Jack slouched his way to the back of the boat while Jill bent to a position in front. Together they maneuvered it toward the opening, where Jill rested her end on the door frame as Jack wrestled the boat sideways to fit through the door. He gave one last wrench to free the top of a seat and cracked his head on a beam.

"Shit!"

"What happened?" Jill said, staring into the shadows.

"I bumped my fucking head," Jack grumbled. He shook off the pain and said, "OK, it'll go now."

They turned the corner with the boat, but Jill lost her footing on the rocks, dropping her end of the boat. Jack was just stepping through the door, but pitched forward with the sudden shift in weight and fell headfirst into the boat. His wife almost righted herself, but in the end tumbled hard onto her butt.

"You clumsy piece of shit!" she wailed at herself.

Laughter rumbled and a familiar voice sang out, "Jack and Jill went up the hill to fetch a paddle boat, Jack fell down and broke his crown, and Jill came tumbling after." It was Rudy, all six feet five, 250 pounds of him, in cutoffs and a sleeveless T-shirt. He offered Jill a hand, pulling her up with ease. She slapped at the back of her jeans and then gave him a hug.

"I bet you guys have heard that before," Rudy guessed, a huge grin creasing his round face.

Jack extricated himself awkwardly from the boat, not willing to laugh the matter off just yet. "Gee, Rudy . . . no, I think you're the first to think of anything so clever," he said, still pissed.

"Ooooh," Rudy said, "do I detect a touch of sarcasm?" He stood with his huge arms folded across his chest, waiting for Jack to compose himself.

"That's never happened to us before," Jack said, shaking his head. He prided himself on his physical skill, hating to appear awkward.

"Well, there's a first time for everything," Rudy allowed. "Let me help you with the boat."

"Thanks," Jack said, relenting. "Good to see you, man," he added, shaking the giant's hand.

With Rudy assisting, they launched the craft in no time. Jill secured it with an anchor, while the men chatted. Rudy had sold his farm in Pennsylvania the same year the Adamsons had bought their cabin, moving his wife and three kids to Maine permanently. The Hamiltons' cabin was a home actually, much larger than the others and equipped with heat.

Jill corralled Nefertiti and joined Jack in the car to retrieve the boat from storage in Waterville, a thirty-minute drive. The dealer had the eighteen foot, emerald and gold bass boat ready when they arrived, attached the trailer to their car, and the Adamsons were off again. They drove to the boat ramp at the south end of the lake, and Jill backed the boat into the water as Jack shouted directions.

"Is the drain plug in?" Jill asked as Jack prepared to disengage the boat from the trailer.

"Yeah," he nodded. "That was the first thing I checked. Since I'm already down at this end, I thought I might fish for an hour." It was more of a question than a statement.

She smiled—her husband was never more of a little boy than when he first got his hands on the boat. "That's fine. I'll take the trailer back and do some grocery shopping."

Jack donned his life jacket and maneuvered away from the ramp with his foot-controlled, electrically powered trolling motor. When he reached deeper water, he fired up his 115 horse power Mercury and motored toward the stream that connected Longawonga to another lake. Jack monitored his depth finder for rocks and shallow bars until he located the old creek channel, which had comfortable depths. After turning off the big motor, he retrieved his fishing equipment from a storage compartment and perched on the elevated seat in the bow, where he could consult another depth finder and move the boat with the trolling motor.

Jack began fishing a slow-falling plastic worm, rigged with a hook in its middle, imparting an enticing wobble to the descent. Soon he'd left the wider portions of the lake and was following the narrower confines of the Longawonga Stream, but no bass had been tempted by his offering. He slapped at a fly buzzing around his head and then his bare arms. The thing landed on the top of his trolling motor, where two more flies joined the first as if they were scouts reconnoitering. They were smaller than a typical fly, green and triangular in shape—like miniature stealth fighters.

The three took off and buzzed him from different directions, greatly impeding his efforts to fish. He slapped at them with one hand and then transformed his graphite rod into a swatter, whipping it wildly in all directions. The insects were too agile by far and began to swarm him as reinforcements joined the sortie—he suffered a bite on the left hand and then a wound to the back of the neck. Without warning, an image began to form malignantly in his mind's eye: the repellent face of Vincent Price spliced to the head of a fly.

"Son of a bitch!" He jerked the trolling motor from the water, tossed his rod to the deck, and danced madly back to the console, waving and twitching like a man possessed. Anyone watching from shore would've concluded he was having convulsions triggered by some regrettable medical condition. He couldn't flee at full throttle because of the vagaries of the channel, but he motored as fast as he dared, still fending off the kamikaze assaults of the resolute flies. He was a poster boy for improper boating: one hand on the steering wheel and the other in the air flamenco style, clacking imaginary castanets.

Finally, he reached the security of deep water and opened the throttle, blasting up the lake at fifty-five miles an hour and leaving the squadron of flies in his wake. A wind had kicked up and clouds were moving swiftly to obscure the late afternoon sun. Out of range of his tormentors, Jack slowed to reduce the chill to his face and arms. Remembering that rain had preceded their arrival, he flipped on the bilge pump and noted with satisfaction the stream of water ejected from the boat. When the spurting continued longer than he would've predicted, Jack pulled back on the throttle and stopped. He lifted the rear hatch and inspected the drain channel in the bottom of the boat. A slight current coming into the bilge signaled that the craft was taking on water, not at a dangerous rate, but he was disconcerted all the same. He continued on his way, staying close to shore and running the bilge pump until it began to suck air. After docking, he helped Jill unload groceries before revealing the problem.

Knowing how she would react, he said as offhandedly as possible, "A little water's getting into the boat."

"Is there a leak?" she asked with alarm. "The boat's practically brand new."

"No," he assured her, "the drain plug needs tightening."

"I thought you checked it—"

He interrupted her to head off the finger pointing. "I saw that it was in and assumed that it had been tightened," Jack admitted. "I'll pull the boat into shallow water, and you can hold the front end so it doesn't swing around. I'm not promising," he said, hedging his bets, "but I should be able to get at it without taking the boat out of the water."

The gauge on his boat showed the temperature of the waist deep water to be sixty-two degrees when he jumped in, promptly regretting it.

"Jesus Christ, my balls will shrink to bee bees," he chattered, shaking uncontrollably. He untethered the boat with trembling hands and pushed it toward shore. Jill waited barefoot on the sandy beach, delaying her baptism, although she'd only be in up to her ankles. The wind was huffing out of the northeast at a steady clip now, the sky blackening as well. Situating the stern with the motor up in water just deep enough for the boat to float, Jack sat down behind it while Jill steadied the bow. After a few false thrusts with a long handled screw driver under the bobbing boat, he finally found the notch in the drain plug and turned it several times.

"OK, it's tight now," he said. He took control of the boat from Jill, who fled to the relative warmth of the cabin. After securing the boat, Jack checked the bilge, discovering to his great relief that no water was flowing in. Then, like Frankenstein's monster, he shuffled stiffly toward the cabin as the wind knifed through his T-shirt and bathing suit.

Later that night they lay in bed, the air tasting thickly of their dead fire, the cabin strewn with the efforts of their unpacking. They both stared at the slanted ceiling beams as Nefertiti burrowed under the blankets.

"We're getting too old for this," Jill said.

"I'm inclined to agree with you," Jack said, staring at a knot. It looked like a cocker spaniel he'd owned—run over by a car when Jack was eleven.

"I talked with Rudy for a few minutes. He said his daughter would clean the cabin and carry the heavy stuff out with her husband."

He knew that Jill had already discussed a price for the service. "It would probably be worth it."

"That's what I think." No sooner had she spoken than rain began to pelt the roof. "We didn't put the blinds on the porch—there'll be water all over the floor," she said, raising up.

It was a two-man operation, so Jack said, "Do you want to go do it?"

She sank back to the bed and buried her head under the covers. "No . . . we *could* be in our comfortable new home right now," she complained in a muffled voice. "I'm freezing my ass off."

Jack wasn't sure if this last was a signal to cuddle or something else. "I hope not—what would I have to grab onto?" He scooted over next to her, his chest touching her back.

"Oh, not tonight, Jack. I don't think I could manage it."

"I don't think I could, either."

"That would be a first."

"Like Rudy said."

Within seconds they slept like the dead.

TWENTY-THREE

Kathy sat with her video cam aimed through the open window of the T-bird, her air conditioning working overtime on the oppressive June morning. It had been raining almost every day now between two and five in the afternoon, monumental downpours that left the air drooping with humidity the next day. Her target on this Sunday was a modest, but well-kept rambler directly across the street from Reverend Sweeny's whiter than white church.

Unlike some other older homes Kathy had seen in Sarasota, the owners of this one had kept the trees and shrubbery at bay and the yard orderly. Fronds were not hanging on the roof, and leaf and limb had not barricaded the windows. There were no junkers or boats on cement blocks cluttering the lawn. She'd spotted eyesores like that no more than a stone's throw from upscale communities such as her parents'. But this unprepossessing little house had made the most of its charms by extending the aura of the church to itself—meticulous landscaping, a white cement block exterior, and a flat, but white roof. Kathy was hoping that the similarities encompassed more than the merely aesthetic. Two days prior to the crime, Elmer Manson had bought a can of white spray paint. It was his house facing the church, and she'd decided to plant herself there on a Sunday morning, hoping to witness a connection with the sinister Sweeny.

Just now, the white door of the bungalow was opening, and Kathy's heart leapt at what she saw: a man about the age of her parents, five eight or five nine, with a balding pate. He was accompanied by a petite woman with tightly coiffed white hair that took on a bluish tint when struck by a shaft of revealing sunlight. Kathy needed some good pictures for her witness, so she zoomed in on the couple. She was taping with a steady hand when a raucous belch erupted in her throat, loud enough for the couple to hear, Kathy feared. But they didn't break stride, and she was able to stabilize the camera, which had jiggled as she burped.

The previous evening Dan had treated her to what he claimed was a local secret, a Mexican dive called La Flatulencia. Kathy had thrown caution to the wind, devouring a bean burrito platter washed down with two Coronas laced with lime. Fortunately, there had been no embarrassing explosions after dinner—although she could've always blamed Kirk or Spock, who released gas innocently and at will. This morning, though, Kathy was paying the price.

As the Mansons crossed the street, she shut off the video cam, making a spontaneous decision as she slid the device into its cover. Why not attend the service and confront Manson in the house of the Lord? She waited until they were swallowed by the church, slipped stealthily from the car, and approached the house of worship herself, noting with interest the topic of today's sermon posted on the sign board: "The Rapture."

She was greeted inside not only by blessed air conditioning, but also a pink-faced, cherubic man with a nimbus of grey hair clinging desperately to the crown of his head. He smiled at Kathy not out of recognition, but by the way of greeting in a vacant, bland manner, suggesting the aftereffects of a lobotomy. She was confident that, given a few more seconds with his mouth open, he would begin to drool copiously. "Won't you please sign our guest book?" he asked robotically. Clearly his programming allowed him to distinguish congregants from visitors.

The open volume was lying on a little pulpit to the left of the next set of doors, and Kathy bent to sign, lest she upset the delicate equilibrium of her greeter. A manic impulse seized her, and she wrote "Mary Magdalene, 3 Rockaway Drive, Bethlehem, PA 66666."

"Bless you, Mary," the vacant one intoned after glancing at her signature.

Kathy nodded incredulously and pushed through the doors, an action she regretted immediately. As near as she could tell, each pew was filled, but her entrance seemed to have turned every head in the assemblage, their faces flashing the same post-surgical smile she'd encountered without. Confronted by so many gleaming teeth, retreat seemed out of the question, but advance appeared to be futile as well.

She was rescued from her quandary by a hovering usher who, as if he were dispensing divine assistance, practically flew to her aid. Grinning vacuously, he escorted her around the left rear of the chapel and down the side aisle for ten rows—much closer than she wished to sit. At the end of the pew were a man and a woman with what appeared to be their son, whom Kathy guessed to be about nine or ten years old. She sat down next to the boy, who regarded her with interest, his face alive with more intellectual curiosity than any adult she'd encountered thus far.

A booming organ note snapped every neck toward the sanctuary as Sweeny and his wife made a grand entrance, he lifting his hands as a signal to the congregation to rise and she directing the choir to readiness. The young boy offered an open hymnal to Kathy, and she realized he meant to share it with her. She was not familiar with the hymn, nor did she think favorably of her singing voice, but she held one side of the book, bending slightly to accommodate the difference in their heights.

It soon became obvious that the boy wasn't singing, either, but he was engaging in a spirited pantomime. Mimicking the fervent faces of those surrounding them, he lip-synched perfectly, his round face, short hair, and animated expression reminding Kathy of a young Wayne Newton. He kept glancing at her in invitation until she joined him wordlessly—a little game developing between them as they strove to outdo each other in zealous facial contortions.

Kathy was actually disappointed when the music ended and Sweeny led the worshippers in a solemn recitation of the Lord's Prayer. Her new friend livened up the occasion by peeking at Kathy to see if she had her eyes closed. She returned the favor, and they engaged in ocular hide-and-seek until Sweeny's somber "Amen."

"Hear the word of the Lord!" he boomed over a microphone at one of the two pulpits, the left. Emanating from his black-clad frame, the magnified voice startled Kathy and set her stomach rumbling ominously.

"Today's scripture reading is from John, chapter three, verse eight. 'The wind bloweth where it listeth, and thou hearest the sound thereof, but canst not tell whence it cometh, and whither it goeth.'" Here Sweeny paused for dramatic effect, but Kathy could no longer restrain herself from audibly passing gas.

The boy's mother glared at him, pinched his arm, and whispered a stern "Jimmy!" Her son accepted his reprimand stoically, such was his loyalty for his new-found friend.

After his mother turned her attention back to the minister, Jimmy grinned sideways at Kathy and mouthed, "Good one."

"'So is everyone that is born of the spirit,'" Sweeny concluded, his tone portentous and his demeanor intimidating.

The communion service followed and Kathy accepted a wafer and a jigger of grape juice so as not to draw attention to herself, feeling strangely like a cannibal as she consumed the body and blood of Christ. Jimmy tried to snatch a second mouthful of juice, but was slapped smartly on the wrist by his vigilant mother. A noisy performance by the choir ensued with Mrs. Sweeny as soloist. Robed in black with a cinch at her waist, she proclaimed mightily, her accentuated breasts slicing the air like the sword points of avenging angels. Finally, the collection plates were passed, Kathy contributing a dollar with her hand closed over the bill to prevent discovery of the size of her donation.

She felt a grumbling in her bowels again as Sweeny strode to the pulpit on the right and shook his head in an attitude of dismay before beginning his sermon. "There is a wind blowing through the world, and it bears a foul smell. It is the wind of moral degradation, pushing upon us the purveyors of drugs in our neighborhoods; the sellers of smut in the film, television, and music industries; the 'artists' who pander pornography in their canvases and sculptures; the deviants who spread sexually repugnant lifestyles; and the infidels who beset our God, our President, and our troops. Satan puffs out his cheeks with the wind of pride, tempting us to succumb to these evils. But I say unto you this morning what is written in Proverbs," the minister thundered. "'He that troubleth his own house shall inherit the wind'!"

Kathy could contain her flatulence no longer, discharging a silent, but lengthy stream from her nether region. Jimmy's mother wrinkled her nose and cast a murderous look at her son before grabbing the flesh of his upper leg in a vise-like grip. But he was a good little Christ, suffering silently for his friend without so much as an incriminating glance in her direction.

Satisfied that he had rammed the fear of God into his listeners' hearts, Sweeny resumed on a quieter note. "But for those of us who are born of the spirit, there is a different wind. For those of us who have accepted Jesus Christ as our savior—in our *hearts*, not in empty words and actions—a gale is coming. In the Acts of the Apostles it is foretold, 'Suddenly there came a sound from heaven as of a rushing mighty wind.'"

Kathy gritted her teeth and engaged her sphincter, clamping down with a ferocity that surprised her, cheeks gripping the pew. Her efforts succeeded as the gaseous impulse subsided and Jimmy was spared another dose of maternal abuse.

"And what is this mighty wind?" Sweeny asked rhetorically. "It is the Rapture; it is Jesus Christ coming for us. First He will take the holy dead, and then we who are holy will be taken from our homes, from our workplaces, and from our planes and trucks and cars—only our clothes left behind. And the unholy will be left behind as well, crying in despair at the chaos and ruin that will accompany our departure and wondering at whole bodies ascending through ceilings and roofs."

Sweeny allowed his gaze to wander over the congregation, so that the full import of his words might have their effect. Kathy flinched as it seemed that he stared directly at her. Could he tell that she didn't believe a word he'd said? Did these people really think that they would be singled out for salvation while all the "skeptics" of the world would be consigned to destruction?

As if he'd read her mind, the minister resumed speaking, a merciless smile deforming his face like an open wound. "For the legions of those who do not believe, hear the holy word of Thessalonians. 'For the Lord himself shall descend from heaven with a shout, with the voice of the archangel, and with the trumpet of God.'"

He lifted his eyes heavenward, inviting the congregation to imagine the scene and hear the formidable sound. Jimmy, who'd been conserving his resources for his new contest with Kathy, unleashed a fart of such volume and intensity that it dwarfed her suppressed efforts, resounding throughout the chapel like a thunderclap. His mother rewarded him with a vicious kick to the shin, and Sweeny rushed on like a mighty wind.

"'The dead in Christ shall rise first: then we which are alive and remain shall be caught up together with them in the clouds, to meet the Lord in the air: and so shall we ever be with the Lord.'"

On a prearranged signal the organist burst into the opening chords of "The Old Rugged Cross," a hymn that Kathy actually knew. As Jimmy offered the hymnal, she whispered in his ear, "You win." His lip-synching was all the more exuberant in victory, and she mouthed the words lustily, having some familiarity with the melody and tempo.

In spite of the sour note sounded by God's trumpet, Sweeny marched in a triumphant attitude down the center aisle during the last verse; the congregation filed out after him as the organist continued the familiar refrain. Kathy slid out of the pew with a backward grin at the boy, who appeared genuinely sorry to see her go. Then she turned her attention toward the Mansons, timing her exit so that she could pass by the minister at the same moment as they.

"Miss King," Sweeny said, taking her hand so tightly that she felt the urge to knee him in the groin. "Visitors are always welcome, even those in league with the Devil."

"I was enraptured by the service," Kathy replied, smiling as falsely as she could manage. "But I actually came to speak to the Mansons," she added, turning to the startled couple.

"I . . . I don't believe we know you," Mr. Manson said, struggling to recognize something familiar about the young woman standing in front of him.

"You don't, sir," Kathy said, finally freeing her hand. "But I know that you bought a can of white spray paint two days before the statue of *David* was vandalized at the Ringling Museum."

"Good riddance," Mrs. Manson said, patting her blue hair.

"If you hadn't been in such a hurry to go at our last meeting," Sweeny interceded, "I could've explained all that. Members of the church are encouraged to add a coat of white paint to Jesus whenever the spirit moves them."

Kathy played her trump card. "As we stand in this church, Mr. Manson, would you swear by the Father, the Son, and the Holy Spirit that you did no harm to *David?*" She thought she detected a flash of panic in Sweeny's eyes. Unfortunately, Elmer Manson didn't hesitate.

"I certainly will, Miss King, and I did use the paint on our Jesus."

"And what about you, Mrs. Manson?" Kathy persisted.

The woman huffed and waggled her shoulders. "I'm glad that nasty statue was damaged, but I wouldn't do such a thing."

"Where were the two of you on Saturday evening, November second, of last year?" Kathy asked, although she grudgingly felt they were telling the truth.

Mr. Manson shook his head. "I can't remember that far back . . . I'd have to look at our old calendar if we've still got it."

"You won't have to do that, Elmer," Mrs. Manson said. She fixed Kathy with stare as if she were nailing her interrogator's limb to a cross. "We were doing what we do every Saturday night, young lady—watching reruns of Lawrence Welk and Ed Sullivan on the cable. They're the only Godly things left on TV."

~

Bernice MacDonald, spry and enthusiastic, was delighted to have a visitor in spite of teasing her husband about finding pretty young women at odd hours of the night. "He hasn't changed a bit—always on the prowl."

Harry took the ribbing good-naturedly, pleased that his sexual prowess was being extolled, inflated or not. They chatted over Scottish shortbread and iced tea, the last in deference to the season. The MacDonalds allowed Kathy to feed small pieces of cookie to Haggis, who took to her as if she were an old friend.

"You smell my dog, don't you," she said, scratching the animal's ears. Looking up as her hostess, she added, "Well, if I eat any more, Bernice, it'll go straight to my hips. Let's get down to business."

Kathy attached her video cam to the MacDonalds' TV, astonishing them with her expertise. They had trouble just programming the VCR, they said, though they were proud of their ability to send e-mail to their grandchildren. Kathy let the tape run for a few seconds and then froze it on a close-up of Elmer Manson.

"Hmm," Harry said. "He's about the right size and build . . . the hair's right, but that's not the guy."

Kathy was disappointed, but not surprised. "What's different?"

Harry considered. "The eyes. His are brown, and the man I saw had blue eyes. The face isn't the same, either, but the eyes are poles apart. Besides the color, there's something else. This fellow on the TV . . . his are sort of expressionless. But that night under the lights, the man's eyes were . . . I don't know, wild, a little crazy. Does that make any sense?"

"Yes, it does." Kathy consulted her notes. "You didn't mention his eyes before."

Harry nodded. "Something about seeing the tape reminded me."

The day hadn't been a complete loss, Kathy thought after saying her good-byes to the MacDonalds. She now possessed some more information about the man's physical appearance, and she'd had a little fun as well. The last time a boy had outfarted her was in the fifth grade.

TWENTY-FOUR

Richard Lovejoy congratulated himself on his patience. He'd been waiting for inspiration, and now a confluence of events was poised to reward him and punish Butcher. As the heavy rains of June had neared record proportions, Richard had watched his neighbor, like everyone else in the community, drain the overflow from his pool. A spigot attached to the base of the filter unit was opened for this purpose with a hose attached, which could run beyond the homeowner's yard to the common ground at the edge of the preserve. Then drains spaced at intervals could carry off the excess water.

Butcher had been disconnecting the hose after each use, but with the persistence of the rain day after day, he'd begun leaving the tube attached. Just now Richard had been observing his foe brush and vacuum his pool, closing off the bottom drain to divert more suction to the vac. Suddenly, a flash of wicked insight, like a bolt of malignant lighting, illumined Richard's path to revenge.

If the pool water were lowered beneath the level of the skimmer and if the bottom drain remained closed and if the pump came on—it would suck air and burn out! If

Richard could sabotage the machinery tonight, Butcher might think it was his own fault. Perhaps he'd left the spigot open a notch and the drain closed the day before. The pump was already set to come on early every morning and run late because the days were so long.

Another circumstance was also contributing to the timing of Richard's scheme. Butcher had recently taken a job at Home Depot—the neighborhood grapevine even reported that he'd gone to a school sponsored by the chain for its prospective employees. Of course, Butcher may have sought work out of boredom, but Richard maliciously hoped that his neighbor had overextended himself with his new home or that his finances had taken a body blow from the last stock market plunge. At any rate, there was a good chance he'd leave for the store the next morning without noticing the last gasps of his pool pump.

The day couldn't pass fast enough for Richard as he obsessed over his plan. As he and Connie drove to the fitness center at the Plumbago Racquet Club to do their workout, he barely acknowledged her attempts at conversation. Because she was usually happy to conduct a running monologue, she didn't notice his detachment. Lately his wife had chattered about the same thing: couldn't they take the Adamsons up on their offer to visit them in Maine? The bad weather there had given way to a beautiful New England summer, Jill had said in a recent phone conversation. By contrast, Sarasota was either unbearably hot, intolerably wet, or both. Richard was actually receptive to the idea; he missed talking to Jack, and a change of scenery would provide a respite from the nasty season that was developing. But before he left, he wanted closure on the Butcher affair.

Richard wandered through the various exercise stations without enthusiasm, not even ogling one of the young instructors, whose form-fitting outfit left little to the imagination. As he and his wife soaked in the hot tubs of their respective locker rooms, Richard was not stimulated by any of his usual erotic fantasies. Instead, he sat limply as the jets pounded his body, imagining the steps he would take in the middle of the night.

Connie normally slept like a stone once she fell asleep, and Tippy wouldn't move from his accustomed hideaway next to their feet. Richard had answered nature's call innumerable times without disturbing either his wife or the dog. Like every home in Plumbago, Butcher's pool machinery was located outside his cage and was identical in operation to Richard's. He didn't think he would need a flashlight, nor did he want to use one. Even if it were overcast, the coach lights on all the garages would shed enough illumination to see reasonably well. And the pool equipment was located on the rear side of Butcher's home, the Lovejoys' side, in enough shadow to prevent Richard's discovery. It seemed an easy task, the longest part of which would be drawing off the water from the pool.

When evening finally came, Connie announced that she was going to skinny dip in the pool and turned off all the lights at the rear of the house. They had high hedges of hibiscus along the sides of their cage, and the only neighbors liable to appear unannounced were the Adamsons, an unlikely event because they were 1,700 miles away. Richard knew that she expected a performance on his part and he was prepared to oblige, but he continued to be distracted as he joined her *au naturel* in the pool.

As he used his hands and mouth to pleasure her, he pictured the knobs and handles on Butcher's pool machinery. And at the climax of his efforts, he couldn't shake the image of the long hose, stretched to its extremities, spouting water from Butcher's pool. In fact, the length of the hose nearly caused his erection to falter, its shortcomings made evident by the engorged rubber tube. But Richard soldiered valiantly on, ending the engagement with a final, frantic thrust of his elastic bayonet.

SIXTY IN SARASOTA

Connie yawned, and though Richard was never certain, he always sensed some vague discontent on her part. He knew from experience, though, that she would sleep readily now. As they settled into bed, his wife's breathing soon took on the deep, regular pattern of slumber, and Tippy's muffled sighs imitated his owner's. Richard was far too excited to accidentally nod off, but he waited another thirty minutes to be absolutely assured of not disturbing the sleepers of the house.

He slid stealthily from the bed, donned a pair of walking shorts he'd left hanging on the door to their walk-in closet, and exited the bedroom. After opening the slider to the lanai, he slipped into his flip-flops and sheathed his hands in work gloves, both stationed in their accustomed spot just outside the door. He began creeping around the edge of the pool to the screen door when a flash of lightning startled him, brightening his steps unexpectedly. Once outside the lanai, he slunk toward the darkened home of his neighbor like Macbeth stealing to Duncan's bedroom.

Richard had taken no more than a few steps when the security system at his house began screeching its deafening wail, as if warning the neighborhood that skullduggery was afoot. He always programmed the mechanism at night, fearing that an intruder might take advantage of them during defenseless sleep. It was an unbroken routine, and foolishly, it had never occurred to him that he would set if off after opening the door.

"Fuck!" He scampered back to his lanai, but in his haste to get through the screen door, snagged his T-shirt on the handle. The shirt pulled over his mouth and nose, so that he looked like a bandito or highwayman come to plunder his own hacienda. After flailing helplessly for a few seconds while pinned to the door, he managed to extricate himself and lurch toward the slider. Inside the house he was immediately greeted by Connie's screams and Tippy's fierce barking.

"It's me," he shouted above the din. "I set off the alarm!" His voice quieted his wife, but not the Chihuahua, snarling in bloodlust, which Richard could hear jumping from the bed. He blundered on through the house, banging a hip on one of the heavy sofas before staggering into the laundry room. After flipping on the overhead light, he reset the security code and silenced the blaring klaxons. He turned in relief to face Tippy, fangs bared, hackles raised, blockading the door.

"It's me, boy," Richard said, taking a tentative step toward the dog. Tippy darted forward like a cobra striking and snapped at Richard's ankle. He withdrew his leg just in time and was saved from further peril when Connie appeared and scooped the dog into her arms.

"There, there, it's just stupid, silly Daddy," she cooed in the dog's ear. Tippy emitted a rumbling growl and then whimpered as the pet finally appeared to recognize its master.

"What on earth were you doing?" she asked, sleep lines etched unattractively in her face.

Reacting quickly, Richard said, "I . . . I thought I heard hogs rooting in the back."

Connie shook her head. "Jesus Christ, Dickey, I thought we were finished with that."

"I'm sorry, I should've ignored whatever it was." Then he added as an afterthought, "I forgot about the security."

"Oh, I thought you were testing the system," she said sarcastically. "And why are you wearing gloves?"

He stared at the floor awkwardly. "The hogs . . . all those diseases they carry—"

"Sometimes I think you've just totally lost it," she said, cutting him off.

She turned, still carrying the dog, and walked back to the bedroom. Richard followed sheepishly, accepting her censure with resignation as they crawled back into bed. Neither of them spoke again, but Tippy snuffled and snorted for several minutes before finally settling down. Lightning flickered at the windows and thunder rumbled distantly, or so it seemed to Richard. It would be just his luck that a storm would strike if he set out again.

It's now or never, he decided, when he heard both Connie and Tippy snoring. He tried to float off the bed and glide to the laundry room, where he double checked the security. Green light—a good omen. He peeked out a window at Butcher's house, finding it dark and unsuspecting. Within seconds he was skulking across the lawn again, mischief on his mind.

A jagged scar of lightning directly overhead accompanied by a sonic boom no more than a second later goosed him into high gear. He ducked under Butcher's overhang, cowering like a wild animal next to the pool works. After gathering his wits, he shut off the main drain and opened the spigot wide to draw water from the pool. The house blocked his view of the enclosure, so he waited a few minutes, gazing nervously at the sky before finally daring the wrath of Zeus.

Peeking through his neighbor's shrubbery, he could see that the water level was still inches above the skimmer. He retreated to his lanai to wait out the process, reasoning that he'd done all that was necessary to sabotage the pump—no need to be discovered at the scene of the crime. Wind was beginning to ruffle the preserve, and Richard feared that he might've miscalculated. If a downpour accompanied all the pyrotechnics in the sky, the pool would fill up with more water even as he was draining it. While he fretted over this possibility, a rustling and crunching in his flower beds blipped across his radar.

"Goddammit, there's always something," he muttered. He grabbed the aluminum utility pole standing at one corner of the lanai and stalked outside to investigate. Rooting in the mulch for delicacies of the creepy-crawly kind, his little armored nemesis had returned. So much for the "smell of fear," Richard thought, recalling Jack's words. He whacked the armadillo on its backside as lightning and thunder exploded simultaneously overhead.

He dropped the metal pole just in time as sparks coursed through the armadillo's body, leaped to the pole, and then jumped to the lanai cage, lighting it up like a jackpot slot. The glow faded, but Richard was able to see the hapless, smoldering creature, flat on it s back, its legs pointing toward heaven in a posture of surrender. He gingerly prodded its tail, but withdrew his finger hastily, as if he were a kid exploring a forbidden object. He was not shocked or burned, though; and Richard suddenly understood that a power whose alliances were often random and never certain had interceded on his behalf.

He seized the armadillo in his arms, cradling the thing like a dead child, and dashed to Butcher's pool works. He arranged the animal lovingly on the altar of the power cable and peeped through the shrubbery again at the water. It was below the skimmer, so Richard returned to the machinery and reset the timer, jump-starting the pool pump. He closed the spigot and prayed for rain, not unreasonably he thought, now that he was in the good graces of some watcher in the sky.

Deprived of water, the pump began to falter, its death rattle a grinding, wheezing utterance, almost human in its despair. He was reminded of an emphysematous patient, sucking on a cigarette through a tracheotomy, lungs swollen with air that they couldn't expel. The end was sudden and desirable as the ghost in the machine was given up and the pump ceased its suffering. As a last rite, Richard grasped the appropriate handle, reopening the drain.

He bolted back to his lanai and waited for rain. Lightning bloomed everywhere, like grenades being lobbed across the front lines of battle. Within minutes, the heavens opened, delivering a deluge that exceeded his prayers. The water in the pool would rise, he thought gleefully, and there would be no evidence of his tampering. As for the timer, clearly the lightning and the armadillo had conspired to start the pump and short it out. A mystical union of electricity and flesh—an act of God! Richard cackled hysterically, his uncontrollable laughter swallowed up in the timpani of thunder.

TWENTY-FIVE

Kathy had never missed a visit to Maine in the summer, even while she was in college and even after her marriage. When she'd told Brett that she needed some down time, his reaction had been supportive. His employers were impressed with her progress and when she returned refreshed, who knows, she might just break open the case. She didn't tell him that she was discouraged in spite of turning up a witness and a more detailed description of the possible suspect. She'd bulled her way through piles of receipts since Harry MacDonald had nixed Elmer Manson, and no other suspects had materialized.

And there was another matter she'd withheld from Brett. Kathy had invited Dan to take some vacation time and join her. When she was a teen, she'd invited boyfriends to the cabin—her theory was that if they didn't like Maine, then she wouldn't waste any more time on them. Of course, those boys had slept in the guest bedroom, and Kathy had almost hung up the phone before finally broaching the topic with her parents. Would they mind if Dan stayed with her? There'd been a pause while she'd imagined expressions of horror, hand signals, head bobbing, and mouthed words before her mother had said, "You're a grown woman." They'd talked for a few more minutes, but her parents had been really cool about it. Arranging for a pet sitter and buying the tickets had completed her plan.

Kathy glanced at Dan, who was snoozing now that the plane was safely in the air. They would be over Portland in about an hour, their second leg of the trip. She couldn't wait to see the lake, and more importantly, Dan's reaction to it.

~

"What if we hear them screwing in the bedroom?" Jack asked. "You can't keep something like that quiet in the cabin, you know." Many summers ago, he remembered coming home from a poker party slightly ahead of Jill. When he'd set foot on the stairs leading up to the porch, the noise from Kathy's bedroom had sounded like troops mustering. His daughter and her boyfriend had appeared on the footbridge, looking down at Jack in feigned innocence, while he'd acted as if nothing had happened.

"I'm sure that Kathy will be discreet, but if we hear them, that's life," Jill said, though she hoped that wouldn't be the case. "They'll be on the other side of the bridge, at least."

"Yeah, if they were in the guest bedroom, they'd hear us. Connie and Richard will be right underneath us when they come up," Jack added, frowning.

"Well, we'll just have to engage in abstinence then," Jill said, irritated at him for harping on the subject.

Jack ignored her as the he read the signs directing him to the terminal. After maneuvering to the correct lane, he said, "What if Simon and Garfunkle's song had been 'The Sounds of Screwing'?" Then he sang out, "Hello, penis, my old friend, I've come to thrust with you again . . ."

"Jesus, Jack, enough," Jill complained. But her tune changed when she caught sight of her daughter and her boyfriend. "There they are!" Kathy and Dan were indeed standing outside the little jetport with their suitcases, waving as the Adamsons' minivan drove into view.

On the hour drive back to Longawonga, Dan kept exclaiming over the hills and forests; it was his first trip to New England. He couldn't get over the July weather, either: eighty degrees at two in the afternoon with only forty-five per cent humidity. When they arrived at the lake, after a brief stop to purchase fishing licenses, Kathy insisted that her father give their guest the boat tour immediately—unpacking could wait until later.

Dan was impressed with the size of the lake, but his eyes really enlarged when he stepped onto Jack's bass boat with all its bells and whistles. Kathy pointed out landmarks and luxurious homes, but Jack knew what the young man really wanted was to get behind the wheel. Jack opened the throttle on the way home, delighted by Dan's open mouth and the way Kathy's hair blew wildly at fifty miles per hour. As they docked, they waved to Jill, who was pumping the paddle boat around the cove while Nefertiti lolled in the sun.

After the three had trudged with luggage up to the second floor, Dan gazed at the lake from the window of Kathy's bedroom. "Wow, what a view. Why didn't you and your wife take this room, Mr. Adamson?"

"When you had dinner at our house, we asked you to call us Jack and Jill," Jack said.

"He's so used to being a police officer," Kathy interjected. "And I got this room because I can sleep through the morning sun. The backside of the cabin stays darker."

Dan nodded and then looked awkwardly at the two beds, which were pushed together on one side of the room. On the other side were bureaus and a reading chair.

"Kathy used to have girlfriends up when she was still at home," Jack said. "The way the roof angles, they had the most fun with this arrangement. But whoever sleeps in the second bed will have to crawl over the first one. No touching is allowed," he said, wagging his finger.

"Dad!" Kathy groaned.

~

Much later that evening when both couples were in bed, Dan whispered to Kathy, "Was your dad serious about the touching?"

"He likes to joke—too much sometimes," she whispered back. After an awkward silence, he said, "How do we do this?"

"We can straddle the beds or bounce up and down on the mattresses," Kathy replied.

"Be serious."

"I have a better idea," she murmured seductively. "You can hear everything in the cabin, so I have another place in mind."

He lay quietly in the darkness for a few moments, considering this revelation. A whippoorwill trilled from the recesses of the woods, and a loon yodeled plaintively on the lake. "Does that mean we could hear your parents if they—"

"Yeah."

"God."

"I know." After a pause, she said, "Anyway, we can take out the canoe tomorrow."

"Do you think your father would let us take out the bass boat?" Dan asked, a little too quickly.

"I think you'd rather get your hands on that boat than me," Kathy responded in mock annoyance.

"You'd be a close second."

She lifted her leg from under the sheet and gave him a good kick in the hip.

"Ow! That hurt."

"Shh, that's what you get for being a smartass," Kathy said blamelessly. "As I was saying, we could go over to one of the islands where this hidden lagoon is."

"Umm," he said, letting his imagination roam freely. "I get the idea."

"So you can wait, big boy?"

"I'll see you in my dreams."

In the back bedroom, Jack put down the book he was reading, a piece of nonsense called *The Da Vinci Code*—flat characters, awkward writing, and inaccurate research. "I don't hear anything."

"Turn out the light, for God's sake, and stop listening," Jill admonished.

Jack complied and snuggled up next to her. "Doesn't seeing the two of them make you feel romantic?"

"No, it's their first night here," Jill said, keeping her back to him.

"Does that mean you'll be in the mood on their second night or their fifth?" Jack asked, challenging her logic.

Jill sighed. "I just don't feel comfortable tonight, Jack. And Kathy told me what you said."

"What's that?"

"No touching."

~

Kathy and Dan enjoyed a successful fishing trip the next morning, with everyone hooking some bass. Jack allowed Dan to operate the foot-controlled, electric trolling motor, so he was in high spirits when he and Kathy donned bathing suits, packing a picnic lunch and fishing rods, and headed for the islands in the canoe.

The spot that Kathy had in mind was tucked into the shoreline of a large island hidden from view by the two islands visible from the cabin. A shallow channel between these land masses and the other discouraged boat traffic, and the lagoon itself was sheltered on three sides by rugged rock formations. They maneuvered the canoe along a narrow gap bordered by submerged boulders and glided into the pool, which was about thirty feet in circumference and five feet deep at its center. A clearing with a well-defined path leading into the pines marked the shoreline where they beached the canoe.

"We can explore the island later if you like," Kathy offered.

"There's only one thing I'd like to explore right now," Dan said suggestively.

She grinned, unsnapping her life jacket, and pushed off into the water, its temperature seventy-eight degrees according to the gauge on her father's boat. After the effort of propelling the canoe, the effect was both refreshing and liberating. He stroked after her until he was within arm's reach, arrested by the deafening noise of motors, something akin to runaway lawn mowers.

A flotilla of jet skiers, six of them on identical purple crafts, roared toward them before banking sharply to avoid the shallows. They circled in the area for several minutes, bouncing over their own wakes and waving at the couple. Pleased with themselves for executing such a remarkable show, they rooster tailed off, leaving the lagoon roiled with waves and the canoe scraping against the pebbly bank.

"You did say this place was 'hidden,'" Dan recalled.

"They won't be back," Kathy promised.

But another boat entered the area, a small whaler with a stand-up console, and advanced directly toward them. The boater, attired in a khaki uniform, zipped though the tight passage as if he were an old hand at navigating these waters. He was stern-faced and stocky, with close-cropped hair showing under his hat.

"It's the game warden," Kathy said in an aside. She was familiar with his tactics after years of fishing on the lake with her father.

"Any luck?" he asked, shutting off his motor and pulling up to the canoe. The question was designed to trap the unwary, Kathy knew. The laws allowed for possession of only one bass, its length between twelve and sixteen inches.

"Not so far," Dan answered wryly.

"Could I see your licenses?" the warden demanded, eyeing the fishing rods. Kathy returned to the canoe and produced the documents from a soft tackle box.

After inspecting them, he asked, "What's in the cooler?"

Another chance to catch them in a lie, Kathy thought. "Our picnic lunch," she replied.

"Would you mind taking the top off?" he requested, when she didn't offer to.

Kathy complied, noting his disappointment as he discovered the mundane food.

"Have a good day, folks." He split the passage neatly and shot off in the direction of the jet skiers.

"Friendly bastard," Dan observed.

"Like you on a traffic stop, I imagine," she said, splashing some water in his direction with the flat of her hand.

He lunged for her and missed, but ceased his pursuit when another boat puttered into the deeper water beyond the lagoon. This time it was a party barge, a flat pontoon boat with an awning on top. Four guys in sleeveless t-shirts were dangling lines over the side while sucking on beers. Unfortunately, they dropped their anchor after each of them began hauling white perch out of the water.

"There's no limit on those," Kathy said. "Any bozo with a hook can catch a hundred."

"You mean these bozos are likely to stay awhile," Dan inferred.

"Yeah, looks like it. Why don't we take our blanket and picnic stuff and find a secluded spot on the island?"

They grabbed the contents of the boat and began trekking inland, the dense pines breaking up the sunlight and stifling the breeze. Each slapped at an occasional mosquito and flicked at perspiration that formed in the close air. Shortly they came to a rocky outcrop with a smooth space at its base—just off the trail and large enough to accommodate their blanket.

"Do you want to have lunch first or skip right to dessert?" Kathy asked, making no attempt to disguise *her* preference.

"Just desserts," he answered, pleased with his word play, a facility that had never been his strong suit.

"You've been around my father too much," Kathy said, drawing him down to the blanket.

They began kissing, working themselves up, but because they were no longer moving targets, mosquitoes dropped in for a bite. The couple swatted at the insects in irritation, but Dan was not to be deterred as he began lifting Kathy's arms out of her one-piece. No sooner had he freed one than a hair-raising scream, seemingly from many voices, pierced the forest.

Kathy adjusted her suit and jumped up. "What the hell was that?"

Her question was answered within seconds as the sound of thudding feet was followed by a steady stream of children pouring along the path. Each was carrying a plastic bag, and they stopped periodically, scanning the ground.

"I'll bet they have some," one of them said, a chubby, red-faced boy with thin dirt ring around his neck. "We're on a scavenger hunt, and I'm looking for soda cans and plastic wrappers," he said, pausing by their blanket.

"We have that, but we're still using them," Kathy said, thinking about the contents of the cooler.

"Who are all these kids?" Dan asked.

"Teams," the boy said. "We came over from the Y camp."

"That's one cove north of our place," Kathy explained

"How many of you are there?" Dan wanted to know, a shrinking feeling in his groin.

The boy screwed up his brow. "Oh, I don't know—there were fifty canoes."

"That's at least a hundred," Kathy calculated. "Check with us later, and if we're still here, you can have our trash." But the look that she and Dan exchanged augured a disheartened retreat.

~

That night as they lay in bed scratching their bites, Kathy said, "What did you think about my father's comment on the case?" She'd finally introduced the topic at dinner, especially her discouragement at being closer to a solution, yet farther away at the same time.

"You mean what he said about thinking outside the box?" Dan replied. He hadn't raised the subject, not wanting to spoil their little vacation.

"Yeah."

"It couldn't hurt—you should explore every avenue at your disposal."

"It occurred to me . . . I've been operating under the assumption that the vandal or vandals had a bone to pick with Ringling or disliked graphic art in general, choosing *David* as a notable example of nude sculpture."

"Uh-huh," Dan said, following her line of reason.

"What if the perpetrator had a grudge—who knows why—against this *particular* statue? In other words, the crime had nothing to do with the museum or all the nude artwork out there. Somebody was angry at this statue *alone.*"

"I see what you're saying," Dan said, excited. "That's a different way of looking at it."

"But does it get me any closer to solving the case?" Kathy said, running a hand through her hair.

"It gives you another motive to explore," Dan said. A chorus of loon calls reverberated around the lake, as if to say "you're onto something."

Kathy reached over and clasped his hand. "How quiet do you think you can be?"

"I'll bust my balls trying."

In the other bedroom, Jack put down *The Da Vinci Code* in disgust and turned out the light. "Did you notice how disappointed Kathy was with their afternoon on the lake?"

"Yeah, too many boaters, too much noise," Jill said.

"None of the great places remain secret, do they?" Jack lamented.

"Just like Sarasota," Jill agreed.

"It's awfully quiet over there," Jack noted, figuring that all the outdoor activity had tuckered out Kathy and Dan.

"Uh-huh."

Jack cozied up to his wife and whispered in her ear, "Hello, penis, my old friend—"

She started giggling before he could finish the verse. A good sign, he decided, nestling closer.

TWENTY-SIX

"I might've given up some time in Maine to see that fried armadillo," Jack said. He flicked out a plastic finesse worm and watched his line as the lure sank slowly in ten feet of water. Ever since the Lovejoys had arrived at Longawonga, Richard had been bursting to tell his story of revenge. Now that they were alone on Jack's bass boat, he'd finally shared his secret with his neighbor.

"Butcher didn't discover the damage until late in the afternoon," Richard continued. He was fishing a surface plug, a lure that imitated a wounded minnow when twitched across the top of the water. "When he returned from Home Depot, he must've noticed that the pump wasn't running. Anyway, he prods the armadillo with his aluminum pole like this."

Richard timidly poked the air with his graphite rod, like an effeminate swordsman fearful of wounding his opponent.

"Then he jumps back when it falls off the power cable," Richard added, flinching melodramatically.

Because Longawonga was only thirty minutes west of the ocean, the lake attracted a resident population of gulls. One of their number was gliding near the boat, gluttonously eyeing Richard's artificial minnow.

"Keep an eye on your lure," Jack warned.

"Yeah . . . so he fiddles around with the pump, the timer, and all the controls, but nothing happens, of course. Man, was he pissed," Richard said gleefully. "The next day the pool guy comes out and replaces the pump. Butcher finally gets up the nerve to touch the armadillo and carries the thing out to the preserve and dumps it—no ceremony, no Christian burial."

"He could've said a few words, at least," Jack said, piously condemning Butcher's uncharitable behavior.

"Poor thing—the turkey vultures made mincemeat of it before the day was over." Richard hung his head in an attitude of exaggerated regret.

"For service in the war on domestic terrorism," Jack intoned. "Struck down shockingly when its armor failed, yet sacrificing its body to defeat the Butcher of Plumbago. May the armadillo rest in pieces."

"Amen," Richard said, closing his eyes and snickering.

"Jerk your line, Richard!" Jack commanded.

Richard pulled back with his rod just as the greedy gull swooped down on the lure. The bird missed, but was not to be deterred, mistaking the sudden movement of the wooden bait for a fleeing prey. The gull hovered just over the water and plunged again, snaring the lure in its beak before winging off with its prize. Line zinged off Richard's reel as the bird soared upward.

"What do I do now?" Richard said, his mouth agape.

"Give the line a tug and maybe he'll drop it," Jack advised.

Richard tightened up on the reel handle and pulled, jerking the gull back toward the boat, but the lure didn't come free.

"One of the hooks must be stuck in its beak," Jack guessed. "Reel it in."

"Can't we just cut the line?" Richard asked dubiously.

It was a legitimate question, but Jack didn't want the bird on his conscience like Coleridge's albatross. "We could, but the bird would probably die if it can't feed properly, or it might snag itself on something since there are two sets of hooks."

Richard accepted this explanation, especially in light of the forfeiture of the armadillo's life. Nature should be repaid for her help. He began reeling and easily towed the gull from sky to water, as if he'd been bringing down a kite.

"The damn thing's light as a feather," Richard noted, staring at the bird, which was about forty feet from the boat.

"What a surprise," Jack said. "Now you've gotta get it over here and work the hook out."

"Me?" Richard had obviously expected Jack, the experienced boater and fisherman, to extricate the animal.

"Well, I could do it, of course, but you bagged him," Jack correctly observed. He would help if necessary, but watching Richard attempt the rescue was too good an opportunity to pass up. Having placed the responsibility on his friend's shoulders, Jack generously offered a little advice, "You'll want needle-nosed pliers and some gloves."

He opened a storage compartment and produced these items, holding Richard's rod as Lovejoy donned the gloves. Richard reeled the bird in, squawking and fluttering, until it was about three feet from the boat and set the rod down. Then he grabbed the line and pulled the gull alongside the bow.

"Pliers," Richard said, holding out his free hand.

"No anesthesia?" Jack posed, challenging the surgeon's wisdom.

"Pliers, dammit," Richard repeated, somewhat testily.

Jack slapped them into his hand and watched as Richard reached down to work on the bird. The lure had treble hooks fore and aft, and one hook on the front treble had impaled the gull's beak. Richard tried to grasp this hook with the pliers, but he'd left too much play in the line, allowing the bird to flap and twist. It rose just upwind of Richard and began excreting milky white droppings, which plopped onto his hat and T-shirt.

"Argh!" Richard said in disgust, dropping the line.

"You'll have to change the writing on that shirt," Jack said. "'Fish fear me, women want me, and birds shit on me.'"

"Let's see what you can do," Richard dared. He moved to the other side of the boat and cupped water from the lake onto his clothing.

Jack took the gloves and the pliers from Lovejoy and set to work by clutching the end of the lure, a maneuver that removed all the slack from the line. The gull was unable to shift, allowing Jack to grasp the shank of the hook with the pliers and twist slightly while lifting the bird from the water. Gravity completed the task as the hook slipped out cleanly and the bird dropped into the lake. Within seconds, it realized that it was free and beat its wings with reckless abandon—flying toward the east and the Atlantic and away from freshwater fishermen.

"Let's try another spot," Richard said, lake water dripping off the bill of his cap.

"How 'bout a different lure while we're at it?" Jack suggested.

"You're the expert," Richard said sourly. So far Jack had caught six bass while his guest had only garnered bird turds.

Jack rigged up a jig and pig, a single-hook, weighted lure with a silicone skirt and a plastic, two-legged trailer. "Believe it or not, this looks like a crawfish in the water," Jack explained. "Let it go to the bottom and give it a couple of hops. If nothing takes it, reel it in, and cast to a different spot."

He moved the boat to a channel with some submerged rock piles, a likely habitat for crawfish, which bass, like Cajun gourmands, dearly loved. On his second cast, Richard hooked something that bent his graphite rod nearly double.

"It won't budge," Richard complained, yanking back mightily. Fortunately, his drag wasn't set too tightly, and some line pulled off from the force of his efforts.

"Maybe you're hung up on a rock," Jack guessed, a common occurrence on Longawonga. Not wanting to lose the jig, he said, "Let's try a different angle."

He maneuvered the boat past the hang-up so that Richard could free the hook, but it wouldn't budge. Then both men saw the line move of its own accord.

"There's something on there," Richard exclaimed, growing excited.

"And it's big," Jack echoed. He was happy for his friend, and besides, it was no fun catching all the fish when he had guests in the boat. He considered it a test of his own prowess as a guide if he could get others to land some bass.

Anticipating the fish's size, Richard began shaking as he fought his quarry, a phenomenon that still struck Jack in spite of all the hefty bass he'd landed over the years. Lovejoy's efforts eventually nudged the fish off the bottom and upward through the water column.

"Take it slowly, he's coming," Jack encouraged.

Richard heaved back mightily on the rod, and the creature finally emerged from its lair. "What the hell . . ."

"It's a snapping turtle," Jack pronounced in disappointment. Larger than the gopher tortoises in Sarasota, but shaped just as they, like a toilet bowl, the ugly snapper eyed his tormentor and hissed. The jig was lodged squarely in the animal's mouth.

"Now what?" Richard asked uncertainly. "And what's that stink?"

"It's the turtle, and we're going to cut off the line," Jack said, grabbing Richard's gear.

"That's not what we did with the gull," Richard asserted, sensing inequity.

"Do you want to try to work the hook out?" Jack asked, offering the rod back to his friend.

Richard shook his head silently. Jack fished a pair of nail clippers from his pocket, reached down as far as he dared, and clipped the line. The turtle moved its legs ponderously and retreated to the green depths from which it sprang.

"What will happen to it?" Richard wanted to know, staring at the empty water.

"They're tough bastards," Jack answered. "There's some corrosive element in their body, so the hook may rust out." After a pause, he said, "What would you like to try now?"

"Let's go in and have some lunch—this doesn't seem to be my lucky day."

Jill and Connie were sunning on the lawn in front of the cabin when the men docked. Nefertiti and Tippy roused themselves and waddled onto the dock, wagging their tails optimistically.

"Where are the fish?" Connie called out.

"Oh, we put them all back," Jack said. "You can only keep one, and I want to be able to catch them again." Sensing Connie's befuddlement, he added, "There are a lot more fisherman than there used to be. If we killed all the fish we caught, there'd be nothing left to catch"

"Jack keeps saying 'we' when he caught all the fish," Richard confessed gloomily.

"You had nothing?" Jill said incredulously. Even rank beginners had success under her husband's guidance.

"I hooked a seagull and a turtle," Richard admitted with embarrassment.

Connie laughed a little too loudly for her husband's taste, and he trudged into the cabin to sulk. Seconds later the phone rang.

"It's Kathy," Richard called to the others. "She wants to talk to everyone."

"We'll put it on the speaker phone," Jack said, as he and the women left the lakefront. His daughter was watching her parents' house again now that she was back in Sarasota and checking the Lovejoys' home as well.

"Catching any fish?" Kathy began.

"It's best we not go into that," her father replied, evaluating Richard's embittered disposition.

"OK, well, the pool guy did his thing—they both look great. The lawns have been mowed... I don't know when he found the opportunity 'cause it's been raining like hell. Your plants are doing fine, Mom."

"Don't worry about them so much," Jill urged. "If they die, I can always get more."

"The people that treat the lawns came," Kathy continued, then hesitated.

Jack sensed immediately that something was wrong. "What is it, Kathy?"

"Well, they stuck those little 'pesticide application' signs in the lawn."

"Yeah," Jack said impatiently, "they always do, what's the problem?" He looked at the others—only Richard seemed worried, as though some catastrophe had befallen his house.

"Like I said, every lawn in the neighborhood has these signs, and every yard looks great... except yours, Mr. and Mrs. Lovejoy."

"Oh God!" Richard wailed. "I knew it."

"What are you talking about, Kathy?" Connie asked, more composed than her husband.

"It looks like they poured all the chemicals on your plants and flower beds—they're all dead."

"No!" Richard screamed with the sort of emotion reserved for a death in the family.

"But why would they make that mistake on our lawn and nobody else's?" Connie asked reasonably.

"I talked to the company," Kathy answered, "and they said there's no way they caused the damage."

"Someone *wanted* us to think that they did," Jack deduced.

"Butcher," Richard declared ominously. He spoke the name the way Jerry Seinfeld said 'Newman,' after discovering any number of times that the scheming, portly neighbor was up to no good.

"But why?" Connie said, understandably perplexed.

"The cat's out of the bag, Richard," Jack said. "I think you better tell her."

"I destroyed his pool pump," Richard confessed, "but I made it look like an accident. I don't know how he figured it out."

"If he asked the pool company to look at the old pump, they'd see it wasn't shorted out," Jack explained. "The pesticide application gave him the perfect opportunity to strike back. There may be no chemical weapons in Iraq, but now we've got them in Plumbago—right in our own back yard."

TWENTY-SEVEN

No doubt about it, she was mired in a crisis of self-doubt. The fiasco with the Lovejoys' yard seemed to have triggered it. Kathy could reason that it wasn't her fault, that there was nothing she could've done to prevent it. But it had happened on her watch, and she felt as though she'd let down not only her parents' friends, but also her parents.

And now she was questioning her handling of the *David* investigation. None of her avenues of inquiry had really produced any fruit. Her theories of who might've vandalized the statue hadn't panned out, and the trail of receipts for white spray paint had led nowhere. There was even no guarantee that the man Harry MacDonald saw the night of the crime was the perpetrator. He could've been a pedestrian who just happened by, she thought. If she believed that to be true, it would really be difficult for her to continue.

The trip to Maine had been curiously disappointing. Longawonga had lost some of its luster, not the picture that Kathy had painted for Dan at all. He seemed to have enjoyed himself, but she wasn't entirely sure. His pleasure could've been feigned for politeness' sake. And Brett had been even more distant toward her (if that was possible) since her return, perhaps signaling a complete loss of romantic interest coupled with a loss of faith in her investigative abilities.

The only thing pressing her onward was her father's suggestion "to think outside the box." That's why she was in the Selby Library this morning pursuing a different tack. Just entering the library had improved her mood; the beautiful building was a landmark in downtown Sarasota. Its white, trapezoidal shapes were supposed to suggest billowing sails, keeping it in harmony with nearby Sarasota Bay and the seashell design of the Van Wezel Center. Kathy liked the multiple, high windows and the openness of the place. She even thought nostalgically of her hours in the libraries of Wake Forest and N.C. State as she began researching her topic: Michelangelo and his *David*.

The more she read the more excited she became. She remembered vaguely somewhere in her studies coming across the belief that the great Renaissance artist might have been homosexual. For most of the sources she now consulted, this was more fact than theory—from his education and training with other boys at the Medicis', his focus on the male nude, his use of nude male models, his disdain for women and marriage, to his love poetry directed toward males.

There was also a recent controversy among scholars in which his homosexuality was contested. And the surprising revelation that a brass wire fitted with copper leaves was provided as a girdle to cover the genitals and buttocks when the provocative statue was first unveiled to Florentines in the sixteenth century. Some things never change, Kathy mused. The thrust of Sweeny's remarks had been the indecency of the statue, not that it and the sculptor of the original were homosexual icons. The minister probably isn't aware of it, she concluded, but someone with a broader education certainly would be. Sweeny had mentioned immoral lifestyles in his sermon, but that hadn't been his objection to the statue. Her vandal could be a homophobe, Kathy theorized, and there was no shortage of such individuals in the current cultural climate. If she could find a gay basher, and if Harry MacDonald could identify him, and if the homophobe had bought a can of white spray paint....

~

Richard Lovejoy was trying to look on the bright side of things. Connie had convinced him to stay the week in Maine because the damage had been done. Rushing back to Sarasota wouldn't have resurrected his crucified flowers and shrubs. And he'd finally caught some fish on Longawonga; in fact, on the last outing, he'd outdone Jack, catching more bass and bigger ones. Now that he and Connie were home, he'd done his grieving over the brown skeletons and moved on. Given so many blank beds, he could start anew, rearranging things and making different choices based on his successes and failures in the past. All the August rain and sunshine were providing a fertile climate for his efforts as well.

But while he planted and mulched—both therapeutic activities—he couldn't help but dwell again on revenge. He'd turned in Butcher for desecrating the preserve, and his neighbor had sabotaged Richard's sprinkling system, ratted on the Lovejoys for over-watering, and befouled their yard with excrement. *I showed great restraint, all things considered*, Richard reminded himself, before burning out my neighbor's pool pump. But the armadillo's sacrifice would be for naught if he were unable to repay Butcher's latest atrocity. Lovejoy cast a sad eye toward the preserve, where no trace of the armored creature yet remained, and felt a tear leak down his cheek—or perhaps it was a bead of perspiration.

Devising a suitable scheme had so far eluded Richard. He could do unto Butcher as he had done unto Richard—but there was no originality in repeating any of his neighbor's mischief. He could intercept Butcher's mail if he kept a close watch—their boxes shared a common post at the property line. But how long could he do that without being discovered and wasn't that a federal crime? What if he sneaked out in the middle of the night and burned Butcher's lawn with fertilizer? He could kill all the St. Augustine grass; then Butcher would have to bear the cost and effort of resodding his lawn. But this reprisal seemed too similar to his neighbor's recent chemical attack on Richard's plants.

It even occurred to him to drive around the area collecting carrion. He'd deposit the dead animals on the sly in Butcher's yard and at the edge of the preserve. The vultures would beset the property—perhaps for days, probably perching on the roof and making a general nuisance of themselves. Richard had seen some residents mount phony owls on the outside of their houses to ward off the unwanted attentions of the ugly birds. This idea appealed to him aesthetically; it singled out his neighbor's property as a house of death. It would be like the raven of Poe's poem, Jack would say, ominous and unsettling by its constant presence.

But would he be able to find dead animals conveniently? It would be one thing to scoop up road kill, but quite another to slog through the woods searching for remains. He would need several carcasses, and handling them would be dicey. Not to mention storing them until he was ready to spread Butcher's table with indelicacies. Connie would want no part of such a venture, and it would be hard for him to fault her for that. There was also the issue of all those vultures hovering right next door—why make things unpleasant for himself and Connie as well?

While the Lovejoys had been in Maine, Jack and Jill had recounted a story about birdseed and squirrels. If Richard could somehow adapt that experience to wreak havoc on Butcher, the inconvenience to his own household would be minimal. It would be an original act of retribution and inexpensive as well. But there would probably be no way to disguise the author or it, if disguise were even a sensible precaution anymore. Whatever damage befell Butcher, he would suspect Lovejoy and vice-versa.

Perhaps devising a method to protect himself against further retaliation would be a more profitable avenue of deliberation. Knowing that Butcher would strike again and probably in the middle of the night were givens. If Richard had a security system in place—one that his neighbor didn't suspect—then Butcher could be stopped and humiliated at the same time. An electrified fence wouldn't get past community covenants. If Tippy were leashed outside, he'd howl and whine the whole damn night. Perhaps there was some kind of booby trap Richard could deploy, but where would he stash it, and how could he be sure that Butcher would spring it? Lovejoy would have to give the matter some thought, because he wanted his anti-missile system in place before he launched another attack.

~

Brett Masterson stared at the phone in his office at the Ringling Museum. He wanted desperately to call Kathy King and arrange a business lunch. Since that spring day when she'd turned down his request for a date, he'd done nothing but feel sorry for himself. He'd never handled rejection well, especially with regard to women, a weakness traceable to the age of eight, when he'd become a ward of the state. That's when his mother had died of a drug overdose, and as for his father, well, Brett had no idea who he was or where he lived. When couples came into the orphanage, Brett was passed over every time. He was too old—he could see it in the women's eyes when they gravitated to younger children, kids who could be raised as one's own.

But he'd been talented in school and won a scholarship—provided by his current benefactors—to Florida State in Tallahassee. Unfortunately, with no family ties and very little extra money, Brett had suffered limited exposure to coeds, other than to eye them wistfully on campus or wherever his part-time jobs led him. So the regular and intimate contact with Kathy had aroused his hopes and fueled his fantasies.

Now there was another complicating factor; his employers were for the first time discussing how much longer they would be willing to fund an investigation. Kathy's initiative and perseverance had impressed them, but she seemed finally to have run out of suspects. Her eyewitness hadn't been able to identify any of her candidates past or present, and searching for vandals in paint receipts was looking more and more like a wild goose chase.

Brett had, in fact, not informed his bosses of Kathy's request for a brief vacation in Maine. They might have ended the relationship on the spot, figuring that the woman herself was out of options. He didn't accept this notion; she wasn't giving up—she simply needed to recharge.

So Brett was in the awkward position of informing her that her services might soon be terminated and working up the courage to ask her out again. The two matters were in opposition to each other, like a funeral followed by a baby shower. But if he didn't work up his courage rapidly, there would no longer be a pretext for any regular contact with her.

~

Jack walked casually along the entry road to Loon Lodges, carrying the mail he'd picked up from the Adamsons' mailbox perched next to the asphalt road. The overhanging trees provided welcome shade from the late August sun, and he'd already had his fill anyway that morning on Longawonga. The fishing had been good, plus he'd had the lake mostly to himself. As he turned into the cabins, Jack noted that he and his wife had the place mostly to themselves as well. Two of their closest friends were still in residence, but everybody else had returned to work. There were a few nearby owners who still popped in on weekends and then popped out just as quickly. The lake was significantly lower as the fall drawdown neared, aquatic plants drooping out of the water and turning brown.

"Anything exciting?" Jill asked from her brown Adirondack chair. She closed the *The Da Vinci Code* with a snap.

"Bills and some of our arts stuff," he replied, handing her the bills. He settled into a chair just like hers, reached down to stroke Nefertiti, and began examining the offerings for the upcoming entertainment season in Sarasota.

"You know," Jill said, her mind still on the book, "the author blames the Catholic Church for suppressing the sacred feminine, and then he conveniently ignores Mary, for Christ's sake."

"Yeah, and that's just one of his sins."

"Here's what I think . . . he's was writing a book tailored to women's reading clubs."

"Uh-huh, capitalizing on the Oprah phenomenon . . . we've never seen *Miss Saigon*, have we?" he asked.

"Don't think so," Jill answered.

"It's playing at the Van Wezel . . . hey, they've got Frankie Valli and the Four Seasons and Willie Nelson." He and Jill loved seeing old groups—the Righteous Brothers had put on a great performance the previous season.

"On the same bill?" Jill asked incredulously.

"Yeah, Philly falsetto meets Texas twang," Jack said sarcastically.

"Well, the way you said it . . ."

"Frankie Valli has Little Anthony with him, and Willie's all by himself." He glanced at another brochure. "The Sarasota Opera's doing *Tosca* and *The Magic Flute.*"

"From the sublime to the ridiculous," Jill noted.

"Don't you have that backwards?" Jack insisted, brow furrowed.

"No," Jill said irritably. "Willie's sublime and the operas are ridiculous . . . you know what I meant." She hated it when he played English teacher with her. "What about the symphony and the ballet?" she asked, moving on.

"Those mailings didn't come, but I'll check on the Internet," Jack promised, excited by the prospect.

"And the Asolo, too," Jill remembered.

"Right . . . are you thinking what I'm thinking?" One of the things that delighted them the most as their marriage had endured and prospered was how often they were on the same wavelength.

"Maybe we should go back sooner than we planned," Jill said. They'd always returned to Maryland by the end of August in the past to fulfill their teaching obligation. This year they'd talked about staying in Maine till the colors changed in late September and early October.

"There won't be anyone here after Labor Day," Jack said, displeased by the prospect. An empty lake somehow seemed as undesirable as one overflowing with vacationers.

"I'm eager to get back to our new house," Jill said in a plaintive tone. "And we need to keep an eye on Kathy and Dan."

"I agree—but it's Richard and Butcher that I'm really worried about."

TWENTY-EIGHT

Kathy King was filled with optimism for a change. She'd just been faxed the information Dan had been preparing for her, profiles of known gay bashers in the Sarasota area. She'd told him not to limit the list to those who fit the description of the man her eyewitness had seen the night of the crime. She wanted to consider any homophobe since there was no guarantee that Harry MacDonald's pedestrian was the perpetrator.

Before she investigated a specific individual, though, Kathy wanted to compare the names in Dan's file to two other lists in her possession: those who'd bought spray paint within a week of the crime, and the members of Sweeny's congregation. She hadn't searched beyond a week to compile the former, uncertain as to the value of poring over any more receipts. And Sweeny had surprisingly provided the latter, smug in an attached note: "The souls of my flock are as white as the paint they lavish on Jesus. Can you say the same for your own?"

Then Brett had called, more animated than she'd ever remembered him to be, proposing a business lunch. She ran her latest theory by him, and he positively brimmed over with enthusiasm, as if her new line of investigation were an antidote for some great affliction. His employers would be impressed, he promised her, with Kathy's imaginative research and the fresh possibilities open to inquiry. Perhaps she was about to crack the case wide open, he gushed.

The doorbell rang. Kirk unleashed a fusillade of barking, and Spock roused himself from the futon. What now? Kathy wondered. She wasn't expecting anyone, and solicitors were a rare, invasive species seldom seen on the resort island.

"Who is it?" she pitched in an unwelcoming tone behind the door.

"Dan."

Dan? He wouldn't have had time to drive here from downtown, and the voice didn't sound right. "I didn't catch that," she said suspiciously.

"Dan Musgrove from De Soto High—you asked me to contact you if I had any information about your investigation."

That was true, but she'd expected him to telephone, not show up at her front door. And she hadn't heard from him in months. It might simply be the young man infatuated with the seductive detective, she thought facetiously, or he might actually have some information. She opened the door.

"You could've called, Dan," she said, mildly rebuking him. At least he was dressed respectably, Docker shorts and a collared shirt. Kirk sniffed at Dan's loafers, and Spock rubbed against the youth's bare legs.

He bent down and stroked the cat, then let the dog sniff his hand. "I wanted to see your place—cool location, Kathy."

"Thanks, my security team is checking you out. Kirk's the one wagging his tail, and the other one's Spock."

"Like the old *Star Trek* dudes, huh," Dan said, straightening up.

"Yeah," Kathy said, feeling positively ancient. "Come on in." She led him immediately into her office so that he wouldn't get any frisky ideas and retreated behind the barricade of her desk. "Have a seat."

"I passed the FCAT," he said, beaming at her from the futon.

"That's great, Dan," Kathy said, genuinely pleased for him. "So are you off to college?"

"That's a long story—I didn't graduate." Although he stated the fact without embarrassment, his face pulled into a shit-eating grin.

"What happened?"

"I flunked English . . . cut too many classes, didn't hand in enough work, so I wasn't allowed to walk at graduation."

"Can't you make up the class?" Kathy asked, fearing that Dan would let the whole issue slide.

"I already have," Dan said proudly, "and that's why I'm here. Here's the thing: I met this girl in summer school—we were in the same boat—and I told her that I was helping you with your investigation."

Kathy couldn't help but smile; Dan had probably used this line more than once to get into a girl's pants. "Was she impressed?"

He smirked. "I know what you're thinking, but hear me out. Seems she had this P.E. teacher up in Manatee County who hated that statue. She said he practically celebrated the day after it was vandalized."

Kathy was interested now. "What was his problem with the statue?"

"Said the guy who made it—what's his name?" he asked, fumbling for the unfamiliar word.

"Michelangelo."

Dan nodded. "Yeah, said he was a faggot, and that queers worshipped the statue."

God or fate or whatever works in mysterious ways, Kathy thought. She was all ears now. "Can a teacher get away with saying something like that?" she wondered.

"She said it wasn't the first time . . . he'd go off on fags getting married, too." He paused and then added, "Buncha Jesus freaks up there, so he was probably teaching family values as far as they were concerned."

"You may be right. That school board was just sued for starting their meetings with The Lord's Prayer." After some reflection, she asked, "Did your friend say how old this guy was?"

Dan shook his head. "But he's been there forever, probably near retirement. My friend couldn't stand him," he recalled. "It was a coed class and he was always joking with the guys and hittin' on the girls. If you flirted with him, it was an easy A."

Kathy took out her notebook. "What's this teacher's name?

"Mr. Bateman . . . she called him 'Master' instead of 'Mister,'" Dan remembered, laughing conspiratorially.

Kathy ignored this. "And the school?" she asked, jotting down the information.

"Claude Pepper High . . . there's one more thing, Kathy," he said, looking even prouder than when he'd told her about stealing the nine kegs of beer.

"What's that?" she said, curious.

"I asked my friend if she thought Mr. Bateman was capable of screwing with the statue. She said he acted like he'd done it himself."

~

Richard Lovejoy had always prided himself on his ability to research a topic. While he was still in the radio business, he'd spent hours and days before tinkering with a successful format or radically overhauling one that was starting to slip. That's why his stations had been so profitable, and why he'd sold them for such a huge profit.

He was applying those same skills now as he researched what he hoped would be his new security weapon. The most important thing was that the creature be pedigreed. That way its uppermost weight might hit 250 pounds, as opposed to a mixed breed, which could top 1,000. He'd already pored over a pamphlet from the humane society on the care and training of the animal. Some owners lavished attention on the pet when it was younger, but were unprepared for the size it would eventually reach. Also, a family frequently absent from the home might incur the wrath of the lonely animal—much like a dog or a cat chews, claws or pees in retaliation against its thoughtless owners. But then again, according to the research, this pet might be smarter than both dogs and cats, certainly the former. He and Connie didn't go away that much, but he thought he could come to an arrangement with the humane society to pet sit for those rare occasions—a sizable donation was likely to overcome any objections on their part.

These were the only negatives that Richard had uncovered. On the positive side, the creature was noted for its affectionate nature. Here was a chance to have a pet that responded to him and not to Connie, like Tippy, who would give Richard the time of day only when his wife was absent. The new animal was imminently trainable—it could be walked on a leash—and because it was territorial, he would train it to protect his property. He allowed himself a rare smile at the thought of Butcher's potential encounter with the creature in the middle of the night. And after he deployed his latest assault on the hated home next door, Richard was sure that his neighbor would retaliate. That underscored the features of the animal that Lovejoy prized above all others. If it felt the threat of foreign invasion, it possessed weapons of mass destruction (perhaps "ass destruction," Richard thought gleefully) and the belligerent personality to exercise them. Traplike jaws and razor teeth would take a bite out of Butcher's counterattack.

Of course, Richard would have to fashion a wallow in the back yard. He would blend it aesthetically with his mulched islands of flowers and shrubs. The creature could root and poot there to its heart's content, providing as it did a wonderful source of fertilizer for the rest of the yard.

Richard doubted that God was blessing the conflict with Iraq, but fate seemed to be smiling on his battle with Butcher. The humane society was now in possession of a mature female that had been potty and leash trained. He would make arrangements and surprise Connie; he couldn't wait to see the looks on the faces of Jack and Jill! In the meantime, he'd purchased birdseed and practiced picking the lock of his lanai. All would soon be in place: the squirrels would come, first descending on the preserve, and then with a vengeance on the house of Butcher.

~

Labor Day had come and gone, taking with it the boys and girls of summer. Lake Longawonga had fallen so far that Jack had been forced to jump rather than step onto his boat from the dock. He'd towed the craft into storage the day before, and now he and Jill were gazing at the lake one last time before departing in their packed minivan.

His wife glanced back at the cabin and shook her head. "It just doesn't look right." The porch windows hadn't been boarded, the replica of Longawonga Light was still on the shore, and the paddle boat was beached, not crammed underneath the cabin.

"Donna and Ed will take care of everything—they're dependable people," Jack said in reassurance. He and Jill had known Rudy's daughter since she'd been a teenager, and he had no reservations about turning over some of the tasks of closing the cabin to her and her husband. The Adamsons had also left out the Adirondack chairs and heavy stepping stones painted with lake and wildlife scenes so that the Bensons could stow everything in its proper place.

"Just think," he added, "it'll look exactly like this next year." The Bensons were going to open and clean the cabin before the Adamsons arrived.

Jill nodded and smiled. "That's the best part—driving up and having all this work already done for us."

They climbed into the car, which calmed Nefertiti, who was whining in the second row of seats. She circled a few times before settling into her bed and blanket, redolent with eau de dachshund.

As they drove past the empty cabins, Jill said, "We could stay for the colors next year." She was obviously having second thoughts about abandoning their original plans.

"Sure," Jack said, knowing that they probably wouldn't. Then, to make her feel more at ease with their decision to return early to Sarasota, he philosophized, "It wasn't in the cards, Jill. Fate obviously has other plans for us."

PART V

TWENTY-NINE

The boys' team meeting room at Claude Pepper High was a malodorous space filled with grimy student desks. The blackboard in the front was overspread with diagrams of football formations arranged around a single, alarming word: "Execution." The walls of the room were covered, literally, with inspirational adages printed in bold black lettering on stiff white paper. "Winning isn't everything, it's the only thing," "Show me a good loser and I'll show you a loser," and "It's not whether you win or lose—yes, it is" immediately captured Kathy's attention. On further inspection, she discovered one saying that she'd never encountered previously, "Before Title IX, a woman's place was in the home."

"Oughta fire 'em up, don't you think?"

Kathy turned to the voice and saw a man who seemed to match the physical description of her eyewitness—thinning hair, sixtyish wrinkles, average height, and slightly mad blue eyes. He was wearing sneakers, athletic shorts, and a gold T-shirt emblazoned with "Pepper Pirates" in black and the logo of a buccaneer, patch over one eye, cutlass in mouth, also in black. She was reminded of her dad's tale of Mr. Lovejoy's meltdown in Publix.

"Max Bateman," he said, offering his hand.

"Kathy King." He held her hand a little longer than customary, and something about the slimy texture of his flesh made her wonder where the appendage had been. She snatched hers away, craving a handy-wipe.

"Have a seat," he said in a teacher's authoritarian voice.

She chose one in the front row, while he propped himself on the corner of a large educator's desk, a piece of furniture remarkable for its barren top. Where are the books, papers, and pens? Kathy wondered. Further evidence that while jock rot might flourish in the room, intellectual growth would go unfertilized.

She also realized that he'd placed himself in a commanding position where he could look down on her. Kathy was the subservient student, her eyes directly level with his crotch. She decided to let the matter pass; if he felt unthreatened and in control, perhaps he'd reveal more than if she pressured him.

"So one of my students squealed on me, huh," Bateman said, eager to address the topic. "You an art critic or something?"

Kathy had told him very little on the phone, only that she was researching Sarasota's famous landmark and the different views local citizens held regarding *David*. "Actually, Mr. Bateman, I'm a private investigator, and I don't reveal my sources."

His eyebrows, an unruly configuration much like President Bush's, raised in alarm, creasing his forehead. "Somebody suing me for expressing an opinion?" he asked suspiciously.

Not an unreasonable possibility in today's litigious climate, Kathy thought. "Not that I know of. Actually, I'm looking into the vandalism, checking every possible angle. Apparently, the statue wasn't your cup of tea."

He laughed, an ominous rumbling that banished the sunshine of amusement. "That's putting it mildly. Every time the media promotes Sarasota there's a picture of the damn thing. Like some badge of honor," he said sarcastically. "Up here in Bradenton we're blue collar and barbarian, and let me tell you, Mrs. King—"

"Miss."

He looked at her guardedly. "You're too attractive not to be married. Are you some dyke working for a bunch of faggots? Have they got their thongs twisted 'cause their queer statue got roughed up?"

Kathy was offended, not by the accusation, but by his language. Still, she wanted him to vent freely, so she said, "I'm straight, Mr. Bateman, and so is my boss." At least she hoped Brett was. "But I'm interested in your thoughts on *David*. I didn't realize that it was considered homosexual," she lied.

"Just look at the way the boy stands there," Bateman said, as if the pose wrought by Michelangelo were obviously homoerotic. "Like an open invitation if you ask me."

"Have you been asked, Mr. Bateman?" Kathy posed innocently.

A vein began to bulge in the man's temple, and his eyes, already manic, enlarged until he looked absolutely pop-eyed. "What's that supposed to mean?"

"Your anger," she answered. "I assumed it was caused by some traumatic experience—such as having been 'propositioned,' for want of a better word, by someone of the same sex."

"Do I look like someone they'd make a pass at?" he asked, not rhetorically, his fists clenched. Not only had his voice risen, but his face had reddened as well.

"I didn't say that—" Kathy began before he interrupted her.

"It never happened, and if it did," he said, the vein throbbing, "I'd beat the living shit out of the queer bastard."

He seemed ready to say most anything now, Kathy thought, pleased with herself. "That's comforting, Mr. Bateman, but let's get back to the statue. What is it that offends you so much?"

"Well, it's nude for one thing," he said, as if only a moron could miss something so obvious. "That kind of art doesn't belong in a public place."

"But nude statues are commonplace," Kathy protested. "What's so distasteful about this particular one?"

"It's a boy, don't you see?" he said with the intensity of a coach furious at a blockheaded player.

Kathy played ignorant. "I don't get it, humor me."

"It's what faggots want . . . a young boy . . . it's what they dream about." He stood up, his arms renting the air for emphasis. "The damn thing practically screams 'molest me!'"

"I never thought of that," Kathy said, the slow student finally grasping the concept. It occurred to her that coaches spent all their time with young boys.

"Well, now you have," Bateman said with grim satisfaction. "And here's something else for you to think about. Besides the museum," he said, ticking the items off on his fingers, "you've got the Asolo and the Van Wezel and the symphony and the opera and the ballet." His voice became more agitated as he recited the list, ending on a high, mincing note. "That's all pansy stuff—they oughta call the town Fairysota."

"Mr. Bateman, where were you last November second at nine p.m.?" she asked, puncturing his rant.

For a few seconds he was speechless, as if the wind had been knocked out of him, or, because of the sickly expression on his face, he'd been kicked in the groin.

"You think I'm the one?" he finally said.

She nodded, and he regarded her first with consternation and then with disbelief that escalated into uncontrolled mirth. She thought the laughter seemed forced, and when he finally gained control of himself, he said, "Let me tell you what I'd have done to that thing if I'd thought I could've gotten away with it. I would've stuck a pipe bomb up its ass and blown it to smithereens." Then he had a more arresting thought. "Or I would've taken a sledgehammer and pounded it into a million pieces."

Kathy wasn't amused. "You haven't answered my question."

"Should've never given you the vote," he said, shaking his head. But he walked behind the desk and opened a drawer. "Yeah, here's a schedule from last year," he said, holding up a sheet of paper. "I was coaching a J.V. football game that evening."

He handed her the list, which showed a four p.m. game on the date in question. "What time did it end?" Kathy asked. She was taking notes now.

"I'm usually outa here by seven, seven-thirty," he answered.

"Where'd you go after the game?"

"Home. Gotta grade papers and make lesson plans," he added, grinning.

Kathy knew that was a crock. Her parents had complained mightily during their careers about P.E. teachers pulling down big stipends for coaching sports, something they had the time to do because they never took any work home. Her dad had coached tennis for a few years, but had given it up because he'd been forced to grade papers into the middle of the night.

"Can someone corroborate that?" she asked.

"I'm not married, so you'll just have to take my word for it," he said, a note of challenge in his voice.

"Were you with someone that night?" Kathy persisted.

"What are you inferring?" he said, his beetle brows twitching on the verge of anger.

"Don't you mean 'implying'?" she said, correcting him.

"Whatever," he spluttered.

"I'm just trying to save you the trouble of the next step," Kathy said ominously, enjoying his discomfort.

"What's that supposed to mean?" he said. The cracks in his composure weakened his stalwart pose, like a statue weathered by the elements.

"I have an eyewitness who saw someone on the grounds of the museum about the time of the crime," she answered.

"The police will want you to stand in a lineup since you don't have a confirmed alibi." She hadn't arranged anything with Dan yet, but she was confident she could. She'd promised him an arrest if she tracked down the culprit, and he'd already used department resources to help her.

"I don't have anything to hide," he said, some of his bluster and bravado returning. "Name the time and place."

"Someone will be in touch with you, Mr. Bateman," Kathy said, rising. Now she had to make good on her bluff.

~

Harry MacDonald wanted very much to please the young woman. She reminded him of a girl he'd bedded in his early life, while he was still sowing his wild oats. There was no chance that Miss King would fancy an old fool like himself, but he could always dream.

He'd been standing in front of the viewing window for several minutes now trying to make up his mind. Only one of the men in the lineup, number four, resembled the man he'd seen back in November. Four's age, shape, and countenance all fit Harry's picture of the suspect, but there was something not quite right. This man's body was too muscled, and the way he stood, defiantly, didn't match the skittish movements of the pedestrian. And the face was harder, almost cruel, not sensitive and soft like the man he'd seen. Harry looked to Miss King for guidance—she was standing to his right with a police officer.

"Take your time, Harry, we want you to be sure," she said, smiling.

He returned to his task and after a few moments made up his mind. If he had to testify in court, he could always say he wasn't sure. "Number four."

"Are you positive, Mr. MacDonald?" the police officer asked.

"Yes," Harry lied. It had been almost a year, so his doubts were only natural, he persuaded himself. It was probably the guy.

"Thanks, Harry," Kathy said, placing her hand on the old man's shoulder. She opened the door for him, then closed it and turned to Dan.

"Well?"

"With Bateman's statements to you and MacDonald's ID, we'll be able to get a search warrant," Dan said. "But we'll need some hard evidence to charge him with anything."

Kathy would keep her fingers crossed, but some doubts were nagging at her. Bateman seemed to be truly certain of his own innocence, or else he was staging one hell of a believable act. And he reminded her of someone else in her investigation—but she couldn't put her finger on who it was.

THIRTY

"What's with the squirrels?" Jack wanted to know. "It's not even close to winter."

In fact, the September day was typical of late summer in Sarasota, low nineties with humidity building toward likely afternoon thunderstorms. Accompanied by Connie Lovejoy, the Adamsons were paddling idly in their pool, waiting for Richard to return from a secretive errand. The squirrels, swarms of them, were chattering and bustling in the preserve, but mainly behind two homes—the Lovejoys' and Butcher's.

"They've been like that for three days," Connie said, floating in a blue floral pool chair. "If I had a gun, I'd scatter their asses."

"I'm surprised Richard hasn't done something about them," Jill remarked. "Isn't he worried they'll climb all over your cage?" She snuggled her back up to a jet, where the pulsations of the ninety degree liquid contrasted to the cool waters of Longawonga.

"You would think," Connie said, shaking her head. "Not only did he tell me not to worry about them, but he seemed pleased they were there."

"What's Richard planning for that new bed?" Jack asked. Lovejoy had created a large oval of fresh dirt and mulch between his house and the Adamsons'.

"He says it's a surprise," Connie replied. "The only surprise is that he didn't create it on the other side to irritate Butcher—not that an empty bed would bother anyone for very long," she added hastily.

Nefertiti and Tippy, who'd been lazing in the shade of the overhang, rose as one, growling as they walked to the side of the lanai cage. The object of their displeasure soon appeared, goading them into fits of barking like small arms fire or a chain of exploding firecrackers. Richard was leading or being led by a leashed and harnessed Vietnamese pot bellied pig, black, slightly taller than his knees, and built like a small tank. The animal had a face that only a nursing sow could love, but was graced with a white beauty mark in the middle of its forehead.

"Jesus Christ!" Connie fumed, losing her balance in the chair and toppling into the pool.

"No, her name is Star," Richard proudly proclaimed. "The humane society thought it best that I use the name given by her previous owners. Besides walking on a leash, she's pedigreed, potty trained, and spayed."

"You mean a feral boar hog won't be sniffing around?" Jack said, disappointed, watching dubiously as Star pressed her snout into his hibiscus bed.

"This beauty will remain a virgin—no porking for her. And best of all, she won't pee or bleed on our tile or carpet," Richard assured them.

"I'm not having that damn thing in the house," Connie spluttered, having regained her footing.

"That's why I went to Home Depot and bought a storage shed," Richard said smugly. "I'll put it up under the trees over there next to Star's wallow." He indicated a spot between a bottle brush and a live oak, close to the house and the oval of dirt and mulch.

"You mean that's not a flower bed?" Jill asked with mounting alarm.

"No, it's Star's wallow," he repeated. "I'll outfit the shed with sawdust and straw, and she'll be in hog heaven. So when I said she wouldn't mess on our floors, I meant the small amount of time that she might be inside."

"For God's sake, Richard, WHY?" Connie screeched.

Her husband put a finger to his lips. "Butcher," he replied. "I'm planning another attack, and when he retaliates—we know he will—my watchhog will be ready."

Jack, who'd been studying the sturdy creature, observed, "With her stomach slung low to the ground like that, she reminds me of Nefertiti."

The dogs, in fact, had ceased barking and were sniffing and snorting at the edges of the cage. Maybe this animal was some kind of bloated dog, they seemed to be thinking. After all, a human being *was* walking it on a leash, and it *did* have its nose to the ground.

"Another stroke of luck is that the previous owners had a dog," Richard said brightly, as if fate had conspired shrewdly to thrust Star the pot bellied sow into the affairs of Plumbago Plantation. "She should get along just fine with Tippy."

"Let's see about that," Jack said, hoisting himself from the pool. He attached Tippy to his leash, which had been lying nearby.

"If anything happens to that dog, I'll divorce you," Connie bellowed, sounding as though she meant it.

Jack opened the screen door, using his foot to block Nefertiti's escape, and ushered Tippy out to his first meeting with his porcine sister. Star snuffed and grunted, lifting her snout from the intoxicating aromas buried beneath the hibiscus bed. For his part, the Chihuahua, so eager to get at the exotic creature before, now circled uncertainly, backing away when the pig extended her rotund head. In an unexpected move, Star then pirouetted rather gracefully, offering her broad butt for Tippy's inspection.

"Now there's a pig who understands doggy etiquette," Jill noted as she climbed out of the pool.

Tippy accepted the invitation, satisfying his curiosity at great length before allowing Star to complete the interspecies pas de deux. The Chihuahua trembled in anticipation, having never experienced the presence of such a large, wet nose in his unprotected orifice. His fear was comparable to that of a human patient who catches sight of his proctologist coming at him with a vacuum hose instead of a sigmoidoscope. Star was mercifully brief, even bestowing an oink of approval.

"I'll be damned," Jack said, studying the pig.

"Good piggy," Richard said, stroking Star behind her large, floppy ears. "That's how you reinforce desirable behavior." Clearly, he now considered himself an expert on the psychology of swine.

Jill had joined the men outside and reached down to caress the animal. "Hmm," she said, finding the experience pleasurable.

Connie emerged from the pool, her anger undiminished. "So . . . am I the only one who still thinks this is a half-assed idea?"

"What are those drops of water on her snout?" Jack asked, pointing at Star's face. "I don't see them anywhere else."

"Pigs don't sweat," Richard said with authority, "except for that one little spot."

"But you sweat like a pig when we play tennis," Jack noted, not unreasonably.

"You can say that again," Connie agreed. She was fed up with Star's mutual admiration society and only too happy to demean her husband. "He's like a furnace in bed—too bad some of that heat doesn't extend to a certain piece of his anatomy."

Richard winced noticeably. Jack and Jill exchanged unhappy glances; this was more than they wanted to know about the Lovejoys' sex life, and not the first time that Connie had humiliated Richard.

He endeavored to ignore the remark. "Because they don't sweat, pigs like to roll in mud to stay cool," Richard continued. He was now a lecturer, and they were his audience—whether they were interested in barnyard behavior or not. "Come on, Star, let's show them."

He led the pig to the wallow and unleashed her. The exposed earth and mulch were still damp from a heavy watering that he'd applied earlier, and Star took to it like a duck to water . . . or a pig to mud. She did a little swan dive, thrust her snout enthusiastically into the rich earth, then flipped over on her back and wiggled ecstatically, like a human ridding herself of an exasperating itch. Tippy dashed around the edges, whining, but couldn't quite bring himself to flop in the muck with Star, who was now pretty well covered with the stuff.

Nefertiti showed her acceptance of the new phenomenon through boredom. She walked away from the screen, found some shade, and settled into a somnolent ball, her head turned away from the pig and the people. Connie was not nearly so tolerant.

"It's filthy," she raged. "I couldn't possibly let that animal through the front door."

Richard came to the defense of his sullied swine. "She's not a dirty pig," Professor Lovejoy insisted in the face of the evidence. "Covering herself with mud helps her cool off," he reiterated. "And it protects her skin from insect bites. Before I ever bring her into the house, I'll hose her down. But that caked mud will mix just fine with the sawdust and straw in her shed. I'll even sleep with her for a few nights until she adjusts to her new surroundings."

"You'd rather sleep with a pig than your own wife?" Connie yelped.

Jack thought of several witty responses, such as "Yeah, Richard, you already have a pig in a blanket—why burden yourself with another one," or "Since you don't shave your legs anymore, Connie, he probably won't be able to tell the difference," but Jill gave him a look so dark that he bit his tongue.

"Like I said, it'll just be for a couple of nights," Richard protested, "until she feels comfortable in her new home."

"Will you sing her a lullaby, Richard?" Jack asked, unable to restrain himself entirely. "Hush, little piggy, don't squeal a word, Papa's going to buy you a mockingbird, If that mockingbird don't sing, Papa's going to buy you a chicken wing," he crooned.

"Enough, Jack," Jill cautioned.

"What *does* it eat?" Connie asked, struck by a sudden vision of this Falstaffian creature eating them out of house and home.

"Ralston Purina makes a pig chow... I've got some big bags of that in the van along with everything else," Richard said. It was obvious that he'd planned this venture carefully, leaving no stone unturned.

"I wonder if it tastes anything like Wheat Chex," Jack said.

"WHO GIVES A SHIT!" Connie shrieked.

They all stared at her in silence for a few seconds. Finally, Jill said, "I think I've had enough sun for today." She returned to the lanai, which roused Nefertiti from her stupor, and woman and dog entered the back of the house.

Richard said to Jack, "Would you mind doing me a favor?"

"Sure, what is it?"

"Help me get the stuff out of the car and put the shed together."

Jack glanced apprehensively at Connie, who seemed momentarily paralyzed, like a character in an absurd play who has no reasonable course of action to pursue. "OK, let's get at it."

Connie disappeared as the men set about their work, but Star faithfully oversaw the operation from her wallow. Jack hypothesized that, denied a boar that could mount her, she'd channeled the remnants of her sex drive into an orgasmic romp in the mud. He'd never seen a creature in such ecstasy; pig and fecund earth were one, a union blessed by the same god purported to have fashioned Adam from a lump of clay.

When the men had erected the shed and provisioned it with sawdust, straw, and pig chow, Richard said, "Let's hose her down."

He enticed her from the wallow with a handful of food, reattached her leash, and "good-piggied" her to a fare-thee-well while Jack gently washed her down. Then the two neighbors dried her off with some old towels before escorting her to her new abode. Star rooted in the straw and sawdust for several seconds before plopping down and falling into a deep, blissful sleep.

"Richard, there's one thing you haven't told me," Jack said in a muted voice, not wanting to wake the pig from its nap.

"What's that?"

"Why did Star's previous owners give her up?"

Richard smiled. "Cant get anything by you, Jack. Always thinking, aren't you? OK, you might as well know—she bit a cable guy and a meter reader, and chased a little brown man with a weed whacker halfway to Tampa."

Jack stared at the sleeping pig with a new appreciation. "Aren't you worried that she'll bite someone?"

"No, that's exactly what I want her to do."

THIRTY-ONE

"So, there you have it—Brett Masterson's dull little life," he concluded. "As I said, this isn't a ploy for sympathy . . . just a way of explaining to you why I've been so distant. And," he added, looking away from her toward the water, "why I was so easily discouraged when you couldn't go out with me on the day that I first suggested."

Kathy was close to tears, not just because of his account, which was heart-rending, but because he'd chosen to reveal his past to *her*. It had to be extremely painful to have endured an unloved, *unwanted* childhood. He'd laid bare his vulnerability, and she just wanted to take him in her arms and squeeze some of her vast stores of affection into his veins. She settled for cupping his hand in both of hers, and they sat in silence for a few moments.

In the background a keyboardist in a commodore's cap was singing covers of Jimmy Buffet, Elvis, and Roy Orbison. Umbrellas strategically placed on the grey deck provided shade for the lunchtime crowd at O'Leary's, their conical shapes mimicked by the cramped bungalow's pointed roof. As for the food, the fried shrimp was delicately battered, the sides of fries and slaw were generous, and the draft beer was cold. Just to the north was Marina Jack with its restaurant and boat slips, which bordered the park of shade trees and spacious sidewalks where O'Leary's overlooked Sarasota Bay. Across an arm of the bay to the south was Selby Gardens, its canopy of banyans dwarfing the adjacent buildings and vegetation.

The singer had just managed to hit the final note of "Blue Bayou" when a voice familiar to Kathy said, "I hope I'm not interrupting anything."

She gave a little start and withdrew her hands from Brett, who looked questioningly from her to the police officer standing over the diners' wooden table and bench seats. The stare that Kathy and the officer exchanged was not lost on Masterson.

"Oh, no," Kathy said, though her face reddened slightly, "just a business lunch." She regretted her words immediately when she saw the hurt flash in Brett's eyes. "Brett Masterson, this is Officer Dan Crouse, the man who's been helping me in my investigation." And the guy who's been screwing my brains out, she thought, as the two men shook hands.

After Dan had sat down, he said, "Since you told me you'd be here, I thought I'd drop by and give you the results of our search of Bateman's house."

"Did you find anything?" Kathy asked eagerly, the awkwardness of the situation temporarily banished.

Dan grimaced. "Nothing. No . . . uh, pieces of bronze anatomy, no white paint, not even any tools that he might've used. There was no literature on the museum and no newspaper articles about it or the statue."

"Wasn't there anything of interest?" Kathy asked, as she experienced a familiar sinking in the pit of her stomach. She'd had such high hopes that she couldn't bear to see them dashed so easily.

Dan snorted. "A mirrored room filled with weight lifting equipment and pictures of barely clothed guys with bulging pecs."

"Oh really," Kathy said, eyebrows raised. "'The lady doth protest too much, methinks.'"

Dan smirked. "Exactly."

"Well, there are other gay bashers I can check out," she said, though her theory now seemed fragile to the point of breaking. "I'll have to admit that I had some doubts about Harry's identification."

"Oh?" Dan said. He took of his hat and dabbed at his forehead with a clean napkin.

"I think he may have been trying to please me," she admitted. "He called me up later and wanted to know what we'd found."

"Perhaps you have that effect on men," Brett said, breaking his silence. The note of bitterness in his voice was inescapable.

Now it was Dan's turn to evaluate the glance exchanged between Kathy and Masterson. "But your witness *did* see somebody that night," Dan said, bringing them back to the matter at hand. "You shouldn't lose sight of that."

While the other man was maintaining an adult, businesslike demeanor, Brett suddenly realized that he was being petulant and childish. He needed to contribute something to the discussion, to encourage Kathy rather than rebuke her.

"Where did Mr. MacDonald say the man went after crossing the street?" Brett asked, tackling the problem from a different angle.

"Into the parking lot," Kathy said, staring at him.

"Well . . . uh, maybe he was attending the play at the Asolo that night. Maybe that was his cover story," Brett said, warming to the idea.

Kathy looked at Dan in what could only be described as a moment of epiphany. "Jesus, that's so obvious, why didn't I think of it? I can get names of the ticket holders for that night, check them against my other lists . . ." She jumped up, leaping before looking, and kissed Bret lightly on the cheek. "You're a genius," she said. With that, Kathy dashed away, dropping a dollar bill in the jar of the grateful singer, and leaving the two men at her table to arrange their own awkward farewells.

~

Under the cloak of night, Richard Lovejoy removed two bags of birdseed from his van and deposited them in Star's shed. He would've preferred to have had the bags on hand well in advance of his attack because he didn't believe in waiting until the last minute. But the squirrels would've sniffed them out, and the nasty little rodents would have been his problem instead of Butcher's.

The pig roused herself and snuffled the seed, then looked quizzically at her owner. This wasn't the tasty pig chow made by Ralston Purina, but humans frequently added or subtracted items from her surroundings without explanation. She returned to a fragrant mound of straw that she'd busily plumped into a pleasing shape earlier in the evening and promptly fell asleep. Her dreams began to fill, as always, with unknown but divinely aromatic objects buried beneath the earth. Richard checked the alarm on his watch, removed his tennis shoes, and slid into his sleeping bag, leaving on his shorts and T-shirt.

At one a.m., his wristwatch chimed him awake; he felt surprisingly refreshed and fearless with regard to the task ahead. After slipping into his shoes, he hefted the first bag of seed and softly opened the door of the shed. Star grunted and twitched her snout, but didn't awake as he closed the door behind him. A bright moon was both a blessing and a curse: he could easily make his way behind Butcher's lanai, but he worried that he might be seen. He tore open the bag and emptied its contents along the outside of the cage before retreating in haste to his own yard. He'd been depositing seed after nightfall for several days, first in small amounts in the preserve behind his house, and then larger quantities directly behind Butcher's property. Now if the little buggers would simply do their thing.

It was only minutes before he heard rustling and crashing in the trees as the bodies of squirrels came flying toward the bait. In the moonlight, their bodies and sprightly, curled tails were silhouetted against the preserve as they descended—like a Biblical plague—on Butcher's yard. Richard retrieved the second bag, hoping that these creatures were no different from their cousins in Maine. The Adamsons had recounted their disaster with bird seed— a bag left inside their cabin had led to a hole chewed through the porch screen, and Jack and Jill had awakened to a house filled with bushy-tailed intruders.

Richard knew that all the screen doors in the neighborhood were made by the same company, and he'd become so proficient at picking his own lock that he could do it with his eyes closed. Remarkably, he sprang Butcher's mechanism on the first try. Before entering, he threw several handfuls of seed onto the top of the screen—like chumming waters to attract fish, he thought. Then he opened the door and set the catch so that he could enter and exit as quickly and quietly as possible.

Once inside he spread the kernels rapidly, along the house side of the pool and under the overhang. He scattered his seed over potted plants and furniture, into every nook and cranny where the forest creatures might wreak havoc. His heart pounding, he clutched the empty bag to his chest, caressed the screen door to a tender close, and reset the lock with his pick. Having done the deed, he dashed to the safety of his own lanai, his heavy footsteps silenced by the thick carpet of grass.

Now he sat, like a hen brooding over her egg, waiting for his plan to hatch and take on a life of its own. After about fifteen minutes, one squirrel scaled the screen and began picking off the seeds that Richard had flung heavenward with all his might. Another followed suit and soon the lanai cage was darkened with furry bodies like a tree swarmed by locusts.

"Yes!" Richard hissed under his breath. But would they go the next step, take that extra base, push for another yard, drive for the basket, and give him 110%? Would his team eat their way into the lanai?

He could see them scrambling over every inch of the cage trying to find a point of entry. Their frustration was mounting, he sensed, and finally he noticed several enterprising fellows working at one spot on the screen. Another group coalesced perhaps ten feet from the first and then a third clot formed, all gnawing with a passion that would not be denied. Richard rejoiced as they broke through, calculating as they climbed in a trickle and then a stream down the inside of the screen how much damage had already been done.

He'd seen enough, he decided. Butcher's reaction would come in the morning when he saw the rodents and their handiwork all over his lanai. And what would transpire inside his neighbor's head: Lovejoy's behind this, but how did he do it? Richard returned to Star's shed and tucked the empty bags inside some already depleted pig chow sacks. They would all go out with the trash in the morning, and any evidence of his treachery would be mashed into a landfill. The sleeping bag could easily have been a bed in a four star hotel as he fell into a deep, untroubled sleep.

Light had been seeping around the edges of the shed's door for maybe half an hour when the racket began. An angry human voice, words as yet indistinguishable, interspersed with what seemed to be the explosions of firecrackers brought Richard to a full state of alertness. Star was awake as well, grunting unhappily because of the commotion and an overpowering urge to relieve herself. Richard snapped on her halter and leash and led the pig out to the wallow, where she did her business on the same spot she'd chosen the three previous mornings. Then he peeked around the back corner of his house, his presence muted by the lanai screening, at the spectacle unfolding next door.

"Take that, you motherfucker!" Butcher screamed, as his double-barreled shotgun recoiled. The report from the weapon echoed along the preserve, scattering squirrels in its wake. Some were scrambling through the holes they'd eaten in the screen, others dashed madly around the pool, and still more skittered along the outside of the screen or jumped to the safety of the woods.

Butcher took aim again, this time toward the sky. "*Hasta la vista*, cocksucker!" The shell blew a hole in the top of the cage, taking a squirrel with it, its broken body splotched in red as it fell to the ground.

Star was trembling and snorting, actually straining at her leash. Richard stroked her tenderly and whispered, "Bad man, bad man, good piggy, good piggy."

As Butcher was reloading, Connie appeared on the Lovejoy's-lanai, staggering and dazed from sleep, wearing a sheer lace peignoir. Why does she wear that when I'm sleeping with the pig? Richard wondered.

"Go back, go back," he said in a stage whisper. Connie saw Butcher with the gun and then turned to her husband's voice. Richard gestured wildly with his right hand, urging her toward the house. She gave a little cry before reversing her direction and disappearing inside. Richard escorted Star back to her shed and filled her dish with pig chow before closing the door and returning to the battlefield.

"*Adiós*, asshole!" This time a potted palm exploded in the right corner of Butcher's lanai, shards of pottery and squirrel splattering the cage.

Suddenly Richard saw how the U.S. might look to the rest of the world. Butcher was the ugly American with his superior firepower; the squirrels, poor Iraqis with no defense but their wits, trying to scratch out a meager existence with a bit of seed.

"*Sayonara*, shit-for-brains!" He fired the second barrel into the pool, ripping a hole in an inflatable life raft that failed its desperate occupant.

"I called the police thirty minutes ago," Jack called out. Richard turned to see his neighbor running in a crouch toward the Lovejoys' house.

"Good thinking," Richard said. The egg had definitely hatched, and the offspring was scampering on legs of its own.

"Drop the gun, sir." Two uniformed policemen, one approaching from each side of Butcher's lanai, had drawn their service revolvers.

"Speak of the devil," Jack said.

Butcher was in the process of reloading, the gun open and two shells in his hand. He seemed to be thinking it over.

"Squirrels," he mumbled, "gotta get 'em, made a mess of the place."

"It would be better if you didn't fire the weapon any more, sir," the officer closest to Richard and Jack said.

There were several agonizing moments of silence before Butcher dropped his gun and slumped to the floor of the lanai. The policemen attempted to open the screen doors, but found them both locked.

"Could you open the door, sir," the same man said. It was an order, not a question. Butcher made no attempt to comply, and Richard refrained from offering to pick the lock. Instead, he watched gleefully as each officer broke through the screens and unlatched the door. Butcher was cuffed and escorted out of his lanai, and he glimpsed Richard and Jack as he stumbled toward a waiting patrol car.

One of the officers, a heavy-set man with a perspiring pink face shaded by opaque Ray-Bans, returned to take statements from the two neighbors. They reported what they'd seen, and he dutifully recorded their observations in a notebook.

"Oh," Richard said, after the officer had closed his book, "when he was violently angry, he started speaking in Spanish and Japanese."

"Really," the man said, eyebrows raised as he added this detail to his notes.

"And using alliteration," Jack remembered. The other two looked at him in bafflement. "You know, starting words with the same letter . . . Peter piper picked a peck of pickled peppers . . . ."

"I think we have all the information we need, thanks," the officer said, tucking his notebook away without adding Jack's final piece of information. He returned to the car and drove off, Butcher glowering in the back seat. Jack and Richard walked over to survey the carnage in Butcher's yard, shaking their heads at the corpses of squirrels and the blood and debris caking the lanai.

"There's one thing I don't understand," Jack said.

"What's that?"

"Why did the squirrels pick Butcher's yard over all the rest of us?"

"That's simple," Richard said. "He's the biggest nut in the neighborhood."

THIRTY-TWO

If anything, October was hotter and more humid than the previous month, but the trail Kathy King was following had grown cold in a mere week. The night of November 2, 2002, a full house had watched the Asolo Theatre Company perform a comedy called *A Flea in Her Ear*. She'd easily obtained a list of the theatergoers and eagerly compared their names to those on her other lists. No gay bashers, no evangelicals, no paint purchasers, no homeless people, no teenagers—nothing.

There had been one surprise, though, the names of two people that she actually knew. But Kathy had dismissed each of them as suspects because she couldn't think of a conceivable motive either would have for committing the crime.

In spite of these setbacks, Kathy was determined not be discouraged—a gut feeling told her that Bret's hunch was right. As she saw it, she had two alternatives now. She could interview everyone who'd seen the play that night, something she was prepared to do, and eliminate the obvious straight-shooters. Then she could do a follow-up investigation of whoever remained, narrowing down the list of candidates until she had a serious suspect or suspects. This approach would take time unless she got lucky, so before she started the interrogations, she was going to give the other alternative a quick shot.

She'd collected the receipts for eight and nine days before the crime, not willing to concede yet that her perpetrator hadn't bought white spray paint in one of the area's major stores around that time. She was barricaded in her office, the air conditioning working overtime, staring at the slips of paper as Kirk and Spock dozed on the futon. They would be her only company until she finished the task.

Kathy crossed her fingers as she began. Here's hoping my guy is anal, she wished, someone who wanted the paint in hand well before the night of the crime.

~

"All he does is stare at our house—it gives me the creeps," Connie whined as she squinted out the aquarium glass. She was wearing a light cotton black blouse, loose-fitting gold Capri pants figured with Egyptian hieroglyphs, and gold flats.

Richard could see the outline of her ass rolling around in the pants; he was both attracted and repelled by the spectacle. The pharaohs were probably turning over in their pyramids. "Star and I are ready. I don't think he'll wait much longer."

She turned away from the window. "And if he does, how much *longer* are you going to sleep with that goddammed pig?"

"It'll be soon, trust me." He checked his watch; Star's nap would be over shortly, and she'd need a walk and a wallow.

"Trust you?" Connie said, her voice striking a sarcastic note. "You said you had nothing to do with those squirrels . . . you expect me to believe that?" Hands on hips, she added, "I could've gotten my head blown off."

Yes, Richard thought, it would've been hard for Butcher to miss that big mouth. Lovejoy imagined her lying there, blood staining the pink peignoir, a meager supply of brains oozing from her open skull. But she was right about the squirrels, and Butcher had made the connection as well. Richard had watched his neighbor clean up for nearly two days after his return from the police station. The man had found bits of seed and rubbed them together over and over in his hands, as if he might enkindle them from inanimateness into speech. Then, as a procession of workers had come to repair the holes in the cage and the chunks in the lanai, Butcher had begun his vigil of the Lovejoys' house.

"It doesn't matter whether I had anything to do with it or not," Richard said. "Butcher has assumed that I did . . . and I don't think he would've shot at *you*. I'm the enemy."

"It's *our* house that he's staring at," she retorted.

"Intimidation, pure and simple," Richard said. "But he doesn't scare me one bit . . . and he doesn't know what I have up my sleeve for him." He pirouetted dramatically and walked toward the front door. Tippy, who'd been cringing on one of the elephantine sofas, jumped down to follow him.

"Where are you going?" she demanded.

He answered without looking at her. "I have to walk Star. I'm going out the front so Butcher won't see me sneaking around the side of the house from the lanai."

"You're more protective of that pig than your own wife," she accused him.

That pig gives me unconditional love, he thought, but he said nothing as he closed the door behind him. Tippy had already slipped through and run ahead—frolicking with his new sister had become his favorite activity, and the occasional pig chow treats weren't bad, either.

Star was waiting impatiently at the door of the shed, which was warm inside in spite of its location under the shade trees. Richard only left her there for short periods when the sun was up. With Tippy nipping playfully at her heels, she headed immediately for the wallow, which the two animals attacked with enthusiasm. It hadn't taken the dog long to get over his shyness, and Richard added to both animals' pleasure by spraying them with the hose, freshening the muck in the bargain. He'd created a little paradise that he appreciated as much as Star and Tippy, or perhaps more, for reasons known only to him.

The pig finally stopped rolling in the mud after caking herself with it and began rooting. Tippy had surprised Richard two days ago by imitating Star, burying her nose in the mire as if searching for a bone. Now and then, the sow unearthed something—a piece of tubing left over from the installation of the sprinklers or a bit of copper wire. On these occasions, she would clamp onto the object with her strong teeth, plod over to wherever Richard was standing, and deposit the prize at his feet.

She was having no luck today when suddenly a rogue breeze funneled between the two houses. The pig lifted her snout, sniffed deeply, and started trembling, just as she had the morning of the shooting. There was no doubt whose scent was borne on the wind, and Richard recognized the teachable moment when he saw it.

He knelt at the edge of the oval and beckoned to the animal. "Come on, girl." She whimpered as she waddled over, as if Butcher's aroma had the power to injure. Richard dug his hands into her matted, wiry hair, enjoying its coarse texture as he stroked the pig.

"Bad man, bad man, good piggy, good piggy."

~

"They're playing in the mud again," Jill said. She was standing a few feet back from her dining room window, spying on Richard and his pets. She noticed with irony that the dark brown floral pattern of her drapes blended nicely with the wallow.

"It'll be old hat after a while," Jack said, fearing his voice lacked conviction. He was leaning against the serving island in their kitchen, chugging a bottle of Yoohoo chocolate drink

"Maybe," his wife replied, uncertain if she could ever accustom herself to the sight of a pig cavorting in the yard next door. She wheeled and faced her husband. "What if Butcher does some crazy thing in the middle of the night, the pig attacks, and he shoots the pig?"

"I'm sure he was fined for firing the gun and placed on some kind of probation," Jack guessed. "He won't use it."

"If he were behaving like a rational man."

"And neither Butcher nor Richard are behaving like rational men," Jack said, completing her thought.

"What if Butcher decides we conspired with Richard to attract those squirrels?" Jill worried.

"You know," he said, sucking on the dregs of the chocolate, "I've been thinking about that. Richard took an inordinate amount of interest in our squirrel problem in Maine ... you remember when we left the birdseed on the porch."

"How could I forget."

"Well, I told him that story on one of our fishing trips. But I don't see how he got the seed inside the lanai—the doors were locked."

"And you said he didn't tell you anything about his plan." Jill found this hard to believe, because Richard generally told Jack everything.

"Not a damn thing." He considered this anomaly for a few seconds. "Perhaps I'm giving him the benefit of the doubt, but maybe he wanted to remove me from any complicity."

"Well, he's not telling Connie anything, either. In fact, I think their marriage may be on the rocks."

"It was never on solid footing in the first pace," Jack agreed.

Jill walked through the archway that joined the two rooms and looked her husband in the face. "This whole thing has gotten completely out of hand. I wake up every morning wondering when the next shoe is going to fall. What if we can't live here any more?"

"The thought has crossed my mind," he said, holding her gaze. "But I have this gut feeling that something big is about to happen. Maybe we'll have some clear-cut answers then. In the meantime, until the shit hits the fan . . . or somebody's pork is roasted . . . how about a swim?"

He placed the empty Yoohoo bottle on the granite counter top and left to change into his bathing suit. Jill removed the bottle wordlessly; she didn't want any rings spoiling the perfection of the dark green finish flecked with veins of white.

~

Kathy rubbed her eyes and scrutinized the receipt for the third time. It was late afternoon—Kirk and Spock were already anticipating their dinners. The dog kept shuffling back and forth between the kitchen and her office, while the cat rubbed first against Kathy's right leg and then the left. She'd been at her desk for seven hours, with only a potty break for herself and Kirk and a bit of lunch.

Having assured herself that the name on the receipt was indeed who she thought it was, she grabbed her list of theatergoers, indexing down until she found the same name. She exhaled mightily; after nearly a year of investigation she had information that *almost* placed a suspect holding a can of white spray paint at the scene of the crime.

Another revelation followed in rapid order: she had pictures that she could show Harry MacDonald. Kathy dialed him at once, finding the old man home alone with highball in hand and no dinner on the table. "Try to get here before Bernice does" was his parting comment. His old goat routine was becoming tiresome; Kathy wanted a correct answer, not one designed to elicit sexual favors for an aging satyr.

She quickly culled some photos from her gallery, including shots of individuals other than her prime suspect. She wanted Harry to have several choices—if he selected her current candidate from the group, she would only need a motive and a confession.

After throwing some food into the animals' dishes, Kathy jumped into her T-bird and accelerated north on Midnight Pass Road. She pushed the speed limit as much as she dared, and then groaned when she saw that the Stickney Point drawbridge was up. Never fails, she thought. Finally, she made her way east to the mainland and Tamiami Trail before turning north again. Unless one was on I-75, traveling north or south in Sarasota was a pain in the ass. Kathy praised the traffic gods that the snowbirds hadn't yet returned to the city in mass migration numbers as she slogged through a succession of lights on the Trail. Thirty minutes later she passed the museum and worked her way to Harry's house.

She sighed in relief when Bernice answered the doorbell—her husband wouldn't be so frisky with his wife around. Mrs. MacDonald greeted Kathy as if she were an old friend.

"You're just in time for dinner, Kathy. We're having brain food—grilled salmon, brown rice, and spinach salad with walnuts."

Kathy's stomach growled in response, and she realized that it had been a long time since she'd last eaten. "I may take you up on the offer, but I have some pictures I want Harry to look at first . . . if you don't mind."

"I don't mind," Harry said, sticking his head around the corner of the foyer. "What took you so long?" he asked in a tone of mild rebuke.

"I was fighting off all my admirers," Kathy said. "I don't know what to do about it, these young men are so impetuous." She regretted the jab almost immediately when Harry's face sagged beyond what gravity's handiwork had already accomplished.

Bernice laughed appreciatively. "That'll put a crimp in his kilt. Show him those pictures now that he's sobered up, and I'll put the finishing touches on dinner."

She left her husband and Kathy alone, and the young woman led the chastened old man into the living room, where she produced a photo from the folder she was clutching like a lifeline.

"Before you give me an answer, Harry, I want to ask you a question."

He looked at Kathy suspiciously, still smarting from her rebuff. "What's that?"

"How certain were you at the lineup? I had the impression you were just trying to please me."

He hung his head in further embarrassment. "I'm a foolish old coot . . . you're right, I gave the answer I thought you wanted."

"Then promise me you'll tell the truth this time."

He nodded his head. "If it's not the guy, it's not the guy."

Kathy placed the photo on a coffee table, an oval of rich mahogany, its top a leather insert trimmed in gold.

"No," Harry said after only a few seconds.

Kathy placed a second picture next to the first.

"No," Harry said, shaking his head.

It was all she could do to keep her hand from trembling when she dealt the third photograph like a playing card next to the others.

Harry reacted immediately by picking up the picture and holding it in front of his face. But to be fair to Kathy's instructions, he said nothing for what seemed to her an eternity.

"That's him, that's the guy. Absolutely no doubt."

She hugged him, and then to his astonishment, kissed Harry fiercely on the forehead. While he was reeling from a fantasy fulfilled, Kathy was already plotting tomorrow's interrogation. Max Bateman had reminded her of someone, and now she knew who it was.

THIRTY-THREE

As Ted Butcher squirmed in his bed waiting to begin his mission, he was once again tormented by the images of squirrels laying siege to his home. It had been Nam all over again, the Viet Cong sneaking closer and closer to his company's position in the middle of the night before all hell broke loose. They were stealthy and clever, like fucking squirrels, and knew the terrain better than the Americans. So when he'd emptied his shotgun into the horde of rodents, he'd been blowing up VC. He smirked now at the memory of his prowess—the smell of gunpowder, fur and blood flying in the firestorm, and the messy retreat. But his frown returned as he recalled the humiliation. Lovejoy and Adamson had witnessed his arrest, and fixing the damage to the lanai had been costly.

Ted had given up trying to figure out how Lovejoy had done it, but it certainly bore his signature. It had all started with the preserve and then the animals living in it, first the armadillo and then the squirrels. It was a free country—he'd helped to make it that way, goddammit—and if he wanted to look at the fucking river, why couldn't he? He didn't like the idea of Charlie sneaking through the jungle and getting the drop on him.

So if Lovejoy thought that Ted would take this latest shit lying down, like a prisoner being sodomized with a nightstick, his neighbor was sadly mistaken. It's going to be a little closer to home this time, buddy, Butcher thought vindictively. Glancing again at the digital clock on his nightstand, he sat up and lowered his feet onto the floor. He was already dressed in camouflage, both shirt and pants, and his face was blackened. All he had to do now was lace up his boots, which were at the ready, and tap his cache of weapons: the pruning shears, the red paint, and the bag of beer bottles. Snip, spill, smash, skedaddle, that was the plan. He'd teach that asshole once and for all to mind his own business.

~

Richard had been tossing and turning since crawling into his sleeping bag. He sensed that tonight was the night—Butcher would brood for only so long. Oddly, Star was experiencing a restless sleep as well. The pig had whimpered softly several times, rolled over in her hay, and snorted so explosively that sawdust had scattered around the shed.

He reached over and stroked her back, realizing with irony but no guilt that he was caressing a pig instead of his wife. Star seemed to be sleeping peacefully at the moment, so Richard wriggled out of the sleeping bag and stood up. Might as well engage in a little reconnaissance, he thought, as he eased out of the shed.

There was a bright sky, illuminated by a full moon and countless stars, the former famous for its effect on hearts and minds of men. Perhaps that heavenly body had caused his agitation, he mused, or perhaps the lunar pull would inspire madness and mayhem before the night was over.

He crept around the corner of his house and peered through the lanai screening toward Butcher's house. After focusing for several minutes, he was unable to detect any movement or noise. Feeling bolder, he rose from his crouch and walked past the end of the cage. With a mixture of disappointment and relief, he again observed nothing out of the ordinary, only a light breeze carrying the earthy scent of the damp, matted grass.

Turning his attention toward the preserve, Richard noticed that even the forest seemed unnaturally quiet. There was no feral boar hog sprinting along the edges, a bobcat in hot pursuit. There were no squirrels rustling in the branches, no armadillos foraging in the soil. Maybe it was the calm before the storm, or maybe it was just an uneventful night.

He returned to the shed, feeling as though he might sleep now, and cracked the door gently. Just as he did so, Richard heard the unmistakable metallic click of a screen door opening. Star snorted and sprang to attention, then advanced toward her owner. There was no question in his mind that Butcher had just walked out of his lanai, probably with evil intent.

"Bad man, bad man, good piggy, good piggy," Richard whispered in the sow's ear. Then he stepped out of the animal's way and let her catapult into the night—without leash or harness.

~

Jack sighed in exasperation and finally slipped out of bed as quietly as possible.

"What's the matter?" Jill immediately said.

"I'm sorry; I was trying not to wake you," he said, remaining motionless until his eyes adjusted to the darkness. The process only took a few seconds as more light than normal seemed to be seeping through the Hunter-Douglas faux wood blinds. "I can't sleep."

"I can't, either," she confessed. She sat up and flipped on a reading lamp built into the headboard. "What are you going to do?"

"Take a look outside, satisfy myself that nothing's going on," he said wearily.

"Don't forget the flashlight," she said, worry lines creasing her forehead.

"And I'll turn off the security," he said, zipping up his shorts and slipping his feet into a pair of sandals.

"Jesus, I would've set that off," Jill said.

"Well, we don't usually go for midnight walks."

When Jack finally opened the slider to his lanai, he heard footfalls to his left, probably coming from the Lovejoys' yard. Their weight and frequency cast doubt on their human origins, and he directed the beam of his flashlight toward the sound to determine its source. A pig flashed through the cone of light just as the animal was negotiating a sharp turn at the corner of the lanai, followed by a man struggling to keep pace.

"Turn that fucking thing off!" It was Richard, waving his hands wildly and hissing like an old-time villain in the footlights.

Jack doused the light and proceeded with caution across his lanai and out the screen door, where he hesitated to get his bearings. If the attack of the domestic swine was in progress, he didn't want to miss it, but neither did he want to risk the wrath of a shotgun if the weapon was in play. Then a hair-raising scream did exactly that to Jack as prickles of fear electrified his scalp.

"What the fuck!"

Jack switched on the light and began running in the direction of the voice, which was now filling the air with a string of expletives. Holding the flashlight steady as he ran was difficult, so he slowed to a fast walk and trained the beam on the struggling figures that were now no more than twenty feet away. Suspended in mid-air, half in the Lovejoys' lanai or half out, depending on one's point of view, was Butcher. His head and upper torso were squeezed through a hole in the screen, but the lower half of his body was dangling in the grass on the other side. He was clutching a pair of pruning shears on the inside, but Star was clutching his crotch on the outside.

"Help me yank him out of there!" Richard shouted above the man's curses.

Jack positioned himself on one side of the pig, and Richard the other, each man grabbing one of Butcher's writhing hips.

"One, two, three," Richard counted off. Now obstetricians, they tugged violently and delivered Butcher from the womb of the lanai. The umbilical shears lodged in the screen, leaving the child with no tools to combat the cruel world into which he'd been born, a pig's snout up his ass. The two men relinquished their grip and considered what to do next, while their unfortunate neighbor thrashed in the grip of the two hundred pound sow.

Jack shone the light in Butcher's face as he squirmed, allowing the downed man a clearer look at his adversaries. His eyes enlarged with fear as he craned his neck and took in the shape of the Vietnamese pig, which was hanging on tenaciously.

"I heard you gooks were using pigs . . . anything to even the odds . . . fucking slants."

"What the hell is he talking about?" Richard said.

"Beats me," Jack replied.

Richard jerked the pruning shears out of the screen and handed them to Jack. "Keep an eye on him while I alert the neighborhood," he said before dashing off.

Jack gripped the handles uncertainly, wondering what he was supposed to do with the tool, but apparently Butcher had no doubts about their intent.

"Go ahead, you rice-eating pussy," he said. "Gut me with the goddammed bayonet... name, rank, and serial number is all you're gonna get." And then he uncoiled explosively, slamming his rump into Star's face. But the pig was up to the task; she shrugged off his butt butt with a flick of her massive head and tightened her grip. Her captive moaned and beat the ground with his fists before his struggles began to subside.

Jack noticed a dark patch on Butcher's pants where the sow had sunk her teeth, and it seemed to be getting larger. This game may have gone far enough, he thought, though he wasn't sure what game Butcher was playing. And why the hell was he dressed in camouflage?

Suddenly the floodlights rigged by Richard flashed on, drenching the combatants in eyeball-searing illumination. Next, a wave of guitar licks and drumbeats crashed into their eardrums at multi-decibel levels—designed to ward off the feral hogs, Led Zeppelin was pouring out of the stereo speakers.

"Play all the rock 'n' roll you want," Butcher screamed, "you won't get me to talk!"

Connie, wearing a bathrobe covered with puffy feathers and flashy sequins, burst with Richard onto their lanai—setting off the toddler alarm—followed by Tippy, who pointed his head at the moon and howled. Jill, wearing a sensible terry cloth wrap, emerged warily onto her lanai with Nefertiti, who immediately joined the ululating Chihuahua in a chorus that clashed dreadfully with Robert Plant's vocals.

"Call 911!" Jack shouted to anyone who could hear him.

Richard began dragging Connie toward the door nearest the imbroglio, and Jill pressed her face against the screen for a better view.

"CALL 911!" Jack shrieked.

Jill shook her head and held up her hands, and the Lovejoys were ignoring him as they made their way to the scene. Jack pantomimed holding a phone to his ear and dialing, which prompted Jill to return to their house.

"What do you think of the pig now?" Richard asked proudly, letting go of Connie's arm.

"I think you're all fucking crazy," she said, shaking her head.

"Careful, Richard, 'pride goeth before a fall,'" Jack admonished, uncertain how the encounter was going to play with the authorities.

Ignoring them both, Richard stuck out his chest. "This man was trespassing on my property and he cut a hole in my screen," he said, indicating the tear. Then he noticed a can of paint and a bag of beer bottles snug against the cage.

"Well, well, what do we have here?" he said, bending down for a closer look. "Going to throw some paint around, were we, and break some glass?"

"Like the vandalism at the community center," Jack surmised. "That would shift the blame away from him."

"Let me see," Connie said, drawn into the plot in spite of herself.

Spitting out a mouthful of grass, Butcher lifted his head as she walked in front of him. "Whores won't make me talk . . . I'm not afraid of yellow poontag . . . you can give me a million doses of the clap, see if I care."

"Did you hear what he called me?" Connie asked, outraged. "Bite off his balls, Star!"

"Is this what you wanted?" Jill asked. She was carrying a cell phone in one hand and covering one ear with another. "For God's sake," she said, taking in the scene.

Jack wasn't sure whether she was commenting on the ludicrous bathrobe or the man with the pig up his ass. "Yeah, thanks."

He walked away from the group and dialed emergency. "We've got a man wounded here . . . my name's John Adamson, 2142 Utopia Run West . . . yeah, that's in Plumbago Plantation, backs up to the river . . . the wound is in the rectal area . . . the rectal area . . . he was bitten in his asshole . . . no, no, not you . . . I'm yelling 'cause there's a lot of noise here . . . you got the phone number . . . OK, we'll be around back."

When the medics arrived, Richard knelt next to Star and whispered in her ear, "It's over now, girl. You caught him, but it's time to let him go." He scratched her behind the ears, and the animal slowly relaxed her grip and backed away. "Good piggy, good piggy."

Released from the trap-like jaws and lifted safely onto the stretcher, Butcher seemed to recover his senses at least partially. "There are no farm animals allowed on the battlefield," he said. "I've read the by-laws, just like my nosy neighbor," he added, nodding at the medics.

"She's been designated a pet," Richard snapped. "Besides, you were trespassing on my property."

"Says you," Butcher replied, as the stretcher was lifted. "I was on guard duty when that damn thing attacked me."

"How do you explain the shears, the paint, and the beer bottles," Richard sneered, gesturing to the evidence.

"I don't have to—I'm reporting that animal to the authorities in Geneva!" Butcher yelled as he was carried away.

"Fuck you!" Richard spat.

"That goddammed pig already did," Butcher managed to say before slumping back onto the stretcher.

THIRTY-FOUR

When Kathy telephoned her mother in the morning to request her assistance, Jill regaled her with a story that defied belief. The private investigator knew, of course, about the feud between Mr. Butcher and Mr. Lovejoy, but she was astonished that two grown men could push a thing to such extremes. However, it did suggest that the suspect she now had in her sights was capable of bizarre, even irrational behavior. She finally interrupted her mother, who was giving an elaborate description of Connie Lovejoy's bathrobe.

"Mom, the reason I called was because I need to talk to Mrs. Lovejoy alone. Is her husband playing tennis with Dad this morning?"

"Well, that's another thing I was getting to," Jill said. "Apparently Butcher already lodged a complaint about the pig with the county commissioners. Richard got a call early this morning, and he's down at their offices right now making his case."

"So she's home alone?"

"I can see her on the lanai fooling with the hole in the screen and minding the pig," Jill said.

"Invite her over, Mom. Tell her I need some advice about the man I'm dating. We can a have a brunch or something."

"OK, no problem, she'll be eager to talk today . . . but what's this all about?"

"I can't tell you yet, but you'll know soon enough . . . see you in a half hour."

When Kathy arrived at her parents' house, her mother and Connie Lovejoy were already on the lanai and her father was kicking in the pool. A front had pushed through in the early morning hours, lowering the humidity and finally dropping the temperature into the mid eighties. The patio table was spread with bagels, cream cheese, grapefruit and oranges, a box of Entenmanns' low fat raspberry pastry, a platter of scrambled eggs and bacon, pitchers of iced tea and lemonade, and a carafe of coffee. Nefertiti and Tippy hovered by the women's chairs, poised to make short work of any morsel or crumb that fell dead from mouth or table. Star lay nearby in the shade of the overhang, back legs splayed, her head resting on the cool Flocrete.

"So that's the vicious pig," Kathy said, taking a chair.

"She's been real subdued since Richard left this morning," Connie said, "but she was a tiger last night."

"So I heard," Kathy said. She wondered why Connie called her husband "Richard" in his absence, but "Dickey" to his face, a pet name he obviously despised. Jack emerged from the pool, and his daughter watched with interest as Connie appraised his lean body.

"Now I get my reward for all that tennis I played this morning," Jack said as he toweled off. "I can eat with impunity." He grabbed a pastry as he left to change.

"Watch the crumbs," Jill admonished.

"Mrs. Lovejoy—" Kathy began.

"Call me Connie, honey," she said. "I understand you want some advice on men." Here she assessed her fingernails, which were blood red, the same color as her lips. Kathy imagined a victim with a neck wound lying close by. "If I do say so, before I tied the knot with my husband, I was a tad promiscuous."

Jill raised her eyebrows and suppressed a smile, but Kathy managed to keep a straight face. "I'd like to take in some of the culture with the man I'm dating," she said as she spread cream cheese on a bagel "Didn't you and Mr. Lovejoy attend some plays at the Asolo?"

"We saw this comedy that had me in stitches," Connie recalled. "It was French—this guy had a twin that no one knew about, and there was a jealous wife and a jealous husband . . ." She stopped in her account to take a bite of pastry, and a blob of raspberry filling oozed out. "Umm," she said, catching it deftly in her napkin. "They had a bedroom that revolved every time . . . I can't remember; there was some trick to it."

"But it was a professional production?" Kathy pressed her. "The acting, the set . . ."

"Oh yes," Connie assured her.

"But here's the important thing—did your husband enjoy the experience?" Kathy asked as if she were hanging on the older woman's every word. "Is it something my boyfriend would like?"

Connie's brows knitted and she frowned. "You know, Richard's reaction may not be the best indicator."

"He didn't like it?" Kathy said. She stopped chewing for a moment as if this revelation came as a shock.

"He has trouble sitting for long periods, says his legs get restless." She pursed her lips. "To tell the truth, he disappeared for an entire act . . . sometimes I just don't understand the man."

Jill, who up to this point had been puzzled by her daughter's questions, suddenly made the connection. Her mouth dropped as if she might speak, but Kathy signaled "no" with a subtle shake of the head. Jack returned and stacked a paper plate with eggs and bacon.

"I like this idea of eating a lot of food in the middle of the day," he said. "You can work some of the calories off and have a clearer head in the evening." He bit off half a slice of bacon and broke the other half into two pieces, which he tossed to the ecstatic dogs, ignoring Jill's frown.

"I'm going to let *you* take the dog to the vet next time, so he can yell at you," she said.

Jack had an inspiration. "I bet Star would like a treat," he said, looking to Connie for approval.

"Go ahead, since Richard's not here to spoil her," Connie said, after glancing at the apathetic pig.

Jack plucked a strip of bacon from the platter and walked over to where the sow was lying. He dangled the ribbon of pork in front of her snout, but she snorted and turned her head away.

"Sorry, ladies," Jack said, returning to the table, "no cannibalism in Plumbago today. I think Star caught a whiff of a distant cousin."

"Did he say why he walked out?" Kathy continued, as her father attacked his food.

"Oh . . . I can't remember," Connie said. After a moment's consideration, she added, "I don't think he said anything."

"What was he doing all that time?" Kathy asked.

"I haven't the slightest idea . . . but what does that have to do with your boyfriend," she asked, puzzled.

Her response seemed natural and unplanned, Kathy thought. She'd hoped to get more out of her before revealing the actual purpose behind the questions, but as usual, nothing ever came easily.

Her tone was more businesslike now. "Mrs. Lovejoy, did you know that your husband was out of the theater at the same time that the statue of *David* was being vandalized?"

Jack stopped chewing his eggs and bacon, his brain scrambling to make sense of his daughter's implication. Jill remained motionless, staring at her neighbor's face for any betrayal of guilt. The dogs despaired as food ceased to move from plate to mouth, and Star plied the air with her snout as if she might sense Richard Lovejoy before the others and warn him of imminent danger.

Connie's face took a turn for the worse. "You little bitch," she said, wagging one of her nasty nails at Kathy.

"There's no call for that, Connie," Jill said, coming to the defense of her daughter.

"You were in on it, too, you Judas," Connie snapped.

"She didn't know anything about it," Kathy said.

"Neither did I," Jack said, finally swallowing. "What the hell happened while I was changing clothes?"

Kathy sensed that she was losing control of the interrogation, so she began firing salvos at Connie. "Why would he want to disfigure that statue? He kept the penis, didn't he? Is it somewhere in your house?"

Connie pushed her chair back in a manner calculated to annoy her hosts, the legs scraping harshly across the surface of the lanai. "I don't have to listen to this shit," she said, rising. But the gears were turning—the anger on her face was also mixed with fear.

Star abruptly sprang to her feet, no small achievement in light of her bulk, squealed joyously, and trotted over to the screen door. Her master was approaching between the two houses, a spring in his step.

"Great news," he greeted them. "Star can still be classified as a pet, but I have to keep her leashed if she's outside. And I have to post a sign warning neighbors that my yard is guarded by a pig. I've already contracted a company to deliver it this afternoon."

Connie turned to meet her husband, a warning note in her voice. "Dickey . . . Richard . . . Kathy's accusing you of . . . of . . . damaging that statue at the Ringling. She knows you left the theater that night."

Richard froze in his tracks, looking very much like a statue himself, albeit one with all its parts.

So much for the element of surprise, Kathy thought. The cat's out of the bag. "I have an eyewitness who saw you climbing over the wall of the museum grounds," she lied. "Why did you do it, Mr. Lovejoy?"

The elation in Richard's face thawed in the unforgiving sunlight, rapidly replaced by growing panic. To his credit, he gazed despairingly first at his wife and then at his pig before wheeling and dashing toward the front of his home.

"Richard!" Connie bawled after him, and Star joined her with a squeal of anguish. It seemed apparent to both that Richard Lovejoy had abandoned the two women in his life. Kathy bolted to the door in hot pursuit with her father close behind.

"Don't let the pig out!" Jill cautioned, her cool voice of practicality cutting through the disorder.

Jack grabbed at the animal's leash and snapped it onto her harness, barely restraining Star before his daughter pushed out the door. Then he looked helplessly at Connie and Jill; he couldn't manage his own exit and maintain control of the sow. For the moment at least the two women put aside their differences and manned the leash as Jack sprinted after Kathy.

"You could've gone out the front door," Jill yelled after him.

Richard was already backing out of the driveway in his Lexus when daughter and father belatedly arrived.

"I'm going to follow him, Dad," Kathy said, panting.

"Count me in," Jack said, more fearful of what Richard might do to himself rather than Kathy. They piled into her T-bird with the young woman at the wheel.

Richard wound his way erratically through the neighborhood side streets, seemingly unsure of his destination, before turning south onto Whitfield Road and leaving Plumbago. Obviously exasperated by the slow speed limit, he ran a flashing red light, narrowly missing a golf cart and its two occupants. Accustomed to bullying motorists at this crosswalk, two men wearing white Titlelist hats jumped from the cart and brandished titanium drivers at the receding Lexus.

"Asshole!" screamed one, extending his middle finger. Kathy and Jack scooted by, but not before getting donked on the trunk with a driver.

"Probably the only thing he's struck solidly all day," Jack quipped.

"He's turning left on University," Kathy said. "I bet he's heading for 75."

That prediction proved accurate as they followed Richard through several lights before he exited north on the interstate. Then, as if he knew he was being followed, he shifted lanes compulsively, dodging in front of sixteen wheelers and RV's before careening into the open again, while never signaling. He was not in select company in this regard because many of the other drivers were engaging in the same risky behavior.

He flew by the two Bradenton exits and over the Manatee River with Kathy and Jack in hot pursuit. Even though she was pushing eighty, that speed was barely fast enough to keep up with the flow of traffic. At the Ellenton exit, cars slowed in anticipation of turning off to the outlet mall, and rubberneckers ogled a convoy of buses coming south from Sun City Center, natives from the reservation of elderly there freed for a day to imbibe the alcohol of shopping. Richard forged ahead and then darted into the right exit lanes for I-275.

"Is he going to St Pete?" Jack wondered aloud.

"Maybe he's going to circle back at Palmetto," Kathy speculated.

The answer to Jack's question was "yes" as Richard ignored the opportunity to return south and blew through the toll booths, tossing a dollar at the toll taker, who shook his fist at the brown car when the bill took flight.

"Oh my God!" Jack exclaimed after they'd cleared the tolls.

"What?" Kathy said, alarmed.

"He's going over the Skyway. We went to a tournament in St. Pete—I was driving—and he closed his eyes. Said he had a phobia about bridges. When the Lovejoys go to the airport, they always go by I-4. There's no way he'll be able to drive himself over that bridge."

THIRTY-FIVE

The Sunshine Skyway, the world's longest cable-stayed concrete bridge, was finished in 1987 and spanned Tampa Bay between St. Petersburg and Bradenton. The original bridge met its demise in 1980 after being struck by a freighter during a sudden storm. Much of the southbound span plunged into the water along with numerous motorists before traffic was halted. The northbound span was later demolished as well, but the approaching causeways were preserved as piers where the public could drive, park, and fish. The state elected to paint the cables of the new bridge yellow because Florida was, after all, the Sunshine State.

Jack could see those signature cables now shimmering in the distance, and he wondered if Richard would chicken out and pull off the road or park on the fishing pier. He'd expressed his dismay on the way to the tournament when he saw those piers end at open water. It didn't help, either, that the view of Tampa Bay was so expansive that one seemed to ascend toward the sky with nothing below except water for a safety net.

"I told him about the design features created to prevent a similar accident from happening, but I thought he was going to pee in his pants before we got to the other side," Jack said, recalling their earlier trip.

"Well, it looks like he's going across," Kathy observed as the Lexus entered the northbound causeway. Richard positioned himself in the left lane and decreased his speed, allowing the T-bird to perch right on his tail.

"He likes the security of having the other span on his left," Jack surmised. "There's nothing but a sheer drop on the right side."

The Lexus slowed even further now, encouraging other traffic on the bridge to pass Richard on the inside lane, some of the drivers shaking a fist at him or honking. Richard responded by saluting them with his middle finger.

"Same old Richard," Jack said.

"Jesus," Kathy said as they approached the crest, "I think he's going to pull over."

Richard abruptly shifted right and turned into the narrow breakdown lane, knocking over one of the plastic barrels spaced at regular intervals along the edge of the roadway. Kathy braked, maneuvering their vehicle to a safe stop between the barrels only inches from Richard's rear bumper. Richard opened the driver's door, stumbled in his hurry to escape the car, then righted himself and headed toward the boundary wall.

"No, don't do it!" Jack screamed as he squeezed out of the car, checking the traffic on his left. The wall was an easy obstacle to jump or climb over with no fence on top—making the Skyway the third most popular bridge for suicide, Jack had read.

"Let's talk!" Kathy pleaded, her head above the door, one leg on the pavement. She began walking slowly toward Lovejoy.

"Stay away or I'll jump," Richard threatened. Both Jack and Kathy froze in their tracks.

"OK," Kathy said calmly. "Would you talk to someone else?" Richard looked away from the wall and the 197 foot drop to the water below. Kathy was encouraged that her question had distracted him.

"I only see my neighbor and his daughter," Richard said argumentatively.

"See that red box up ahead," Kathy said, pointing beyond Richard. "There's a phone in there." He stared dubiously at the box.

"She's right, Richard," Jack said. "It's connected to a crisis center." When Richard failed to react, Jack added helpfully, "The phone's solar powered."

"Oh, great," Richard said sarcastically, "does that mean it won't work if a cloud comes over?" They all glanced reflexively at the sky, which was bluebird clear at the moment.

His curiosity piqued, Richard approached the box and opened the cover. He lifted the phone off the receiver and pushed a red button.

"Hello . . . Richard . . . Hi, Dorcas. What kind of a name is that . . . Uh huh, I see . . . Well, I'm afraid of crossing the bridge because it might collapse, you know, so I thought I'd jump before that happens . . . My neighbor and his daughter are here. She wants to question me about a crime . . . My wife's at home with the pig . . . Yes, I love her, but I've been sleeping with pig lately . . . No, I haven't been having sex with the pig. What kind of question is that? What kind of pervert do you think I am?" He slammed down the phone in disgust. "Would I get a different person if I tried one of the other phones?" he asked, looking to Kathy and Jack for guidance.

Before they could answer, a Florida Highway Patrol car, lights flashing, pulled into the breakdown lane above Richard's position. An officer stepped out, removed his sunglasses, and began talking rapidly in a familiar manner.

"Hi, Richard, my name's Newt. Why don't you step away from the wall. You don't want to do anything rash. It's a long way down and the death isn't quick and painless—you break all your bones and organs and slowly bleed to death. Let's talk."

"OK, *Newt*," Richard said, arching his eyebrows as he glanced at Kathy and Jack. "That young lady back there thinks I broke a prick off a statue, tattletale Dorcas thinks I'm screwing my pig, and I think this bridge is going to collapse any minute. Otherwise, I'm having a good day."

Traffic was slowing now with the appearance of the officer, drivers rubbernecking as they inched by, fascinated by the possibility of a jumper. In one car a child plastered his face against the window, giving him the aspect of a cretin or an astronaut squashed by G forces. A silver Sebring convertible idled momentarily, driven by a young woman wearing a straw sun hat and a breast-baring bikini top. In the passenger seat was her dog, a boxer, sitting just like a human and sporting a captain's hat and pair of mirrored aviator sunglasses.

"I know the women outnumber the men down here, but that's ridiculous," Richard said.

Her suspect seemed to be his old irascible self, so Kathy said, "Officer Newt, I think he might let one of us drive him home now."

"And who might you be, ma'am?"

"We're his neighbors," Jack broke in, lest his daughter elaborate on Richard's allusion to the Ringling caper. "He's having some problems at home, and he has a phobia about this bridge. If we can get him into the car, he'll close his eyes, and I can drive on across."

"What do you say, Richard? It's no fun busting up your body and bleeding to death like Chinese water torture."

"OK, you've convinced me, Newt," Richard said, rolling his eyes. He began walking away from the wall and toward his Lexus. Officer Newt interposed his body between Richard and ledge, matching him stride for stride.

"You won't regret this decision, Richard. You would've fallen in three point five seconds and hit the water at seventy-five miles per hour."

Jack opened the passenger door of the Lexus, and his neighbor climbed in, curling up into a fetal ball. "I'll see you back at the house," Jack called to Kathy, who was climbing into her T-bird.

As Jack drove off, Officer Newt yelled after them, "Even if you'd survived, you would've looked like a piece of meat!"

At the first opportunity to reverse direction, Jack did so, crossing the Skyway for a second, but blessedly uneventful time. Kathy was right with him and finally they were on level ground again, heading south toward Sarasota.

"It's all right now, Richard."

He sat up silently, took his bearings, and slumped morosely in the bucket seat.

"Would you like to talk about it?" Jack asked.

"No."

They drove in silence the remainder of the distance to Plumbago. In the rearview mirror, Jack could see his daughter busily engaged on her cell phone.

As he pulled up to Richard's house, Jack asked, "Do you want to put the car in the garage?"

"No, it may be used shortly," he answered cryptically.

Kathy parked in her parents' driveway and wasted no time in joining Richard and her father. "I let Mom know how things turned out, and Brett and Dan are on their way over," she said. "One is my boss, Mr. Lovejoy, and the other is the policeman who's been helping me in my investigation. I think it would be a good idea for you to give me the whole story right now."

"Let me see how Connie's doing with Star," Richard said, his face betraying little emotion.

Kathy shrugged. "I wouldn't deny the condemned his last cigarette. Call a lawyer if you like."

Richard sized her up—his neighbor's daughter was a tough little cookie. "What have you been feeding her, Jack?"

"She gets it from her mother," he said, his pride untainted by facetiousness. It was clear to him who had all the backbone in his family.

The trio walked around the side of the Lovejoys' house, where they discovered Jill and Connie huddled at the door of Star's shed. Connie embraced Richard awkwardly and then backed away.

"You weren't really going to jump, were you?" she asked.

"I don't think so," Richard said. "I just enjoy *high* drama," he added, attempting to lighten the prevailing mood. The others, except Kathy, indulged him with wry smiles. "What's the problem here?"

"Star was butting against the shed," Jill said. "She seems to have stopped for the moment."

Richard opened the door and knelt down to greet the sow, who squealed with delight. As he scratched her behind the ears, it was obvious to the onlookers, including Connie, that there was more affection in this reunion than the one between husband and wife.

"You'd like a good romp in the wallow, wouldn't you?" he said, moving aside. Star needed no additional encouragement, making a beeline for the oval of mulch and muck.

"What about her leash?" Jack said, remembering the guidelines from the county supervisors.

"Let her enjoy the cigarette without the Surgeon General's warning attached," Richard said.

"Might as well let the dogs join the fun," Jill said, sensing that Star's future with the Lovejoys might be uncertain. She walked over to the Adamsons' lanai and liberated Tippy and Nefertiti. The former dove right into the wallow, but the dachshund whined around the edges before gingerly stepping onto the soggy earth.

"Mr. Lovejoy," Kathy said impatiently, "there's no good time for a confession, so let's get on with it."

"What do you want to know?" Richard said, his tone impenetrable.

Kathy couldn't conceal her exasperation. "How did you do it? *Why* did you do it?"

"I don't know what you're talking about," he said stubbornly. "So I skipped out of the play, so I took a walk on the museum grounds. There's no crime in that."

"Then why did you take off in your car as soon as you heard the accusation?" Kathy countered.

The looks on the others' faces begged to hear his answer as well, but Richard said nothing. Uncomfortable, the onlookers turned their attention to the animals, which were now rooting with abandon.

"Star's going to wind up in China," Jill said. In fact, the pig's head had disappeared below the ground and mud was flying furiously from the pit she was mining. Without warning she stopped, dug her hooves into the mess, and shook her head from side to side. Then she rose from the hole, a thing of beauty as pigs go, her black hair spiked to cool nonchalance by the gel of mud. In her mouth, which was ringed by lipstick of earth tones, was a rigid, black object a bit shorter than a ruler but with the circumference of a bratwurst. As was her custom, Star trotted from the wallow and deposited her find at the feet of her master.

"Good piggy, good piggy," Richard said as he hugged her, but then he broke into tears.

Kathy snatched the thing off the ground and brushed the dirt from it like an archeologist uncovering an artifact. "It's *David*'s penis!" she exulted, holding the bronze phallus out for the others' inspection.

"She said he was hung like a horse," Richard sobbed as Connie's face contorted in horror. "And she couldn't stop talking about his ass. But I was 'Dickey' this and 'Dickey' that . . . couldn't satisfy her when we fucked . . . why wasn't *I* built like that statue . . . I couldn't stand it any more, so I . . ." He lifted his right arm as if he had a hammer and then let it fall before burying his head in Star's coat, his chest heaving spasmodically.

Two men approached just in time to see Richard reenact

his crime, one in a business suit, the other in a policeman's uniform.

"This is my boss, Mr. Masterson," Kathy indicated. "And as my parents know, this is Officer Crouse." She stepped toward Brett as if she were about to present him an award. "I believe this is the property of the museum," she said, handing him the penis.

Brett accepted it without blushing, a rare feat for him, and then gave her a hug, so emboldened was he by the trophy. "I knew you could do it," he said at her ear.

Not to be outdone, Dan embraced her as well, "Nice work, Kathy."

She beamed, basking in the successful completion of nearly a year of tough, frustrating investigation, and the attention of the two handsome men.

"We'll want that as evidence," Dan said, reaching for the bronze remnant. For a moment both he and Brett had a masturbatory grip on the penis—the pose resembled two boys grappling a bat handle for first "ups."

"My employers at the museum deserve to see this," Brett said firmly. "You can borrow it when you need it."

Dan let his hand drop. "That's only fair." Then he hardened his demeanor as he directed his comments to Richard. "Mr. Lovejoy, will you come peacefully, or am I going to have to cuff you?"

His tears spent, Richard disengaged himself from Star and stood up, a fatalistic expression on his face. "I won't give you any trouble." He looked despondently at Jack, but avoided eye contact with his wife. "The leash is in the shed."

Jack retrieved the leash and attached it to Star's harness as Dan escorted Richard to the squad car and Kathy and Brett walked toward the street. Jill comforted Connie, who was still snuffling and whose carefully plotted makeup had been ravaged by the tracks of tears.

Star pulled toward the receding form of her master, pathetic little squeals issuing from her throat. Jack maintained control, but let her advance far enough to see the cavalcade depart. As she stared in almost human bewilderment, he considered the year that had just passed—a year of pigs and men, of armadillos and squirrels, of wars at home and abroad, of statues and women—it was a year that he would not soon forget. And because his birthday was only a few days away, Jack knew he would always remember this time as the year when he'd been sixty in Sarasota.

A bright red pickup truck slowed in the front of the Lovejoys' house and parked in the street. Printed on its cab door in brilliant white was "Acme Lettering, Signs of the Times." The driver, a young man in jeans and a red shirt bearing the same logo, stepped out carrying an invoice.

"I have a sign for Mr. Lovejoy."

"This is the place," Jack said.

"I'll install it for you," he said as he unlatched his lift gate.

Jack didn't hesitate. 'Put it right here," he said, gesturing with his free hand. "At the corner of the yard next to the driveway."

The man extracted a two by three metal sign affixed to a sturdy metal pole and pounded it firmly into the ground with a mallet. Jack shifted his position with Star so that he could read the warning that Richard had ordered. The bold white letters against the red backdrop read "BEWARE OF HOG."